In Lieu of a Plot Synopsis . . .

"To say that the plot defies synopsis is an under-statement; that is a major part of the book's charm. You keep waiting for the hero to trip over the author's loose ends; when he doesn't, you end up cheering. With such an un-predictable story line, it would seem impossi-ble to create a surprise ending. Yet Farmer manages to achieve that too . . ."

—PENTHOUSE

PHILIP JOSÉ FARMER
THE
UNREASONING MASK

BERKLEY BOOKS, NEW YORK

Portions of this book have appeared in *Playboy* Magazine.

This Berkley book contains the complete
text of the original hardcover edition.
It has been completely reset in a typeface
designed for easy reading, and was printed
from new film.

THE UNREASONING MASK

A Berkley Book / published by arrangement with
G.P. Putnam's Sons

PRINTING HISTORY
G.P. Putnam's edition / September 1981
Berkley edition / January 1983

ISBN: 0-425-05551-5

A BERKLEY BOOK ® TM 757,375
Berkley Books are published by Berkley Publishing Corporation,
200 Madison Avenue, New York, New York 10016.
The name "BERKLEY" and the stylized "B" with design are trademarks
belonging to Berkley Publishing Corporation.
PRINTED IN THE UNITED STATES OF AMERICA

For my parents, George Farmer (1895–1950) and Lucile Theodora Jackson (1899–   ), who gave me love and the best of care.

"What I saw in the mirror was not what the mirror saw."

—*Lord Ruthven's Prisoner*

"Where there is only one, there is also another; where two, always three."

—Nur el-Musafir

"All visible objects, man, are but as pasteboard masks. But in each event—in the living act, the undoubted deed—there, some unknown but still reasoning thing puts forth the moulding of its features from behind the unreasoning mask. If man will strike, strike through the mask! How can the prisoner reach outside except by thrusting through the wall!"

—*Moby Dick*

THE UNREASONING MASK

1

"THE *BOLG* KILLS ALL BUT ONE!"

The voice was weak, whispering, and wet. If a shadow under water could have a voice, it would sound like that.

Then the voice boomed like a giant's in the sky, like a rocket exploding near his ear. It propelled him far up into a grayness. Then he was falling down a well the glimmering walls of which sped slantingly away from him but were always visible.

Ramstan had never been so terrified.

He hurtled in the twilight past two naked giants shaped like men but sexless and suspended upside down by chains attached to ankle bands. Harut and Marut? The fallen angels punished thus forever because they had had no compassion for the children of Adam and Eve?

They flashed away into the darkness above, and the well opened out into Space in which myriads of bits of Matter glared. Stars? Eyes?

Suddenly, he was skimming the surface of a white star. He held a bucket, and it was scooping up the thin stuff which burned with a cold light so strong that even when he turned his head away from it the light filled his skull and blinded him.

Then he was in darkness and squeezed by something neither dry nor wet, hot nor cold, moving nor unmoving.

The voice whispered.

"God is sick. Unbreakable flames fall from the black sky.

The earth ripples. Oceans charge. Blood blazes. Flesh fries. Bone burns. Wicked and innocent flee. All die. Where to go?"

Now he was the lone survivor of the shipwreck but was clutched by darkness and cold. He was struggling up towards light, warmth, and air.

"Run, Ramstan, run!" the voice shrieked.

Run? He was drowning in an element that permitted no running.

But he surged from the black, the cold, the deep. He was a fisher who had hooked the fish, himself, and had reeled himself up and out. The oily, icy abysm drained from him as he gasped like a fish on land.

That voice. Where had he heard it before? Long ago? Had it spoken then in Terrish or in Arabic, his natal tongue? What had it spoken in just now? He did not remember.

"I dozed off! In all this noise!"

He sat on a chair of stone covered with thick leather. The top of the table before him was a hard, shiny, brown wood shaped into a symbolic bird, a flat crescent body, the tips upturned to represent wing feathers. On it was a double-stemmed goblet cut from the green-and-red fossilized bones of a reptile. It was half full of a thick yellow wine in which swam blood-red worms, thin as the veins in a drunkard's eyes.

He sipped the wine, which tasted of honey and grapes and faintly of almonds. The latter, he supposed, came from the worms. These were so thin and fragile they slipped unfelt by the tongue into the throat. There was always in the sweetness of Kalafala a barely perceptible bitterness.

Life could be good sometimes, but evil was sure. The end of any life, good, bad, or good-bad, was death and corruption. Everything Kalafalan, in all its airiness and delicate involutions, nodded to the Destroyer.

The interior of the tavern was shaped as if it were a coliseum built by drunken Romans. Seen from above, the edges of the tiers of seats formed sine waves. The seats were separated by translucent clamshell-form partitions three meters high. They held the same customers as when he'd fallen asleep. No one had left; no one had entered.

Ramstan's booth, on a middle tier, faced the entrance, which was beyond the top level of the row of tiers. The floor of the central area was smooth and glistening and sometimes used for dancing and sacrifices. In its center was an oval counter. Within it were four bartenders. Around the oval area were four slender columns of white-and-black stone, fluted vertically but banded with jagged rings. At the flaring top of each column was a chair, and in the chairs sat the harpist, the flutist, the violinist, the bassoonist. They were playing the insane-Mozart music of Kalafala.

"The *bolg* kills all but one!"

If that voice came from his unconscious, where did the name of *bolg* come from? What flowers of the dark mind had been pulled up from even darker earth and assembled to make the bouquet of *bolg*? Why would that dark part of himself speak in a code?

Bolg.

A waitress walked by him. He glimpsed multitudes of himself in the oval-shaped mirrors forming a belt around her waist. His ruff-necked cloak and cockaded hat, his long curving nose, thick black eyebrows, and large black eyes, and the mask now slipped down around his neck made him look like a great bird. He was a huge, handsome-ugly eagle crouching over the stone-bone goblet, dipping now and then to suck in the liquid and worms.

Doctor Toyce stepped out of the shadows of the hall entrance. Her mask hung below her chin, giving her a puff-throated appearance. She was short, though taller than any Kalafalan, blonde, bronze-skinned, and pug-nosed. She paused to squint through the green-blue currents of smoke and the shallow, sea-bottom-green light floating down from the stained glass ceiling. She waved her hand at Ramstan and walked down the curving ramp, disappeared behind a tier, and came out of a dark, oval doorway two booths from Ramstan's.

There were no straight or obvious routes for getting in or out of the tavern. All was twist and turn, retwist and return. The mind of the Kalafalan was a Möbius strip; everything they said, did, or made was inturn of outturn. Yet, all was beautiful, if tinged with the sadness of the inevitable.

Toyce gestured at the bartender. He grinned with two rows of shark teeth. Even the Kalafalan face reflected the inner person. Humanoid, its bright red lips were connected to the nose and the chin with two triangles of red cartilage which made the face circus-clownish. The black eyebrows curved around the eyes to the prominent, almost pyramid-shaped cheeks. A clown until he smiled, the Kalafalan, then he flashed teeth like Death's own.

"The *bolg* kills all but one," Ramstan said in Urzint.

Toyce's pale eyelashes flickered. She sat down and said, "What?"

"The *bolg* kills all but one."

"What in hell is a *bolg?*"

"I don't know. I heard somebody say that just as I was waking up from a catnap. But whoever said it was gone. Did you see anybody leave here just as you came in?"

Toyce shook her head and crooked a finger at Wilimu, a bartender. Wilimu tapped a small gong in the shape of a butterfly and pointed out the new customer to a waitress. She disappeared in a doorway beneath the two Earthpeople and presently came out of the doorway which Toyce had used. In a delicate, three-fingered, very long-thumbed hand, she held the bottle of black liquor which Toyce loved. It glittered in the goblet like obsidian under an Aztec sun. It tingled like a dying electric eel in the throat. It shot flaming stars in the belly and comets in the brain.

Toyce sucked in the waitress with her eyes.

"Answer my question," Ramstan said.

"What? No. I saw no one."

Ramstan wrote three *X*s and a spiral on a chit and stood up. "I'm going back to the ship. That was no dream. I feel . . ."

Toyce said, "I thought maybe we could get stoned. You could forget whatever's troubling you and maybe . . ."

"I'm not troubled or in trouble, Aisha."

"Whatever you say, Hûd. Or are you now in your official persona, and I call you Captain Ramstan?"

"Just try, for once, to keep your nose out of the glass and your hands off alien flesh. There might be an emergency."

"Then you are expecting trouble. But, if you won't tell anybody what's up, how can you expect . . . ? Look, either we're on shore leave or we're not. Which is it?"

"I'll . . . as of present, shore leave. Meanwhile . . . never mind . . . forget it. That voice . . ."

2

HE PUT THE MASK on his face. Its edges clung to his skin, sealing in the nose and the mouth. He walked through three halls and four doors, bathed in sonic waves that were automatically beamed if a door opened. This was for the safety of non-Kalafalans.

Outside, the sun, much like Earth's, was riding out the late afternoon. It was midsummer in the temperate zone of the northern hemisphere, but a cooling west wind flapped his cloak. The spaceport, built by the natives for visitors long long ago, was on the plateau-top of a small mountain. Ramstan could see past the houses and down the slope to the great city on the plains.

Two hundred kilometers east, a dark-purple mountain range loomed. The Kalafalans called this 20,000-kilometer-high mass *Tha'ufukwilala*. The Westering Beast.

Overhead, perhaps a hectometer up, two purple creatures floated toward the purple range. They were shaped like humpbacked boxkites with thick disks on the lower side. Born on the low hills of the west coast, they were now being pushed in their final form toward their final home by the west winds.

When they struck the face of the Westering Beast, the gas in their humps would explode, and the thin, brittle skeletons would shatter. The bone shards would add their tiny amount to the trillions preceding them. Their scattered flesh would feed larvae that would eat their way out of the rubbery capsules hurled from the explosions.

The larvae would creep down the jagged face of the range and begin the slow journey to the coast. There they, like their ancestors, would metamorphose into the floating death-pregnant form.

In a few thousand years, the Westering Beast would have crept up to this mountain and the city in the valley. In a few centuries after that, this area would be covered. Before then, the cities, towns, villages, and farm buildings now stretching from south coast to north coast would be moved 200 kilometers to the west.

"Why haven't you killed the larvae long ago and stopped this burial of your land and of all living things?" asked many visitors from many planets. "Why didn't you do this 2000 years ago? Why didn't you destroy the nests on the western seacoast hills? The time will come when you will be pushed into the sea."

"Oh, no," the Kalafalans replied. "You do not understand. The bottom layers of bone are decomposing and forming the basis for a very rich soil. When the time comes, we will clear off the top layers and plant vegetation and form a new world. By then, the *awawa* will be buried under the bones of their ancestors, and the Goddess will have ended them, and we will have a land richer than the rich land we now have."

"By the time you get around to doing that, you won't have enough population to do the required work. And you, too, will be buried," the Earthpeople said.

The Kalafalans smiled. They trusted in their Goddess and Her designs.

Ramstan had discussed this attitude with Klizoo, the spaceport administrator. Now he saw Klizoo coming out of a nearby park. Holding up his thumb and forefinger in the broken *O* of salutation, Ramstan called out in the spaceport lingua franca, Urzint.

"Klizoo, length and pleasure! Pardon my abruptness, but have you recently seen any non-Kalafalans you didn't recognize?"

Klizoo laughed, revealing his sharklike teeth. Ramstan

could see the slender stalactite of flesh hanging from the roof of his mouth. It was this organ that aided in forming two buzzing consonants which made it impossible for non-Kalafalans to speak the language. Urzint was, fortunately, simple in phones and relatively easy for most sentients to master.

Klizoo stopped laughing. "I haven't seen any I didn't recognize, though, to be frank, all aliens have a look-alike likeness. But an Earthwoman has just come into the city. From the northern coast. She registered at the hotel not more than an hour ago. Her name is Branwen Davis, and she is a crewmember of Irion's ship."

"Irion? But *Pegasus* left months ago! What's this woman doing here?"

"Ask her."

Ramstan was exasperated. The Kalafalan authorities must have known that this woman, Davis, had been left behind—for scientific research?—yet they had never thought to mention it. Also, the hotel staff had probably—no, undoubtedly—never mentioned to Davis that Ramstan's ship was in port. Surely, if she'd known that, she would have reported to him at once.

He just did not understand Kalafalans, and he never would.

But then the Kalafalans said the same thing about the Earthpeople.

"Oh, yes," Klizoo said. "The Tenolt are here. They just landed."

Ramstan jumped as if he had stepped barefoot on a scorpion. His interest in the mysterious Earthwoman evaporated.

"The Tenolt?"

He lifted his right hand, its back close to his mouth, and spoke through his mask into his skinceiver.

"Alif Rho Gimel speaking. Alif Rho Gimel. Come in, Hermes."

Lieutenant-Commodore Tenno's voice said, "Hermes here, Alif Rho Gimel. A Tolt ship, looks like the *Popacapyu*, landed thirty minutes ago. She made an unconventional approach, must have descended on the far side of Kalafala and stayed low until she came over the mountains. The port authorities were upset, but the Tolt captain said that the ship was having drive problems and he had to bring her in quickly."

"Why didn't you notify me at once?"

"It didn't seem necessary. No sooner did the *Popacapyu* land than her ports opened and out came a number of crewpeople. They went immediately to the control tower, and then some went to the hotel and the tavern. That didn't indicate hostile motives, sir. Besides, we have no reason to suspect hostility."

Was there a questioning tone in Tenno's voice?

He added, "Sir, more Tenolt have left the ship. They're unarmed—like the others."

Ramstan had continued walking. He stopped under a tree on the edge of the field. He could not see his ship, *al-Buraq*, because she was on a lower-level berth in the center of a great concrete basin. But the upper part of the oyster-shaped Tolt vessel was visible. Most of the ship was concealed by a triple-row of giant, poplarlike trees. Only Kalafalans would plant trees and flowers in the middle of a landing field.

The ship had to be the *Popacapyu*, which had been berthed near *al-Buraq* on the Tolt port on the night that *al-Buraq* took off so suddenly, uncleared by the Tolt authorities.

Now that the *Popacapyu* was here—and how had the Tenolt found *al-Buraq*?—her captain would, sooner or later, be visiting Ramstan. He would ask why the Earthship had made its unauthorized departure. Or would he? He knew why.

Ramstan started walking again. When he came to the limit of the field, he left the trees to continue southward. After going down the hill far enough so he would not be seen from the Tolt ship, he walked east across the face of the hill. He took a half-hour to circle until he could approach *al-Buraq* from the east.

He paused to lean against the slim, corkscrew-shaped flying buttress of a government building to catch his breath and to admire—for how many times?—his ship.

From this side of the field, he could see her upper part. The vessel lay in a depression the opposite wall of which was deep and vertical. On this side, ramps led up from the craft for the passage of crew and supplies. Many Kalafalans stood along the edges of the depression gazing at *al-Buraq*. She crouched in her berth, glowing with a bright-red wax and wane, breathing light. A monstrous starfish-form bright as a hot coal just fallen from a fireplace, her five arms sprawled out from the fat central body. She was now in this form so that the loading and unloading of cargo and supplies and the entry and exit of personnel could be expedited. For take-off, she could shift to space-form in two minutes, though she did not have to metamorphose to do so. The five arms, covered with hundreds of thousands of small armor plates, would shrink in length, swell in circumference, draw up, become part of the saucer-shaped body. Or, if she were to travel in the atmosphere, she would become needle-shaped. There was no danger of personnel being crushed in corridors or cabins during the shape-change. The bulkhead sensors detected that which must be uninjured or undamaged. Only if the captain—or a delegated authority—overrode the inhibitions with a spoken code could the shape-shifting be harmful to the crew.

Ramstan crossed the field and gently moved through the hundreds gathered to admire the ship. They smiled and spoke to him in their native tongue or in Urzint. Many reached out to touch him lightly. Their fingers scraped off dust of meteors, powder of comets, light-exudations of stars, and also the texture of all the fleshes of Earth. Or so they claimed.

Ramstan smiled diplomatically when the fingers touched him. He smiled at a baby held up to him and at a particularly pixyish female. She gestured with one hand, thumb and a finger curved and touching to indicate she'd like to rendezvous with him.

At that moment he envied those of his crew who would have accepted her invitation. But he had to behave as the representative of the best on Earth. Whether or not he liked it, he was clad in moral armor. It was not that of Kalafala but of Earth. And his own.

The natives did not understand his behavior. Some of it repelled them, though they had not told him so directly. Despite this, they touched him with wondering, wonder-netting fingers. He might be as cold as interstellar space, but this, too, was thrilling. Cold burned in beauty.

"Kala!watha! Kala!watha!"

The murmurs flowed around him. *Kala-* indicated "person" or "sentient" or "speech." *-!watha* was as close to "Earth" as their language permitted them to approach. The Terrans could not pronounce at all the buzzing consonant designated by *!* in the phonetic transcription used by the Terran linguists.

Here and there arose murmurs of *p + hawaw!sona.* *Double-*

mask. Earthpeople here wore masks to strain out the psychede-
ligenic spores. Also, no matter how expressive or uninhibited
his or her features seemed to the other Terrans, to the Kalafalan
the Earthperson was masked with slow-flowing concrete.

Ramstan stepped past the sign which bore the ideogram
warning the natives to go no further. He went down the ramp to
the bottom of the depression and up the nine stone steps to the
slab on which *al-Buraq* sprawled. Normally, the stone was
gray. Now it seemed to blush lightly. A moment later, it
blushed deeply.

The ship panted red light through the semiopaque hull. The
lower part of the disk-shaped body and the five arms bulged
out against the slab, like a behemoth pressed down by its own
weight.

Ramstan halted before the two masked marines at the port,
gave the password—though both recognized him, of course
—held out his right hand so one could read through UV glasses
the code printed on the palm. He entered the port, air under
pressure blowing from it, and went down a short corridor. The
bulkhead before him smiled; he stepped through the lips. For
about seven seconds, he stood still while supersonic beams
disintegrated spores that had been killed in the corridor.

A whistle sounded; the bulkheads flashed red. He removed
his mask, folded it, and stuck it into an inner pocket of his
jacket. He went on into a corridor twice as tall as he, round,
and curving toward the center mess hall for the third-level
crew. The floor was cartilaginous and springy. Round and
lozenge-shaped shining plates alternated along both sides of
the corridor. Opened or closed irises were spaced at irregular
intervals along the corridors. The light was white within the
ship; Ramstan moved shadowless. The glow on the circle to his
right dulled, then became a mosaic of partial views of
operational-important places in the ship. Eight triangles, separated by a thin black line, composed the circle and showed him
three slices of the bridge, the chief engineer's post, chief
gunnery officer's post, two laboratories, and the chief medical
officer's office.

"Cancel V-1," Ramstan said, and the mosaic died out in a
burst of light.

A whistle shrilled. A lozenge on the right bulkhead showed
the face of Lieutenant-Commodore Tenno.

"No orders now," Ramstan growled. "Cancel A-1."

Tenno disappeared in a glory of light. That was one of the disadvantages of replacing metal and plastic with protoplasm, cables with nerves, computers with brains. Like a dog wriggling and fawning with frenzied love at her master's return home, *al-Buraq* was overexcited at seeing him after his long (ten-hour) absence.

The chief bioengineer, Doctor Indra, was working at the inhibition of *al-Buraq*. At least, he was thinking about the problem or should be. Ramstan had seen Indra squatting cross-legged on the floor, immobile, even the eyes unblinking, one skinny brown arm extended to the bulkhead and holding a mentoscope against a sensor plate.

Ramstan left the corridor for an elevator passageway.

At its end was a port which became a hatch as he neared it. He stepped onto the gray disk which rose up through the hatch, said, "One-three. C-C," and waited. An iris opened in the bulkhead, the disk moved into the iris, carrying him with a motion which he could barely feel. The bulkheads rounded to form a shaft, the disk rose, the flesh-colored bulkheads glowing, and then stopped with a slight chuffing sound. The shaft bent overhead, the bulkhead behind him curving over, the rest of the shaft quickly shaping itself into a corridor.

Ramstan stepped off the disk, walked three paces to where the shaft curved upward again, and waited. In three seconds, the bulkhead just before him split, and he walked into his quarters. This was a small room which was expanding now that the master was home. It was hemispherical, and the only visible furniture was a table on which stood an electron microscope. The deck was bare except for a prayer rug, three meters square, near a bulkhead by the iris. It was made of woven wool, as required by the al-Khidhr sect, and was dark green except for a red arrowhead design in one corner. This was the *kiblah*, the symbol which was to be pointed towards Mecca when the worshiper knelt on the rug. Here, of course, there was no means for determining where Mecca was. This made no difference to Ramstan. He had not prayed since his father had died. He did not know why he had not left the rug on Earth, and he had not cared to wonder why. Most of the time he did not even notice it. Now, looking intensely at it, he thought it moved.

One of the superstitions of the sect was that prayer rugs, if rolled, unrolled themselves just before al-Khidhr, the Green One, appeared. If unrolled, the rug moved its edges to indicate the coming of al-Khidhr.

Ramstan turned away. He was getting too nervous, he told himself. Next, he'd be hallucinating al-Khidhr himself.

The bulkheads had been bare and glowing faintly yellow. Now, murals appeared on them, ship's electronic reproductions of paintings by Ramstan. Most were geometrical abstracts, but there was one naturalistic St. George slaying the dragon and another of Aladdin during his first encounter with the *djinn* of the lamp. These two were his most recent works. It had taken him a long time to overcome his early conditioning against the representation of living things in art.

Ramstan, though he'd abandoned the faith of his ancestors, still could not eat the flesh of swine, regarded dogs as unclean, and wiped with the left hand after defecating. But he had overcome his conditioning against drinking alcohol.

He stood before the St. George and dragon, spoke a code phrase, and the bulkhead opened, its central point of distention the dragon's eye. Within was a large globe open at one end. It contained two plastic boxes, one larger than the other. The smaller held top-secret records, little spheres, each set in a hollow. The other—that held the reason why he had ordered *al-Buraq* to leave Tolt so quickly and why the Tolt ship was now here.

He struggled with the desire to open the larger box and look at its contents. He sighed, shuddered slightly, and told the bulkhead to close up. He patted the bulkhead, and it quivered. *Al-Buraq* was watching him, and she had interpreted the pat as a touch of affection from her master. Somewhere, in the dark chamber in ship where the synthetic brain floated, a complex of neural circuits, unanticipated by the designers, had grown. The "obedience" configuration now had an "affection" annex.

Ramstan turned away and uttered another code word. A viewplate on the bulkhead across the cabin widened, and it began to run off a film of the cabin since Ramstan had left it. He watched it with his mind on other things: the Tenolt, Branwen Davis, and the bodiless voice in the tavern.

His indrawn breath was a knife-edge scraped across a whetstone. He cried, "Hold it!"

The film continued running. He said, "Freeze it!" and the film stopped. In one corner flashed 10:31 ST, the time of the photographing.

Ramstan groaned, and he said, "Run it back," and then, again, "Freeze it."

The screen had showed an empty cabin. Then, suddenly, the figure had appeared. It had not entered through the iris; it had just popped out of nowhere like a ghost materialized.

Its back was to Ramstan, and it was facing the mural of St. George and the dragon. Its head was concealed beneath a green hood, and the body was covered with a green cloak. The back of the hands were very wrinkled and bore huge blue veins and dark liver-spots.

He groaned again. He had seen such a hood and cloak and such hands once before. A long time ago on Earth.

At Ramstan's command, the film began running forward again. The figure stood looking at the mural for three minutes, then it turned. Ramstan was looking into a face that he could not see clearly because it was deep within the hood. But he recognized it. It was ancient, ancient, carved with wrinkles, and it could have been the face of a very old man or woman.

The shadowy eyes seemed to be looking into his.

Then the person in green vanished.

Ramstan cried, "Al-Khidhr!"

3

RAMSTAN SAT BEFORE the table in his quarters. Canceling all shadows except those in his mind, light pulsed faintly from the deck, bulkheads, and overhead. His only communication with the outside was the audio from the first-bridge, and that was one-way.

On the top of the table was an egg-shaped object below the electron microscope. To the unaided eye, the egg was faintly yellowish-white. It was smooth to the touch. Looking at the screen while he turned the controls, Ramstan felt as if he were in an aircraft descending toward a large albino elephant with a very wrinkled hide.

The wrinkled blank expanded, carrying the ends of the egg out of sight. Tiny figures appeared, indistinct at first, then, suddenly, sharp. The surface was as crowded with sculpture as an ancient Hindu temple.

Ramstan moved the controls so that the view swept to the figures at the end to his left. Here, rising up from the surface of a choppy sea, was a multitude of forms: a twelve-tentacled squid with a bony, serrated fin; a vast fishlike creature behind it, its leviathan mouth filled with curving teeth and open to suck in the desperate mollusk fleeing via the double propulsion of jet and sail; a gigantic amoeba which seemed to pulse, its pseudopods reaching out to encircle and ingest a sharklike creature; the gap of the shark's mouth about to close on a bulbous, fat-lipped fish the jaws of which were clamped on a bulging-eyed thing, half lobster, half conical shell; the claws of the hybrid opening to release in its death agony an eel-like creature with a cockatoo crest; a school of things like animated flowers fleeing into the shallows; a band of fish with fins that could swim in the sea or pull them along like cripples on the beach sands, two of the crutch-fins lurching across the beach toward low-growing plants.

Ramstan adjusted the controls again, and the sea surface became translucent. Seemingly far below, though the distance must be an illusion, were many things of many forms that crawled on the muck of the ocean floor, eating the torn parts and the bodies that sifted from the carnage above, eating the carrion and each other, dying, themselves being eaten, while eggs spurted from mothers and fathers, eggs hatched, the young darted out in all directions to escape the eaters, some of whom were their own parents.

Dimly, through the murk, the outlines of a long-buried city advanced and receded, a shattered ziggurat topped by an altar and a leaning idol, a pillar, a broken arch, an upside down trireme ragged with living valves clinging to its hull, the hint of a huge and fearsome creature with burning eyes quivering in its hollow, the granite head of a massive statue up to its mouth in mud mixed with bones and shells, its long curving nose and fierce eyes stonily proclaiming terror, arrogance, and invincibility to an uncomprehending thing of a hundred skinny legs and a beak like a vulture's.

Another turn of the controls. Beneath the mud? He could not determine what it was. Something batlike and grinning.

He turned the controls back and moved the eye past the shore and into the jungle. Here was a strange creature which seemed to stretch for miles, which was, actually, a procession of beasts and birds sequentially advancing, progressing, and retrogressing from the crutch-creature that had achieved a total land life. It was many beings making a single being, flowing out from the other, branching, flowering, sometimes a branch curving back to enter the sea, a many-bodied, many-limbed, many-headed flow of flesh.

Ramstan reached out to turn the egg slightly, stopping his

fingertips short of it as if he feared that it might burn him or cling to his flesh and suck him into it. After a few seconds' hesitation, he felt it, and it was, as always, cool and smooth. But he could feel the squirm of life and the suddenness and soddenness of death and the tingling of tiny voltages of terror and pain and laughter and joy and triumph and despair.

So he sat, turning the ovoid, adjusting the microscope, tracing the slow spiral of sculpture.

Here was a city, proud and high-walled, about to be destroyed by barbarians from the mountains, a horde that had wandered for decades over desert and now coveted the milk and honey, the gold and the jewels, the furniture and the trinkets, the women and the herds.

Here was another city destroyed only by time. The rains had gone, the land had dried, the people had died or gone seeking a place where the soil was wet and black and thick and the skies were wet and cloudy. A jackalish beast crossed the wide street, now covered with sand, where victorious armies had once marched down its length, dragging captives behind chariots piled with loot while the citizens cheered and the band played loud martial music. Now the only sound was that of the wind through empty dusty rooms, the hoot of an owl, the hiss of a serpent. Beyond, the descendants of the refugees pushed their herds across vast steppes, headed toward a distant land of walled cities, many rivers, and easy pickings.

And here were rockets poised for the first manned leap to another planet, helmeted figures working around it.

And there was the first starship, and beyond it the first confrontation of explorers and natives.

And here was a sculpture which had puzzled Ramstan the first three times he had studied it. Now he understood that it was composed of symbolic figures representing the universe, or *a* universe, collapsing, every bit of matter from giant red stars to free hydrogen rushing back toward the point of origin. Beyond that was another easily interpreted figure: the single primal colossal star exploding. Beyond, stars forming. Beyond, planets. Beyond, the thick sea with life forming.

And here and here and here were figures that filmed his skin with cold. In the midst of the life and death of universes was a tiny, often-repeated, egg-shaped object. Always with it were three hooded figures.

Ramstan understood what their ubiquitous presence meant, or he thought he understood, but he could not believe it.

The river of birth and death and rebirth spiraled around the egg. But on its one end was a blank area. Either the sculptors had not lived long enough to complete their work or they had intentionally left it unfinished. If the latter, why?

The *glyfa* could tell him, but it was silent and had been for some time.

Ramstan had taken the *glyfa* out of the bulkhead-safe, moved it easily to the table since the a-g units on its ends reduced its 500-kilogram weight to five grams, and asked it to speak to him. But the voice was still.

Was it mute because it wanted him to study the thousands of sculpturings, to learn from them something that it could easily tell him but which he would believe only if he had taught himself? Or was it occupied with its own thoughts or with whatever went on under that impenetrable surface?

Though the *glyfa* had never hinted at it, Ramstan felt that the egg hid inside it a world as thickly populated as a dozen planets. Within that white compress was a seething, a ferment. Sometimes, he imaged a nest of jam-packed writhing and hissing snakes, sometimes a multitude of angels on pinpoints, sometimes snakes with angel wings.

More than once he envisioned a tiny sun hanging in the center of the hollow egg. It glared down upon the curving surface, a closed infinity of living sculptures a million times more intricate and extensive than those on the exterior. Through them wandered a tiny old man, creator of the egg-world, self-exiled, self-enclosed, nomadic and monadic.

Why did he see an old man there? Why not an old woman or a nonhuman male, female, hermaphrodite, or neuter?

Ramstan thought he knew why. The adult tended to use the mental images he'd lived with in childhood. He had been raised and educated in a Muslim sect which was orthodox enough except for its focus on the mysterious al-Khidhr. The Green One, talked of but not named in *Surat 18* of the *Qu' ran*.

But al-Khidhr had been a figure of Arabic folklore long before Muhammad became the voice of Allah. He was supposed by scholars to be, in fact, Elijah, the Hebrew prophet. Certainly, many identical tales were told of them, and they were often equated in the people's minds. Late twentieth-century scholarship, however, had indicated that the legends of al-Khidhr existed before Elijah had been born.

Ramstan didn't know the truth about the Green One nor did he care. When he was a child, he had believed that there truly was at least one immortal with magical powers. But, in his early adulthood, he had decided that al-Khidhr was only one of the legion of folklore figures, no more real than the Mullah Nasruddin, Paul Bunyan, or Sinbad the Sailor. He also became aware that the Khidhrites had incorporated many of the elements of that other mysterious person of Muslim legend, Loqman, with those of al-Khidhr.

Still, though his mind denied its verity, his emotions, connected to and powered by the child buried in him, were ready to evoke the image of the Green One when the proper stimulus touched him. Within him, as there seemed to be within the egg, an old man—Melchizedekean, pre-Muhammad, pre-Kaaba, pre-Mecca—wandered the lion-haunted, lion-yellow deserts, coeval with Ishmael, that "wild ass of a man," when Ishmael was a senile great-great-great-grandfather babbling of Ibrahim and Hagar and of the lover of his youth, the divine Ashdar. The adult Ramstan classified al-Khidhr as a myth, a symbolic figure, or an archetype fleshed only in dreams.

But there was that puzzling and disturbing encounter, if it was such, which he could not forget. . . .

He was a third-year cadet at the space academy at Sirius Point, Australian Department, and on this day, the star pitcher, he was in the ninth inning during a game against the University of Tokyo. The score was 6–6, and he had just struck out two men. Next up was Jimmy Ikeda, the best batter Tokyo had. Daishonin Smith had just stolen second. And then, while Ramstan was winding up to pitch the first ball at Ikeda, he had been stopped. A messenger from the commandant told him that he was wanted immediately in the commandant's office.

Ramstan had been furious, then he became frightened. Only a few minutes ago, the commandant had been in the first row in the section reserved for the higher officers. Now he was gone. And what terribly serious event had made him halt the game at this moment? Ramstan could think of only one thing. He was numb as, still in his player's uniform, he hurried to the commandant's office.

"Your father has died," the commandant said. A moment later, his mother's stricken face was on the phone and she was sobbing and telling him of the heart attack. His father had been rushed to the hospital, which was only half a kilometer down the corridor in the megabuilding. But his father had insisted that he be taken home, and he was now there in his own bed.

A half hour later, Ramstan was on the shuttle to New Babylon. Eighty minutes after embarking, he was on the twentieth level, which held the university and the staff residences. On opening the door to his parents' apartment, he found his entrance blocked by someone who was just leaving. He or she was tall, only half a head shorter than Ramstan. Under a green hood was the face of a centenarian, deeply wrinkled, the lips absent as if they had chewed themselves away on the hard edge of time. The nose was long and sharp, ground thin by a remorseless grindstone. The chin was bony; a few long hairs bristled from it. Under prominent brows were extraordinarily large eyes, set very far apart, their color indeterminable in the shadow of the hood. The body and legs were under a loose green robe from which protruded wrinkled spotted feet in sandals. Under one arm was a very large black book, the old-fashioned printed kind, a collector's item. The arm covered part of the large Arabic letters on the cover.

At any other time, Ramstan would have given the ancient in his or her long-outmoded clothes his full attention. But now, after the stranger had passed by, he strode into the apartment crowded with relatives and friends.

They were chanting the *Surat Ya-Sin* as he walked through them and into the bedroom where the gaunt eagle face of his father was still uncovered.

"When We sent to them two, and they denied them both, so We reinforced for a third, and they said: We are messengers to you.

"They said: You are only mortals like us. The Merciful has not sent down anything. You are lying!"

After the funeral, Ramstan asked his mother, "Who was that old man who left just as I entered?"

By then he had decided that the stranger was male.

"What old man?"

"He looked as if he must be a hundred years old. He was

dressed in a hooded green robe, and he carried a huge black book under one arm."

"I didn't see him," his mother had said. "But there were so many people there to mourn. He must have been a friend of your father's."

She gasped, and she held her hand to her mouth, her eyes very wide. "An old man in green robes and holding a black book! Al-Khidhr!"

"Don't be silly."

"He came to record your father's name in his book!"

"Nonsense!"

Ramstan had had to leave soon thereafter for the shuttle to Sirius Point. But the next evening his mother phoned him.

"Son, I asked everybody who'd been there when your father was dying, and nobody saw the old man in green carrying a large black book. *You* were the *only* one who saw him! Now do you believe that it was al-Khidhr? And since you alone saw him, it must be a sign! A good one, I hope!"

"It's a sign that you hope I'll return to the faith."

"But if you were the only one to see him!" she had wailed.

"Then it was my grief. When the father dies, the son becomes a child again, if only for a little while."

"No, it was al-Khidhr! Think about it, Hûd. Your faith isn't dead after all! Allah has given you another chance!"

Ramstan had never told his parents how he had seen an old man—the same?—bending over him when he was twelve and sick and had just awakened from a dream. The old man had been, of course, the tag-end of a fever-inspired hallucination. Thus, when he had been stricken with grief for his father, somewhere in his brain a switch had closed, and the old man of the sickbed dream had been imaged forth again in a circuit. That was all there was to it. Certainly, he was not going to say anything about him at the academy. If the authorities heard about it, they would suspect mental instability. Even if he were then run through another battery of PS tests and still came out with a high score, he'd not even be an alaraf-ship crewmember, let alone be an officer.

At that time, the first alaraf ship was not yet built, but it was known that she would be and that more were planned. Ramstan was fiercely determined to be an officer on one and then, someday, the captain.

He had achieved his ambition, and he had, in effect, then thrown it away.

"Was it worth it?" he said out loud, though it wasn't necessary to speak to be heard.

There was no answer.

"Speak, damn you!" he cried, and he struck the egg with a fist. He yelped with pain. The egg was as hard and unyielding as Death itself.

He heard a chuckle—or thought he heard it. Was that himself laughing at himself? Had he been talking to himself? He did not think so when the *glyfa* spoke or when he thought it was speaking. But, when it was silent, he wondered if he talked for both himself and it.

When a man thought that he might be splitting in two, and that man was responsible for the lives of four hundred men and women, he should turn over his command and commit himself to the care of the chief medical officer. But if Ramstan did, he could no longer conceal the *glyfa*. No, he would *not* give it up. He could not let Benagur take command. Benagur would search the ex-captain's quarters and would find the *glyfa*. But perhaps Benagur, like Ramstan, would keep silent, knowing that once the others learned about it, they would lock it away or study it. Then Benagur would also be denied possession of the *glyfa*—or vice versa.

The silence undulated from the egg, curved back from the overhead, deck, and bulkheads, and thickened like abyssal waters around a bathysphere.

"I speak!"

Ramstan started, his heart beating as if struck by a fist.

When the *glyfa* had spoken to him while he was carrying it from the Tolt temple, it had used his father's voice. Now, Ramstan heard his mother's voice. And, like his father's, it spoke in his familial New Babylonish, basically a creolized Arabic but with at least half of its vocabulary borrowed from Chinese or Terrish.

Ramstan said, "It's time . . . far past time . . . that you did speak."

"Immortality," his mother's voice said. "I offered it, but you neither accepted nor rejected it."

"Two forms of immortality," Ramstan said. "A choice of one of two. One of which is not true immortality. I may live for billions of years, but I will eventually age, though very slowly. And I will eventually die of old age. Though, probably, I'll die long before that. In such a long lifespan, accident, homicide, or suicide will put an end to me. The statistical distribution of events will ensure that.

"As for the other form, it's also probably not a true immortality. I can live forever—*you* say—as a magnetically shaped complex of neural waves existing inside you. Which means that I'll be under your control. . . ."

"No! I promised you that you may live as you wish. Any and all of your fantasies will be fully realized—forever."

"How do I know that your word is good? Once I'm in your power . . ."

"What would I gain by betraying you?"

"How would I know that until it was too late for me to do anything about it?"

After a long silence, Ramstan said, "Has it occurred to you that I might not be interested in living forever or even beyond my natural lifespan?"

Silence.

Ramstan broke it. "Somehow, you stimulated in me an overpowering desire to steal you from the Tenolt. I became a criminal. I abandoned my duty, betrayed my trust, lost my honor. Threw away everything I've worked so hard to get as if it were rusty old armor. How did you get me to do that?

"Was it because there was in me a criminal impulse, however slight, and you detected it and amplified it until I couldn't resist it? The impulse which should have died became an obsession because you brought it from a dying flicker to a roaring blaze?

"But, if you could do that, why can't you overpower me to the point where I agree to do what you want me to do in return for immortality? Is it because you did not detect that, unlike most people, I have no desire to live forever? That I want something else?

"Or don't you care whether or not I want immortality? You can and you have manipulated me enough to use me as your agent, and that's all you're concerned about. You've succeeded so far, *glyfa,* but you've gone as far as you can with me. My back is up. I won't do anything more for you unless I know what your goal is and maybe not then. What do you want me for? What do you *want*?"

"What do *you* want?" his mother's voice said.

Minutes of silence passed. He would not reply because he had no answer to that question, and the *glyfa* was done with this conversation. But not with him.

4

MASKED, CARRYING SOME CLOTHES and the *glyfa* in a small suitcase, Ramstan left *al-Buraq*. He had hesitated a long time before he had decided to take the *glyfa* with him to the hotel. Perhaps it was not too late to return it to its worshipers. He was sure that the Tenolt would see him leave ship, and they would quickly find out that he had checked into the hotel. They would approach him, carefully, of course. They would have to do that since there were many Earthpeople staying in the hotel during shore leave. Or would they? They were fanatics, and they wanted their god back. But they did not know that he had the *glyfa* with him. They could, however, seize him or try to do so and hold him as hostage until the *glyfa* was returned to them.

He did not know what they would do. All he did know was that, at this moment, he felt as if he would gladly be rid of the *glyfa*. And if he could somehow negotiate its return and also keep his people from knowing what he had done, he would never again, never, forget his duty.

Did he really believe that? He did not know.

When near the hotel, he passed Warrant Officer Deva Kolkoshki. She saluted him despite his order not to do so outside ship during leave. She was defying him subtly or perhaps not so subtly. In some way which she probably could not define, she was showing her hatred for him.

He passed her, and his back rippled with cold. Daggers of ice seemed to pierce his heart and genitals. Deva was very passionate, and Ramstan felt sure that only her basic stability and morality and years of naval discipline kept her from thrusting a knife into him. Perhaps he was wrong. Just because she was Siberian and her culture was as violent as the Americans' had been was no reason to assume that she had to suppress a desire to stab him. He might be projecting his feelings of guilt upon her.

No. He felt no guilt. Why should he? He had had an affair with her, as he had with twenty or so of the women of *al-Buraq*. Then she, like so many others, had accused him of not loving her, of not even thinking of her when they were making love. His mind, she had said, was on something else. What was it? What was he thinking about when he should have been entirely enfolded with her, become one with her? Whatever it was, it offended her and made her feel more like a thing than a human being.

Ramstan had not been able to explain. But all his affairs ended in this manner, though not all the women seemed to hate him as intensely as Deva did.

That was the trouble with the sensitivity techniques and raising of consciousness disciplines that were part of the education of all Earthpeople. He sometimes wished that his century had the same casual attitude towards affairs that twentieth-century people were supposed to have had. The trouble with his own time was that love was force-fed to the citizens. Not all gavaged geese kept the food down and grew fat. Some vomited it up.

Thinking thus, he went up the broad stone steps of the hotel, walked across the big portico, and went through two rooms, each with heavy, thick doors that shut automatically behind him. These would not open if another person wished to enter a few seconds after him or if somebody else was already in one of them. Again, he went through the spore-killing process.

Passing through a wide oval portal, he entered the lobby. The floor was of polished chrysanthemum-white and poppy-red stone. Pillars with curved flutings jetted up into the shadows of the ceiling. Beyond the stone forest, against the far wall, was the sea-green desk of the clerk. His name was Biza!a, and he was the only other person visible. Ramstan removed his mask, but the clerk, recognizing him under it, had Ramstan's keys ready. He had been notified by a crewmember that Ramstan wanted a room.

Biza!a smiled, but he managed to convey a shadowy dislike as he handed the keys to Ramstan.

The dislike was for the keys, not Ramstan. Until the first space visitors, the Urzint, had landed, keys were unused on the planet. Biza!a had to perform a ritual cleansing at the end of each shift because of his contact with these.

Ramstan looked around the empty lobby. Most of the chairs were monstrously huge and sprawling and had some unfunctional grooves in the arms. Unfunctional for humans, anyway. They had not been built for any beings now lodged here. Like most of the other furniture and furnishings of the hotel, they had been constructed for the Urzint. Six of their ships had used this field for a long time. Then, one day, they had failed to show up as scheduled, although they had promised that they would be using the field for millennia to come. Why had they disappeared?

Ramstan walked up the broad, curving ramp to the third floor—there were no elevators—and quietly unlocked the door to his room. He pushed it inward swiftly, leaped into the room and looked around quickly. It was empty and still. The sunlight slanted through the single enormous window onto the gigantic bed. The bathroom, so large that he would not have complained if it had been the bedroom, was empty. A movable platform of glistening yellow hardwood stood before the washbowl, which he used as a bathtub. There was another platform with steps before the toilet bowl, the top of which was a contraption of yellow hardwood. The Kalafalans had made various adjustments for the smaller size of the recent guests. However, if those for whom this hotel was built should return, they would find everything ready for them.

Ramstan set the electronic traps on the suitcase and put it inside the cavernous closet. After locking its door, he went into the hall and locked the door to his room. Returning to the lobby, he asked Biza!a if any new guests had registered in the last twenty-four hours.

"Six Tenolt."

"No one else? An Earthwoman, perhaps?"

"Ah! She did not register, though she had intended to. She inquired about you, and I said you were in town. She left immediately afterward."

"For my ship or for town?"

"She did not say. There is, of course, the possibility that she had a third destination. Or none at all."

Bizala was correct, but Ramstan was nevertheless annoyed. These Kalafalans! They spent so much time in considering all possible methods and avenues of action, they seldom accomplished anything. However, as Toyce had pointed out, they seemed as happy as Terrans or any species they had met so far. Progress in science and technology was not necessarily the index of a high civilization.

Ramstan walked back to his room briskly. His bootsteps sounded hollowly in the vast untenanted lobby, staircase, and corridor. Before arriving at his room, he spoke into the back of his hand. "Alif Rho Gimel. Come in, Hermes. Have any strangers contacted you since I last talked to you? Any other news to report?"

"Hermes, here. Negative to both inquiries."

"Anything to report on Dogfaces?"

"GL reports contact with four where the action is. Negative animus." (*Translation:* Our men on ground leave in town contacted four Tenolt, and they didn't seem unfriendly.)

"Did Dogfaces inquire about me?"

"Positive."

"Were Dogfaces looking for me?"

"Not specifically, Alif Rho Gimel. They did ask if you were in town."

"What did GL say?"

"They said they didn't know."

"Alif Rho Gimel out."

Although it was not suppertime, he took his meal from the suitcase. He had meant to remove it before setting the traps but had been too occupied with more important matters. He unset the traps by playing a beam of canceling frequencies from his pocket pseudo-pen over the case. After taking the package out, he reset the traps. Cooking the meal took three seconds after he set the dial on the bottom of the package. He ate without much appetite. He did not dare to order wine sent up. A little drug in it would put him out of the way while the Tenolt went through the suitcase. He did not really believe that they would use poison, since they had the best of reasons for wanting to keep him alive. At this time, anyway.

However, there were other forces operating in the shadows, and what their wants and wishes were he could not know. His death might be one of them.

He dumped the cups and dishes into the toilet, where they dissolved within ten seconds. He returned to the chair and moved its huge body on its six wheels so that he could see the sunset. He sighed with delight at the beauty. There were magnificent sunsets on Earth, on Tolt, on Raushghol, but Kalafala's paled them. Dust from volcanoes on the northern and western fringes of the continent supplied colors, but this alone was not responsible for the high beauty.

Golden stars, tiny and bobbing, drifting from west to east, were, in actuality, far-off boxkite things, dancing lenses for the sun. A pinkish cloud drifted upward, putting out reddish fingers, greenish heads, silvery shoulders, orange-and-emerald-green-streaked ragged eyes, serrated buttons of yellow turquoise, misshapen mouths with carmine lips, and broken irregular teeth of velvet-black and flamingo-pink.

Briefly, a comet the color of cigarette smoke formed against a sky banded with decaying sine waves of pale violet, blood-red, and carrot-yellow. It rose, head downward, tail spreading out until the colors faded, as if washed out by God, and the comet had collided with an ephemeral sun of amethyst-green and both had died.

Twelve kilometers to the west, millions of varicolored diaphanous-winged insects were leaving their feeding grounds to fly to the great spindle-shaped communal nests in which they slept, safe from the crepuscular and nocturnal birds and flying animals. But the preyers were harrying and eating now. Although they were not visible at this distance, they were causing the momentary formations. The beauty of the sunset was a byproduct of hunger, terror, and death.

Then the sun slipped its moorings to the horizon; the sky became black. It was unclouded but starless. Kalafala was on the edge of the universe, and, when on this side of its sun, the night sky was empty.

BOOOONG! One hundred thousand bronze gongs struck

once to weld into a single clang. In the yards of the houses on the plateau and in the city in the valley, Kalafalans hammered the household gongs to announce the departure of the sun. The single note rose like a bronze bird, the beat of its wings shaking the hotel and rattling the windows.

Torches flared in the spaceport town; thousands of torches would be lit in the unseen city in the valley. A drawn-out, shuddering cry wailed at the window, and the torches danced toward the temple to the northwest of the hotel. Ramstan felt a twinge of longing for Earth. The cry reminded him of the evening call of the *muezzins* from the loudspeakers in his level of New Babylon. Though he had peeled off belief in Allah or in any gods as if it were a coat on a hot day, he still responded at times to the Pavlovian bell: his emotions salivated. A cry like a *muezzin*'s became an angel's hand squeezing the heart, a piezolelectric flexing.

There was still light in the upper sky. The field was dark except for the now-yellow pulsing of *al-Buraq* and white lights from two open ports in the Tolt ship. Figures appeared in one, cutting off most of the beam, and then the Tenolt had become one with the shadows.

He rose from the chair and walked around in the darkness until his muscles were no longer stiff. Returning to the chair he sat for a long time, his eyes on the dark-and-white vista beyond the window. He shifted uneasily. He should return to ship, but he was not going to. By staying here, he might entice those who lusted after the thing in the box in the suitcase to try to get it now.

He waited for an hour and then moved the chair away from the window to the blackness of a wall. He placed two olson beamguns in the grooves on the arm of the chair and sat down. Now and then, he heard little creaks and slitherings he could not identify but which did not alarm him. The interplay of the pull of the sun and moons, shifting temperatures and humidities, and settling of the ground stretched and squeezed the hotel as if it were an accordion. He ignored the tiny sounds and waited for the click of metal in the lock and the cautious turning of the knob.

And then, as time and night hobbled by, he had a fantasy. What if the key were inserted, not in the little lock at his waist-level but in the huge lock at the level of his head? What if the ponderous door swung open, and a turret-headed, neckless, bone-ruffed, triangular-bodied and column-legged Urzint was silhouetted by the hall lights? And the ancient guest clomped in with steps as heavy as a rhinoceros's straight to the closet, opened the suitcase, put on the tepee-sized nightgown, and went straight to bed with never a word to its little roommate? What then?

He was in a dark woods and running desperately but slowly and heavily, the air thick against him, while a dark, unseen, unnamed thing loped behind him. The thing snuffled. Ramstan tried to howl with terror, but he could force nothing through his throat, which had turned to stone. Then he put his hand in his pocket, and he drew out a small comb. This he threw behind him, knowing that the stiff teeth of the comb would become a thickly tangled forest of trees. His pursuer bellowed with frustration. The crash of its body as it hurled against the great trees and interwoven branches of underbrush was like the toppling of a mountain.

Presently, the thing was breathing raspingly behind him. He reached into his pocket and drew out a small mirror and threw that behind him. There was another bellow of frustration and rage and a splash as of the toppling of the face of a glacier into the sea. Ramstan drove on against the heavy air. He was on a flat plain, hard dirt with no vegetation, and the air was becoming even grayer. Then there was the slap of wet paws on the plain, and the breathing was once more behind him. Ramstan pulled from his pocket his third and last gift—from whom?—a whetstone, and he threw this behind him. Though he did not look back, he knew that this had turned into a high mountain range. The thing's bellow reached him as a faint sound, but he heard its claws digging into the stone slopes and its labored breathings as it pulled itself up and up. And then, as he sped on, he heard its howl of triumph as it topped the highest peak and began to slide down the other side.

Moaning, sweating, Ramstan awoke. Near the door, against the wall, a wavering figure stood. It was in a dark robe, its face shrouded by a hood. The face was as pale as moonlight and gave the impression of being that of a very old man or woman. It was either human or remarkably humanoid.

Ramstan blinked, and the figure shimmered and then was gone.

It was the glowing tag-end of his dream, appearing just as he awoke, and he had seen it as an afterimage. Al-Khidhr, the Green Man? It had been pointing at the lock. He rose, and, automatically picking up an olson from a chair arm, walked swiftly toward the door. He saw the ghostly tube projecting through the keyhole, stopped breathing, turned, and ran to the window. He started to turn its lock, which kept the two sections tight against the outside air, when he remembered the mask. Still not breathing, he groped around in the seat of the chair until he found it and then put it on. Only then did he swing the two sections of the window open, and, leaning far out, breathed deeply.

When his lungs were full, he ran back to the tube. The slight hissing from the open end of the tube had told him it was not an olson but a gas-expeller. It would not do to fuse the tube-end with a blast from the olson. The gas might be explosive.

Ramstan went back to the window and leaned out of it backwards, his eyes on the tube. Presently, the tube was withdrawn. There was a series of clickings as a tool was worked on the lock. He crouched behind the chair. As the door started to swing open, he put his back against the wall, drew up one leg, and shoved the gigantic chair with it. The chair sped toward the doorway on its six wheels, making only a slight squeaking. The door swung open. The chair rammed into the figure momentarily silhouetted in the light. The figure crumbled and went over backward under the impact of the chair.

Ramstan had run, crouching, a few feet behind and to one side of the chair, his olson ready. He stuck his head out of the doorway, ready to yank it back. But he saw nothing threatening in the hall. An arm with a human hand extended along the floor from behind the massive bulk of the chair.

Ramstan duckwalked around the side of the chair, moving quietly. The man on the floor might have an olson in his hidden hand. But that, too, was open and still, and he was looking into the red-streaked and glazed eyes of Benagur.

5

BENAGUR'S HEAD was massive. His hair was as black and as coarse as a bear's and fell past his shoulders. His beard was long and square-cut. His face looked like the half-mad, half-divine face of a stone-winged bull-man in front of an ancient Assyrian temple.

Benagur groaned and rolled over on his right side. The back of his head was bloodied. On the floor by the chair, attached to a plastic cylinder, was the tube which had been shoved through the massive keyhole.

Ramstan helped the commodore to his feet but released him when he growled, "I'm O.K."

Ramstan shoved the chair back into the room and turned the lights on. Benagur staggered in and sat down on an inflatable chair. Ramstan brought in the tube and cylinder and locked the door. "What happened, Benagur?"

"When I came down the hall I saw two cloaked, masked, and gloved persons at your door. They looked up and saw me . . ."

"You didn't shout?"

"Yes. Didn't you hear me?"

"No. The walls and the door are too thick."

"The two ran away down the hall from me. One dropped the

cylinder or whatever it was. They didn't run exactly as humans do . . ."

"Tenolt?"

"I don't know. I started to push on the door, and that's the last I remember until I woke up on the floor. My head hurts."

"There must have been a third. Maybe he was behind the door of the room across the hall. He stepped out and hit you on the back of your head. You regained some consciousness, got to your feet, and then I came through with the chair. It knocked you down again."

Ramstan remembered that he had left the window open. Swearing, he shut it. His own mask was still on, but Benagur had breathed in the spores. He would begin to feel the effect of the psychedelics in about three to four hours. It would be eight to ten days before his body would get rid of them.

Ramstan shut the door to stop the flow of breeze-borne spores from entering the corridor.

"When you get back to ship, Benagur, report to sickbay."

"No! I won't be hospitalized again! I just got out! There's too much . . ."

"Too much what?"

"Too much going on. The Tenolt, everything . . . Why would they want to gas you?"

Ramstan said, "I doubt we'll ever find out. What I want to know right now is why you came here."

"Shouldn't you call for the sanitizers?" Benagur said.

Ramstan didn't like being told that he should do so. But Benagur was right. He called ship and was put through to Chief Petty Officer Wang. She said that she and a squad would be up in five minutes. Ramstan ordered her to bring along a medic and a squad of marines.

Ramstan looked hard at Benagur, who was still on the inflatable.

"I'll ask you again. Why did you come here?"

Benagur straightened, and he winced.

"I wanted to have it out with you."

"Yes?"

"You know why," Benagur said loudly.

"You tell me," Ramstan said softly.

"I want to hear your explanations, privately, before I take action. That is, if I have to do it. I hope I don't have to."

"I don't know what you're talking about," Ramstan said. "You sound as if you're going to make charges against me. Is that it?"

"Why did you order the marines? So you can put me under arrest?"

"You keep sidling away from my questions. I decided that you should be escorted to sickbay. There's no telling how fast the spores may affect you. You might even . . ."

"What?"

"Become violent. It's for your own good."

"Sure it is!" Benagur cried. "Of course! Listen! I've been very much disturbed—and puzzled—by your strange behavior on Tolt. You were missing for some time from ship. Suddenly, there you were, like a thief in the night, carrying that bag and shouting that the ship must take off at once. And you've never given a word of explanation. No one has dared to ask you what was in it. But, believe me, everybody has been talking about it. And I've not had one good night's sleep."

" 'Like a thief in the night,' " Ramstan said. "Well, out with it, man! Exactly what do you suspect?"

His face was expressionless, but his heart was thumping like an imprisoned animal trying to butt its way through a wall, and he was sweating.

"I don't want to do this, Captain! That's why I came here, so we could talk alone and solve this matter without the crew knowing about it. Maybe it's not too late to rectify matters. Maybe we could go back to Tolt and just leave it there and take off, hoping the Tenolt would be so happy to have it back that they wouldn't bother us."

"What is *it?*" Ramstan said.

Benagur's face was red now. He shook as if his bones were crumbling. Ramstan had seen him angry before, but he had never seen him fearful. Or was he reading him wrong? Was it fury possessing him?

"It, it!" Benagur shouted. "You know what it is! The *glyfa!* The *glyfa!* The Tolt idol!"

"You're accusing me of having stolen the *glyfa?*" Ramstan said. He was surprised at the steadiness of his voice.

"I'm not accusing you!" Benagur said. "I'm telling you what you and I know!"

"I wonder if you haven't accidentally breathed in some

spores before tonight. There's no other way to account for this crazy accusation."

Benagur ground his teeth. He stood up, swaying, and took three steps toward Ramstan. His huge hands were closed, but he did not raise them. His voice was clotted with phlegm.

"What I'm telling you to your face is what the whole crew is saying behind your back."

"I don't know why the Tenolt are here," Ramstan said. "Listen. Has it occurred to you and those other idiots that I might be on a secret government mission and that your idle curiosity is endangering it?"

He trembled. For the first time in forty-two years, he had lied. Al-Khidhr forgive him. Allah forgive him.

Nonsense. Neither existed except as concepts. But concepts were as real, as alive, as the person who thought they were real and alive.

"May God forgive you," Benagur said.

"May He forgive us all," Ramstan said, but he did not know what he meant by that.

Benagur closed his eyes and moved his lips soundlessly. He was either praying or using mental techniques to locate the injured cells on the back of his head and then to summon the healing forces of his body. Perhaps he was doing both.

Ramstan, hands locked behind his back, paced back and forth. When he passed the ceiling-high mirror made to reflect behemoths, he saw a hunting falcon whose hood had slipped onto the beak. His eyes were wide and shot with madness and desperation. He must regain his composure or at least the appearance of it. Otherwise, when the marines came to pick up Benagur, they might think that he, too, had breathed in the spores.

A knock on the door. Ramstan used his skinceiver to make sure that it was the ship's crew outside the door. He admitted Lieutenant Malia Fu'a, a biochemistry officer, Chief Petty Officer Wang, and the PD and marine squads. Fu'a was a pretty Samoan who'd parted with Ramstan on good terms after she'd left his bed. She was the only ex-lover who didn't seem to hate him. But she *could* be an excellent actress.

The marines were instructed to take Benagur to ship's hospital after he'd been externally disinfected. Fu'a's squad sprayed his rooms and the hall with a liquid which smelled like new lavender. Ramstan stripped and showered while his clothes were sprayed. He put on pajamas and lit up a cigar while the squad ran a scanner over the room and the hall. The little pistol-shaped device flashed a red light now and then, and the infected spots were then resprayed. By then, the liquid had dried, but the lavender odor hung in the air.

Benagur had not spoken during the entire proceeding. When told by a marine that he must come along now, *sir*, he walked out without a look behind. Fu'a, the last to leave, carried the gas-expeller in a plastic bag. Its contents would be analyzed before morning.

Ramstan explained that unknown persons had tried to shoot the gas into his room and that Benagur had chased them away but had been hit on the head. He said nothing about conducting an investigation later. Though Fu'a had looked curious, she had not, of course, asked him questions. And all the party had been ordered not to say a word to anyone else about the affair.

It would have been wise to station a guard at his door, but Ramstan did not think that the Tenolt—he was sure they were Tenolt—would be back.

A few minutes later, just as he was about to fall asleep despite resonating nerves, he heard a banging on his door. He picked up the olsons, rolled out of bed, and walked to the door.

He spoke through the keyhole in Urzint and then in Terrish. "Who is it?"

A woman's voice, speaking Terrish, came thinly. "Lieutenant Branwen Davis of *Pegasus*, sir. I *must* speak to you. May I come in?"

She spoke with a lilt that seemed . . . what? . . . Irish?

He looked through the keyhole, straightened up, unlocked the door, and backed away. The door swung open, and a very beautiful woman entered.

6

SHE WAS APPROXIMATELY two meters tall, a little over average female height. Her black, coarse, and straight hair was in a pageboy bob. Her eyebrows were thick and dark. The wide-spaced, slanting eyes were large and as green as the Persian Gulf. Her skin was a soft golden-brown. The facial skin below the eyes was paler than that above. The contrast gave her features an almost clownlike appearance.

Al-Buraq's crew, when on Kalafala, wore green masks in the corner of which was a silver-winged mule with a woman's face. The scarlet mask that hung around her neck was the regulation color used by *Pegasus*'s crew. In its lower right-hand corner was a silver-winged horse.

She wore a shimmering light-green dress, knee-length, flaring out at the waist. The sleeves came to the elbow, and the V-neck was wide and plunging. He did not need her to tell him that she had gotten it from a Kalafalan. Her legs and feet were bare and dirty. She carried a small leather bag in her left hand. Her right hand was heavily bandaged.

She put the bag down and saluted. His return salute was sloppy, resembling a gesture for her to go away.

"You look tired, Davis. You must've had a long hard

journey. Sit down before you fall down. Before you report, would you like a drink?"

She smiled, showing beautiful white teeth. Sighing, she dropped onto the inflatable chair as if her legs had given up the ghost.

"I'd love a drink, thank you."

He gestured at the bar, installed by the hotel for its smaller and more recent guests. "There's plenty of native liquor there. But I have a bottle of Scotch in my case."

"Scotch will more than do."

"On the rocks?"

"Rocks? Oh, you mean . . . It's been so long. I mean . . . I've been talking Urzint so long that I forgot . . . Yes, Scotch on the rocks."

He asked her when she had discovered that *al-Buraq* was in port. She said that she'd found out a few minutes ago. She'd returned to the hotel, gotten a room and had fallen asleep at once, hadn't even bothered to wash. But she'd awakened about fifteen minutes later and had seen some Earthpeople on the street through her window. She'd gone downstairs at once, and the clerk had told her that Captain Ramstan was in his room. She'd come up at once.

He handed her the drink and sipped on his *Djinn's* Delight. Then he said, "So what happened?"

"I'm a marine biologist. I was left behind, at my request, to continue experiments at a Kalafalan station on the northwest coast. When it was close to the time for *Pegasus* to return from the Raushghol system, I packed up, said good-bye to my Kalafalan scientist and technician friends, and drove off in my jeep. It's a-g generator malfunctioned about a thousand kilometers north of here. The jeep fell, but fortunately it was only two meters above the ground. Unfortunately, it was on the edge of a cliff. It went into the sea. I jumped out when it struck but almost went over the edge, too.

"I tore up the skin on my hand, enough to put my skinceiver out of operation. My NI transceiver went with the jeep, and so I couldn't call the spaceport. Also, I lost my TR box. I also lost my clothes. I like to sunbathe, and so I was nude when the accident happened. I borrowed a dress from a farm woman and started walking. After a week, I came to the Kurodan River. I got passage on a fishing vessel which was returning to the capital. And here I am."

"Pegasus hasn't returned," he said. "She was supposed to rendezvous with *al-Buraq* at Sigdrauf. We waited a month for her. Then we went to Tolt, her stop before going on to Sigdrauf. She had not showed there."

She was pale, and her voice was very low.

"What do you think . . . ?"

"I don't know. We can only assume that *Pegasus* is lost or has been delayed for some reason. Perhaps she is having or had biochemical troubles, and she may be on any of a hundred planets. In any event, *al-Buraq* isn't staying here long. You will transfer to my command. What were your shipboard duties?"

"Only those concerned with the biology laboratory."

"It's only routine and ridiculous in these circumstances," he said. "But regulations require that your I.D. be checked."

He lifted up her left hand with his. With his right hand he pulled from his jacket pocket a round piece of glasslike material rimmed with metal. Holding it over his right eye, he looked through it at the hand. He could see the pale violet symbols invisible to the naked eye.

"Branwen Sacajawea Davis," he read aloud.

Born A.D. 2238/1616 A.H. in the Cymric division of the Northwest European Department.

He looked down at the upturned, dark, lovely face. Her green eyes were wide and bright. Too bright.

He dropped her hand and said, "I'll send for a guard to conduct you to ship. By the way, your hand feels very warm. Do you have a fever?"

"I feel a little feverish. But I didn't, as far as I know, come into contact with any sick native. Of course, you never know."

He phoned ship via his skinceiver. After he'd signed off, he said, "You realize you'll be court-martialed?"

Davis paled but said nothing.

"It's just more routine. Any time loss of naval property is involved, a court martial is automatic. I'm sure that you weren't negligent. Don't worry about it."

A few minutes later, the marines appeared. Davis picked up her bag, saluted him, and marched off. Ramstan watched the long, slim legs and swaying hips, and he sighed. He went up a movable staircase and crawled into a bed half the size of a basketball court.

Halfway through a dream about some shadowy sinister whispering thing, he awoke. His door was shaking under furious knocks, and the skinceiver was shrilling. He put his wrist near his mouth and said, sleepily, "Alif Rho Gimel. What is it, Hermes?"

"CL Waw reported in with an urgent message. She wants to speak to you."

"I think she's here," Ramstan said. "Hold a minute."

He rolled out of bed and dropped off without using the staircase. He looked through the keyhole and unlocked the door. Toyce reeled in, causing Ramstan for a moment to think that she was hurt. But she was only near-falling-down stoned.

"CL Waw's here," Ramstan said. "Out, Hermes."

Toyce fell into the chair that Davis had used. "I need a drink, Hûd."

"Of water," Ramstan said. "What's the trouble?"

"You know that barmaid I was interested in. Well, she told me the Tenolt had come into her place. They were asking about you and getting, as usual, indirect answers to direct questions. Thima, that's the barmaid, said one of the Tenolt was either drunk or about to have a nervous breakdown. He suddenly started babbling about the *Klakgokl*, and . . ."

"The *Klakgokl?*"

"Yeah. It's some kind of monster in Tolt eschatology. It will appear near the end of time and wreck the world, eat up all life. That sort of nonsense. Anyway, he hadn't spoken more than a few sentences about it when his companions dragged him away. The barmaid knows some of their lingo, just enough to understand that something terrible had happened on Tolt. She also caught some references to you when the Tolt was carried off screaming. She didn't know what was said exactly. But she got the impression that the crazy Tolt was swearing vengeance."

"Anything else?"

"No. But whatever it was, it played hell with my plans for Thima. I had to bring you the news, whatever it means."

Ramstan spoke quickly but calmly into the skinceiver.

"Alif Rho Gimel. Come in, Hermes."

"Hermes here."

"Burning Troy! Repeat, Burning Troy!"

There was a pause, and then Hermes said, "Acknowledge! Burning Troy, sir!"

Before they got to ship, Ramstan received a report from the chemical laboratory. The traces of the gas in the expeller had been analyzed. Even in the quantity contained in the cylinder, the gas would not have done more than put him to sleep for several hours.

7

AL-BURAQ HAD LOST her starfish-shape and bright-red glow. She was a cylinder, flat on the underside, emitting yellow pulses. Flashes of light revealed spacers entering many ports.

By the time Ramstan was on the bridge, all posts had reported in, the drunk and drugged were in the various sickbays, and the general-alert alarm was turned off. The crescent-shaped bridge pulsed whitely from its spongy deck and those bulkhead areas not having indicator/control plates. The six commissioned officers and seven warrant officers were seated in their chairs. Ramstan took his chair in the center of the crescent. The chair was, like the others, a pseudopod of the deck, extended by the ship, shaped to fit him as near perfectly as possible.

On Ramstan's right was Lieutenant-Commodore (acting full commodore) Jimmy Tenno. On his left was Commander Erica Hannay. Five meters before them, the IC panel curved up to a height of 2.8 meters. Thirteen black-lined circles, extending from the deck to the ceiling, filled the panel. A CO and WO sat before one.

"All secure?" Ramstan said.

An octagonal in the lower left-hand part of the circle directly before him flashed *yellow-yellow-yellow*.

"Drive ready?"

Two tiny arrows flashed, one *green-green-green* and one *scarlet-scarlet-scarlet*.

"Alaraf drive on," Ramstan said.

The green light ceased pulsing.

"Activate Reverse Jump Number One—RJN1."

There was no motion, nothing to indicate that the vessel had left Kalafala behind at a distance of googolplex parsecs and perhaps at a distance of googolplex millennia.

The scarlet light ceased.

"EV and coordinates."

The circle became black, and Ramstan was looking into space. Stars flamed white, red, orange, green, blue, yellow, violet. A spiral galaxy, seen from "above," was a dying albino octopus that had been wounded by a shotgun loaded with jewels.

The scanners traveled across the circle, and the octopus drifted out of view on the right side. More stars, a giant red sun, not more than three light-years away, traveled across a nebula bright as a movie screen. The upper edges of the gas cloud formed the ragged silhouette of a crouching and grinning wolf.

Ramstan did not need the pulsing yellow letters that appeared near the bottom of the circle to know where he was. There had never been any doubt anyway.

"EV off. M-GD, Walisk window," Ramstan said.

The view faded. The scarlet arrow came to life, pulsed, and would continue to pulse until Ramstan ordered it to stop.

Ramstan looked to both sides and caught a few officers looking at him expectantly. He frowned, causing them to look straight ahead. All in the bridge, everybody in ship, in fact, obviously hoped to hear an explanation for their sudden departure. He did not have to give one, and he would just as soon not. If they were not informed, however, they would resent it, and good morale would boil away. He would have to tell them something. Fortunately, Branwen Davis and Toyce had given him enough to shape a half-truth.

He sat brooding while the silence in the bridge stretched like a wire between two winches. There would be no breaking point because no one would dare to ask him when he would give the order to resume normal operations. Nor would any voice the question clogging their throats and making some cough nervously.

Suddenly, he stood up. Erica Hannay sighed. Tenno, his dark-brown face oily with sweat, grinned, showing blocklike white teeth. Chief Warrant Officer Vilkas, at the far left, began coughing violently.

Ramstan waited until Vilkas had regained control. He said, loudly, "All posts stand by for an announcement."

His voice boomed out from the panel, was booming out throughout the ship. Three clangs of a bell and a short whistle followed.

"You're all wondering why I issued the Burning Troy," he said. He had turned by then and was looking at the officers. Most just continued to stare at him, but a few nodded.

"Before I tell you why I ordered the ship to leave Kalafala, I must remind you of one thing. That is, we are primarily a scientific survey expedition. Though *al-Buraq* is a ship of the line, we use our weapons only in self-defense. And then only when no other action is open to us. As you all know, I have been ordered to avoid military conflict even if *honor* is involved.

"Until today, we have confronted no sentients with overt hostile intentions. But the sudden appearance of the Tolt ship, her unorthodox approach, using Kalafala as a shield to avoid our detection equipment, a maneuver which required enormous energy, and her recklessness in flying in at treetop level and literally dropping into the spaceport, are strange actions."

Ramstan knew what they were thinking. Why then did you not call a Burning Troy immediately? Why did you go to your quarters at the hotel instead? And what about our precipitate departure from Tolt?

"Though the actions of the Tenolt were suspicious," he said, "I did not believe that they implied attack. If they had wished to attack us, they could have caught us wide open, unprepared, when they appeared at the port. Yet they made not the slightest move toward us. I judged that the Tenolt intended no overtly hostile moves.

"On the other hand, it was evident that they were up to something. I have no idea what that is. But it might derive from the incident which took place during our brief stay on Tolt."

That widened the eyes of those on the bridge.

"As you know, Benagur, Maija Nuoli, and I were the only personnel invited by the Tolt religious authorities to the *anuglyfa* ceremonies. That the captain and the second-in-command would be invited was expected, but it was a mystery why other officers were skipped and a lieutenant invited. I made some delicate inquiries of the Tolt high priest—I had to be sure not to offend any religious prejudices—and he replied that the *glyfa* itself had asked that we three be honored. Our rank had nothing to do with it. He would add nothing further except that we three must have the required *sensitivity*. I asked him what that meant, but he did not answer.

"And so we three were conducted with an honor guard into the holy of holies, a large room constructed of ivory and lacking ornamentation or paint. The only furniture was an altar in the middle of the room, a nine-cornered block of solid ivory high as my waist—it was taken from the tooth of an extinct beast—and on the altar was a diamond. It was twice as big as my head, and on top of it was the *glyfa*. This looked like an egg shape carved out of ivory. It was white and between 14 and 15 centimeters long. Tzatlats, the high priest, said that it was so heavy that four men could not lift it.

"Tzatlats told us that the *glyfa* had been dug out of the earth some ten thousand years before, that it had been the god of the stone-age tribe that found it and was now the god of the whole planet. The *glyfa* had fallen from the skies long before the Tenolt had evolved into sapiency. It was older than the universe; it had survived the birth and death of many universes.

"We found it difficult to believe that a species as highly developed scientifically as Earth's could worship an idol. We thought that we must have misunderstood Tzatlats. It must be that the *glyfa* was a symbol of the creator, just as a crucifix or a statue of Vishnu are only symbols. But no. Tzatlats said that this *was* the god, not a symbol nor an embodiment but the god itself. And it ruled the planet. Tolt was a true theocracy.

"We stood in a corner and watched a ritual which was not explained to us and which I won't describe, since it is available in a report. The ceremony was interrupted when Commodore Benagur suddenly fell to the floor. Though he seemed to be unconscious, he struggled when I picked him up to take him to the ship. Two priests helped me carry him out, and he was still struggling violently while we did so."

The bridge personnel were uneasy, no doubt wondering why he was describing what was well-known.

"The commodore was examined, but no evidence was found that he had suffered some kind of epileptic seizure. He himself reported that he had been overwhelmed by a white light, a light that should have blinded him but did not. After what seemed like hours, but which I can testify were only a few seconds, he began to see something in the center of the whiteness. This was not clear, but he had an impression of a huge blue eye. It became larger, and, as it grew, he felt an increasing heat. Not all over his body, but inside his head, seemingly concentrated in a tiny spot. When the heat suddenly became unbearable, he felt as if he were falling into a bottomless well.

"Nuoli later reported experiencing subjective phenomena, too. But these differed in intensity and kind from the commodore's. She could detect pulsations, variations in air pressure, and then the pulsations became visible as multi-colored square waves. They disappeared simultaneously with the commodore's collapse."

At the time, Ramstan had reported that he had neither seen or heard or felt anything describable as unusual subjective phenomena. Only Benagur had questioned that report. Benagur had accused him of lying after Ramstan had ordered ship to leave Tolt. Ramstan had continued to deny experiencing anything unusual. He had also said that Benagur was still obviously unfit for duty and that he would remain on sick list until he had proved otherwise. Benagur had stormed out of Ramstan's quarters. But there was nothing he could do about it. Ramstan had not reported this incident nor had Benagur, as far as Ramstan knew, said anything about it to anybody.

An hour after returning to ship, Ramstan had left it. He had, of course, told Tenno, now second-in-command, that he was leaving, but he had not said why. He had walked unchallenged out of the port, down the long street that led to the temple, walked past the guards, who obviously were not *aware* that he was present, and half an hour later had again boarded ship. Five minutes later, *al-Buraq* had taken off.

"I was convinced that the *glyfa* was dangerous," Ramstan said after a few seconds of silence. "Despite which, under other circumstances, our scientists would have been directed to study it. As far as I know, it's unique. But when I went back to the temple to discuss what had happened with the high priest, I was told that we were no longer welcome on Tolt. The priest made no threats. He just said that the *glyfa* wished us gone."

Ramstan assumed that the officers were wondering why he had not logged the conversation. However, none dared voice the question. He proceeded to tell them what had happened in the hotel. He omitted his conversation with Commodore Benagur.

"There is no proof that the masked people were Tenolt, but there are no other suspects. I have no idea at all why the Tenolt have followed us here or why they should have made an attempt to anesthetize me. Doctor Toyce's report of the breakdown of the Tolt sailor in the tavern suggests that something horrible has happened to their planet. Obviously, they don't want to tell us what it is. I don't know why.

"However, the disappearance of *Pegasus* is the number-one priority now. For all I know, that might be tied in with the Tenolt's strange actions. In any event, we are backtracking with the hope of finding *Pegasus*."

He paused and said, "Or some trace of it."

A long silence, punctuated by pale faces, followed. Tenno was the first to crack it.

"Captain, will we run away every time a Tolt ship appears?"

Ramstan did not like being questioned, but he said, "We're a scientific mission. And we must at all costs—almost all —avoid anything which might lead to war."

He scanned the faces. "All right. Normal operation."

Two ship's days passed. Ramstan was in his quarters, considering taking the *glyfa* out for another effort to get it to talk, when a whistle sounded. Ramstan spoke the code word which activated a two-way communication. Tenno's dark-brown, slant-eyed face appeared on a screen.

"Captain, we've just rasered some debris at 45,000 kilometers. It might be from a spaceship."

"I'll be right up," Ramstan said.

He felt cold and sick. Could it be what was left of *Pegasus?*

8

WHEN *AL-BURAQ* CAUGHT UP with the debris, she was 600,000 kilometers from the planet Walisk. The pieces of the ship were spreading over a wide area, though going in the same general direction. What attracted Ramstan's attention most was a globe with a diameter of 14 meters. Ship matched pace and path with those of the globe to catch up with it. Meanwhile, other debris had been identified as of Raushghol origin. This was done chiefly through furniture torn loose from the deck in the explosion which had rent the ship. Only the Raushghol, in the Terrans' experience, had three diamond-shaped holes in the backs of all their chairs and sofas.

A screen showed the sphere as a slowly rotating object with a surface of black-and-white squares. *Al-Buraq* had transmitted signals of its own—perhaps unintelligible to the receiver —informing whoever was in the globe, if there was anybody, that help was coming. No acknowledgment had been received.

Al-Buraq jockeyed around, matched, opened a port, swallowed the globe easily and softly, and closed the port. Air hissed into the chamber, which held the globe in a depression fitting the lower third. Antibacterial and antiviral gases mixed with the air for five minutes, then a spray of weak acid washed the globe, followed by high-pressure sprays of liquid helium and then boiling hot water. A few minutes later, crewmembers in spacesuits entered, Toyce among them.

Toyce said, "Never saw anything like this before, sir. I can't find any exterior mechanism to open it up for us. If there's a *shet* in there, the *shet* will have to open it."

Shet was the Terrish nongender, singular and plural, definite and indefinite third-person indicator, a combination of she/he/it from English. An alaraf-drive ship, however, was referred to as *shet-fim*, *fim* being the female indicator.

"Can we cut into it?"

"Won't know until we try, sir."

"It's not likely, but it might contain explosive gas," Ramstan said. "Everybody out. Let a *yeoshet* cut it."

The crew walked through the port into ship; a moment later, a wheeled robot passed through. The port was shut, but the robot waited until ship had built up armor-plated layers to enclose the chamber. When *Task Completed* was flashed on the screen, the CPO directing the party gave the command. A laser beam shot out from the tip of one of the robot's arms, and a thin slice of the equator of the globe fell off.

"I'll be damned!" Ramstan said. "Water!"

It spurted out, then the pressure inside quickly eased off, and it flowed down the side for a few seconds before trickling out.

"Cut out a hole at the equator," Ramstan said.

This was done quickly. More water poured out, but the flow ceased within thirty seconds. The robot moved forward and extended an arm with a tiny TV camera at its end through the hole. Light flared. The lower half of the globe's interior was filled with water, darkened with what looked like blood. In the center floated a dark, shapeless thing.

The sentientologist said, "It's a native of Webn. A seal-centaur. I've never seen one in the flesh before, but I've seen Walisk photos of one. The globe would be the Webnite's self-contained cabin while it's being transported in the ship. It can also be used for a lifeboat. And it evidently has. I've heard that . . ."

Toyce stopped. Like Ramstan, she'd been watching the globe on the screen and so was also taken by surprise. But her reaction came from forgetfulness, whereas Ramstan's came from novelty.

The globe drooped, collapsed, ran together, poured over the

being in the center, and broke away from it with a pop like bubble gum. Bloodied water cascaded over the deck, and the globe had disappeared. The body sprawled in the center of blackened wetness.

"The Raushghols told me that a Webn sphere dissolves in its own water once it's been broken open by force. Believe it or not, that's what they said. The stuff it's made from is supposedly woven by a giant half-sentient sea creature, and . . ."

"How can a thing be half-sentient?" Ramstan said.

"I'm just quoting the Raushghol."

A party rolled the 227-kilogram body onto an a-g sled. The sled rose into the air, and one man directed it toward sickbay. Ramstan watched its progress down the corridors and into the ward. Toyce supervised the three physicians delegated to treat the Webnite. Ten minutes later, she reported.

"Something small but hard and sharp passed entirely through her body," she said. "It must have been going at such a speed it passed through the sphere, too. A tiny meteorite? Anyway, the sphere must have closed up within microseconds after being penetrated on both sides. Otherwise, the air and the water would have boiled off."

"Is she dying?" Ramstan said.

Toyce looked again at the oscilloscopes registering the overall state of health of the finned and armed mass lying on its back in a shallow basin on a broad temporary table.

"She's holding her own—I think. How would I know? I don't know anything about the physiology—or anatomy, either —of an aquatic sentient from Webn. Hell, what's her blood pressure supposed to be? And what's her blood type? You should see the vanadium and magnesium content. Enough to make you drop dead on the spot if it were in your bloodstream. I'm exaggerating, of course, but it would make you sick."

The Webnite was exactly 3.2 meters long, and covered by a sealy chocolate-brown fur. The flippers extended straight out from her body and made up one-third of her length. The belly was huge, though she was not pregnant. The breasts were pendulous and small in proportion to the size of the body. The arms were long; the hands, very broad and flat; the fingers, webbed to the first joint. The head was humanoid. Her eyes were deeply sunk and, at the moment, covered by a transparent inner lid.

"The lids are far enough away from the eyeballs to form a sort of goggle," Toyce said.

She also reported that the Webnite's nostrils could be closed tightly. She had no external ears, and this added to the weirdness of her appearance.

"See, she has a pouch—much like a kangaroo's," Toyce said. "She may be of a species that's regressed, anatomically speaking, gone back to the sea. But a reversion to marsupialism? Doesn't seem likely."

She forced her hand into the tight opening, looked startled, and withdrew it. She opened her fist.

The three flat objects were no longer than Toyce's thumb and seemed to be greenish soapy stones. One formed a circle; the second, a square; the third, a triangle. All had circular holes about three centimeters wide in their centers.

"What the hell?" Toyce said.

"Put them back," Ramstan said. "They're her personal property. Notify me as soon as she regains consciousness—if she does."

Al-Buraq moved into a landing orbit for Walisk. Toyce reported that the labtech computer was making artificial blood for the Webnite, and transfusion should be started in several hours. She had uttered a number of words even though unconscious. Toyce had never heard the language before. But hadn't *Pegasus* been on Webn? Might not Branwen Davis know some Webnian?

Ramstan called sickbay. Davis said that she could carry on a limited conversation in Webnian.

"I doubt we'll be getting into science or philosophy," Ramstan said. "Stand by."

Her green eyes widened, and it was not until after her image faded that he realized why. She had been hurt by his sarcasm. He cursed himself and then wondered why he had spoken so. Was it a defense of some sort? Why did he need a defense?

He did not have long to think about that nor would he, he realized later, have done so even if he had had time. His attention was needed for something much more pressing than delving into his psyche. *Al-Buraq* was close enough to the planet Walisk for visual, thermal, radioactive, and raser observations. The entire planet, from pole to pole, was under black clouds which were mainly carbon-derived smoke.

The smoke came from vast fires raging over thousands of large areas.

"My God!" Nuoli said. "What could have caused *that?*"

It was not from atomic warfare. The radioactive readings testified to that.

The chief geologist reported detection of an unusual number of active volcanoes on both sea and land.

"Twenty-four thousand. The dust from them alone is enough to cover the planet for many years. By the time the dust settles, most if not all the plant life will have died. As for the life that depended upon the plants . . ."

The chief meteorologist reported atmospheric disturbances that could not be explained by the firestorms and volcanoes.

"Something has pulled the atmosphere up into space in the recent past. There are too many traces of atmospheric gases above the normal upper boundary. And there's a phenomenon I've never heard of before. I don't know what caused it, but there's a—how shall I put it?—an oscillatory humping of the air. As if it's still reverberating, reacting to a tidal effect. Let me call you back on that. I'm just giving you my first impressions. I need more data and more time to put them into the computers."

A little while later, the chief geologist reported again.

"Something has made Walisk a hotbed of earthquakes. We're detecting thousands of temblors on land and the sea bottoms. I'd estimate that there are fifty thousand macroseisms occurring at this moment. They're all equal to or exceeding 12 on the Neo-Mercalli scale.

"Also, it's evident that colossal tidal waves have inundated the coastal areas and still haven't subsided. These can't be accounted for only by the seismic activity, immense though these are. Walisk has no moon, as you know, sir, but I'd say that the quakes and the tidal waves and the atmospheric tides could have been caused if, say, Walisk did have a moon the mass of Earth's and it suddenly changed its orbit to one not very far above the exosphere. Anywhere between 10,000 and 50,000 kilometers above the planet's surface. Of course, that's only a fantasy speculation. I won't be bound by that statement."

"Of course not, Doctor," Ramstan said. "Thank you."

Al-Buraq orbited Walisk in a descending spiral, repeatedly crossing all of the four continents, each having approximately the surface area of Africa though not its shape. The readings indicated that the smoke and volcanic dust were so thick that little if any multicellular life survived. Ramstan doubted that much had survived the quakes, tidal waves, and firestorms before the clouds began spreading over the planet.

Two of the continents were on the equatorial line. Their interiors were masses of firestorms so bright that they could be seen through the clouds. Here and there were darker areas which the scientists said were the results of heavy rains. The fires had been put out there, but the bordering regions were so hot that the moisture would quickly be dried up and the vegetation reignited.

"There were vast rain forests there," Toyce said. "Much like those in Africa and southeast Asia before they were cleared and became deserts."

Ramstan decided to investigate at close range one of the continents in the southern hemisphere. It had a great interior desert but had been heavily populated on the coastlines. Though the fires were still raging along the shores, extending sometimes to 300 kilometers into the interior, there were temporarily extinguished areas. The clouds had moved in from outlying areas, carried by the very strong winds, but space-suited personnel could fly in jeeps a few meters above the still-quaking ground.

Al-Buraq poised above an area where rain was falling heavily. The stony desert was only 10 kilometers to the north, but ruins of buildings indicated that the region directly beneath ship had once been thickly populated. Not that there were many objects detectable by the probers. Most of the wooden materials and trees and bushes had been burned entirely and their ashes swept away by the winds and rains. If there were any bones left of the sentient and animal inhabitants, they could not be detected by the probers.

The chief meteorologist reported again.

"The winds have a velocity of 150 kilometers per hour. They're mild, though, compared to the winds in the northern area."

Ramstan knew this because he could read the indicators on

the tec-op panels. He thanked the scientist, anyway. What interested him was the detection by the fine-discriminator probers of thousands of golfball-shaped and -sized objects on the ground or half-buried in the mud. He ordered that the investigators in the jeeps secure some of these. Then, impatient, he commanded *al-Buraq* to get close enough to the surface to extend a suction pseudopod and bring in some specimens immediately.

While waiting, he ordered a launch sent to the northern shoreline to determine if there were similar objects there. "And if you find them, proceed to the continent above this in the northern hemisphere and look for them there."

Al-Buraq headed into the wind at 5 kph. It was not easy for her to scoop in the spheres. The ground was subject to shock after shock, many strong enough to toss the spheres a meter into the air. A few times, fissures opened, and the spheres fell into them. *Al-Buraq* did not try to obtain these. If she had inserted her pseudopod into the fissure, she might have been trapped if the fissure closed.

At another order, ship brought in some pieces of what had been stone columns and some twisted and dented steel beams.

The chemicophysical laboratory reported that there were many smaller spheres in the mud which had been carried in. These had a diameter of three millimeters.

Al-Buraq continued sampling, and she began to trace a spiral path over a twenty-square-kilometer area.

The launch left ship with two pilots and six scientists aboard. It shot northward at 300 kph, its probers scanning the area for 100 kilometers on both sides.

The laboratory chief reported again.

"The larger spheres have a diameter of four centimeters. Each weighs one kilogram. Each has a shell of nickel-iron five millimeters thick. That's estimated, since the shell has been partially melted and some of the nickel-iron has evaporated. Burned off. The core is some black, unknown substance, though it looks like metal. It can't be X-rayed. It's unaffected by the strongest acid. It won't bend or break under a pressure of 500,000 tons per square millimeter, and that's the greatest force we have. It won't melt at 100,000 K. It resists the most powerful laser—so far, anyway.

"The smaller spheres are of the same substance or seem to

be. They only lack the nickel-iron shell of the larger. They've been subjected to the same tests with the same results."

Wendell Tong shook his head. "I've never seen or heard of anything like it."

The screen split into three sections, and the heads of the chief geologist and the chief astrophysicist appeared by Tong's.

"We've been listening in," the geologist said. "May I ask a question?"

Ramstan gave his permission. However, the question was not directed at him but at Tong.

"You say that the nickel-iron shells were partially melted. I doubt that the firestorm could account for that. Wouldn't you say that the melting could only have come from great velocity through the atmosphere? That these spheres are, in effect, meteorites of some sort?"

Tong nodded. "Yes, I'd say so. I'm not competent . . ."

"It's a matter of common sense, of logic," the geologist said. "Only . . . damn! . . . whoever heard of meteorites like this?"

Ramstan said, "The hot nickel-iron shells could have started the worldwide fires, right?"

"That's the only explanation we have at the moment."

Two days later, al-Buraq left, the jeeps having returned the day before. The launch was over the northern continent now and sending in reports. Al-Buraq proceeded to the western coast of the southern-hemisphere continent, spiraled over a hundred-square-kilometer area, then flew to one of the continents in the equatorial region. Another launch was sent to the third continent. After a six-day sampling of the second continent, al-Buraq plunged into the ocean and spiraled over the bottom. When she emerged five days later, she went to the fourth continent. At the end of the sampling there, she was joined by the two launches.

The results of the investigation were both puzzling and mind-numbing.

The spheres were undoubtedly of meteoritic origin or, it would be more accurate to say, they had been launched at high velocity from outside the atmosphere. Both the large and small spheres had been found embedded in trees that had not entirely burned and even in stones and steel beams. They were everywhere from pole to pole. Whatever had shot them had covered the planet by making many orbital sweeps and by missing neither land nor sea.

Walisk was slightly larger than Earth though of less density. Its surface area was approximately 518,000,000 square kilometers. Estimates based on the samplings indicated that approximately one of the larger spheres and twenty of the smaller had struck every square meter. Or they had been intended to do so, but atmospheric and oceanic variations in density and current had resulted in variations in the number of meteorites or missiles per square meter.

"Five hundred and eighteen billion of the large spheres," Tenno had whispered when he heard the report. "Ten trillion, three hundred and sixty billion of the smaller."

Each of the smaller weighed 50 grams. Twenty together weighed 1,000 grams or one kilogram. This suggested that the large spheres had hollow centers.

The total mass of the missiles was an estimated 1,026,000,000,000 kilograms.

"No spaceship would be large enough or have power enough to deliver and launch such a mass. She'd have to be as large as . . . what? . . . the Earth? Larger? Let's get a computer readout."

"An object with that mass and coming so close to Walisk would cause cataclysmic earthquakes and tidal waves," Ramstan said. "But . . . you're right, Tenno. It couldn't be a spaceship or even a fleet. Unconceivable. Anyway, if the thing or things were directed by intelligence . . . what sentient would use such inefficient means as the spheres to kill life? Neutron bombs would be far superior. What good would this destruction be for warmakers? Unless they were so vicious that they wanted only total destruction. I can't believe that."

"The *bolg* kills all but one. God is sick. Unbreakable flames fall from the black sky. . . . All die. Where to go?"

9

AL-BURAQ WAS IN ORBIT over Walisk and awaiting orders from Ramstan for the next destination. He was wondering where this would be when he got a call from Doctor Hu.

"The Webnite is well enough to talk for a while. She wants to talk to you. Lieutenant Davis will interpret."

Ramstan thanked her and said that he would be in the sickbay as soon as he could get there.

"Does that mean right away, sir?" she said.

"Of course!" Ramstan said. "What the hell did you think I meant?"

Hu's face became rigid, but she said nothing. Ramstan regretted having blazed out at her. His nerves were crawling like a mess of worms. He had to get better control of himself. Walisk . . . the *glyfa*'s continued refusal to answer him . . . the Tenolt . . . everything. . . . They were conspiring to crush him.

He walked out of his quarters shaking his head. *Conspiring* was not the correct word. It sounded as if he were becoming paranoiac.

He concentrated on the Webnite. She might be able to tell him something of what had happened, though if she had been in the self-contained chamber when the Raushghol ship was attacked, she might know very little. It was luck that Davis was aboard, since she was the only one who could speak Webnian. *Al-Buraq* had not been to Webn but *Pegasus* had. During her six-month stay there, Davis, as a marine biologist, had been in intimate contact with some of the native scientists and had taken the opportunity to master as much of the language as she could. She also knew the coordinates for navigation to Webn or at least had enough data so that *al-Buraq*'s astrogators could extrapolate the rest needed. In fact, if it were not for Davis, there would have been no way to get to Webn except by going to Raushghol and getting the data from its alaraf navy.

The Webnite and Davis were in the same sickbay. The Earthwoman was there for two reasons. One, to interpret if the Webnite should recover enough to talk. Two, she still had a fever, the cause of which was unknown. She had been probed by machines and had conducted a self-probing, but the fever continued to keep her body temperature above normal. Hu had told Ramstan that she suspected the fever was psychosomatic. It did not seem to be infectious or contagious, and there was no valid reason to isolate her. That had been determined within three hours after she had entered *al-Buraq*.

Ramstan entered the sickbay. The Webnite was floating in a large plastic tank. A technician-nurse, Hu, and Toyce were also there. Branwen sat in a chair by the tank. Her left hand was enfolded in the huge webbed hand of the Webnite. The creature watched Ramstan with large, soft, dark eyes.

"We're ready to record," Hu said. "But I'll be watching to make sure she doesn't tire herself out."

Ramstan bowed to the creature, hoping that she would understand that it was a gesture of respect. Davis spoke to her in a language with many sibilants and stops. She then said, "I explained what your bowing meant."

"You aren't reading my mind, are you?" he said half seriously.

"I'm just trying to anticipate."

The Webnite spoke for perhaps ten seconds. Davis said, "She will address herself to you, since you are the captain. The Webnites are very formal in certain situations. She believes this is a special situation; she believes that she is dying."

Ramstan looked at Hu. "Is she?"

Hu shrugged and said, "I wouldn't have thought so. But

maybe she knows more about herself than I do. Most patients do, even if they aren't aware of it."

Ramstan bowed again, made a coded gesture, and a few seconds later sat down on the chair-shaped protuberance that had formed from the deck.

There was a burst of dialog between the creature and Branwen Davis. Branwen then said, "Her name is Wassruss. She had been picked up by a Raushghol ship and taken from Webn to Raushghol. The Raushghols wanted her knowledge of sea-farming techniques. In return, they would give the Web-nites some deep-sea craft and technological artifacts. Wassruss says that the reasons for her visit are not important. On the way back, the Raushghol ship took a sidetrip to Walisk. Or she started for it, anyway."

Wassruss spoke again at some length.

Davis said, "Wassruss was in her cabin when she heard a peculiar, penetrating, and agonizing whistle. It didn't come over the electronic equipment; at least, she heard the captain say it didn't. She had turned on the intercom connecting her cabin to the bridge. The whistling lasted for about two minutes, and then it abruptly ceased. The ship's detectors showed a huge mass nearby. There was no warning of its appearance. It just was there all of a sudden. The captain said that it couldn't be there. But there it was."

"How big was it, and what did it look like? Was it a spaceship?"

"It was a sphere with a diameter of 13,000 kilometers. At least that's what she overheard the detector-people report. But . . . she does have a word for it. *Tssokh'azgd*."

"What would that translate as?"

Branwen spoke some more with Wassruss.

"It's the Webn name for the Chaos-Monster in their religion. Wassruss says she had abandoned her faith. But now that she has actually seen the *Tssokh'azgd*, she isn't so sure that the religion is false."

Ramstan said, "Ask her how she knows, or thinks she knows, that the thing was the whatchamacallit."

Branwen Davis spoke again. Then, "She says that it is the *Tssokh'azgd*. There is no argument about it. As soon as it's seen, it's known, though that does the knower no good, because she'll soon be dead."

Suddenly, Wassruss began talking so swiftly that Branwen had difficulty interpreting and had to tell her to slow down.

"I am going to die soon. I wish to die on my native world and to be buried according to the custom of my people. If you can get me to Webn before I die, I will pay you well."

Ramstan was flabbergasted, but he did not show it.

"It is not necessary or even desirable that you pay me. In fact, it would be illegal for me to accept money or gifts of any kind."

Toyce said, "Not quite so, Captain. There is a clause which says that you may accept gifts if the refusal would insult the giver or cause ill-feelings of any sort. You will then place the gifts in the storeroom as government property."

Ramstan said, "Ah, I didn't remember that."

Davis had already translated for Ramstan. Wassruss, forgetting Davis's request for slowness, broke into a torrent of phrases. Ramstan did not know what she had said, but he could not mistake the appeal and the desperation in her voice. Her facial expression looked to him like a threatening snarl but was no doubt a smile to her species.

Davis said, "Her people are real homebodies. She is the first to leave her planet, and she isn't sure that what happened to her isn't a judgment of her God. You see how quickly she abandoned her atheism, how superficial it was. She is scared, though. To her it's a terrible thing to die far away from her native sea. And a worse thing not to be buried, not to sink down into the depths and be taken back into the bosom of the ocean."

Wassruss spoke.

Branwen Davis listened, then said, "She wants to know what I told you. She wants to make sure I'm translating correctly. It isn't easy for me; there are so many phrases I don't know or which may have subtleties I didn't grasp when I was learning her speech."

Branwen replied. The Webnite seemed to be thinking for a minute, then rattled off another train of phrases.

Branwen said, "She insists that you accept her gifts. But she says, and I'm not sure I understand her, that these gifts are unique. They do not have their like anywhere in the world."

Ramstan snorted and said, "How would she know? Has she been throughout the cosmos?"

Branwen translated before Ramstan could stop her. He felt his face warm. He was embarrassed, but he was also angry at Branwen.

She must have guessed what he was thinking. She said, "I only asked what the gifts were. She says that she is very tired now and would like to sleep."

Ramstan bowed to the Webnite and left. So, the monstrous but somehow attractive seal-centaur was going to bestow upon him certain treasures. He did not expect them to be overwhelmingly valuable or beautiful. He was, however, curious about them and about the real reason for her giving them, though it was possible that she was not concealing any motives.

Their uniqueness did not mean that they would be interesting, desirable, useful, or any combination thereof. Many artifacts could be unique and yet of little significance except to the owner. Or to a sentientologist, who was theoretically interested in everything non-Terran.

At one time the concept of God, which concept was a mental artifact, could have been of value only to its owner.

That was a strange intrusion of thought.

What was it doing, sidling in through a crack in the wall of thinking?

And why the crack?

Never mind. He could not dwell long on that, though it might not be as irrelevant as it seemed. Nor could he ponder long upon the promise of Wassruss. What seized his mind most of the time, awake or dreaming, was the destruction of the Walisk natives. Had this been done by the thing that the whisperer had warned him of, the *bolg?*

There was one who might have the answer. Who might even have been the unseen warner in the Kalafalan tavern. But it had spoken once while he was carrying it from the Tolt temple and a second time after he had heard the voice in the tavern.

He had since sat down before the table seven times and looked through the microscope at the surface of the egg. His eyes roved over the sculptures of some microbe Michelangelo who had worked them how long ago, perhaps eons? Whatever dwelt inside that impervious shell surely had to extend an antenna to transceive thoughts. Or, perhaps, one of the figures crowding the surface of this little world was an antenna. Or perhaps he was not thinking in the correct category. It might not need an antenna.

Or, and at this a chill skipped up his spine like a cold stone thrown by a clammy hand over a frozen lake, perhaps the egg *was* an antenna?

In which case, who was the transmitter of the thought he received?

He didn't know. One thing all worlds shared was a super-abundance of questions and a poverty of answers.

Seven ship-days after leaving Walisk, while walking to the bridge from his quarters, he was startled by a loud piping noise and the change of a circle on the bulkhead from a pale yellow to a flashing orange-yellow over which rotated a scarlet spiral.

He began running, at the same time calling out, "Bridge! What is the alarm?"

Tenno's face appeared on one of the circles keeping pace with him.

"The EVD has detected a USO, sir. It suddenly appeared from behind the asteroid we passed three hours ago. Raser is checking it out now, sir."

By the time he'd reached the bridge, the raser report was in. The EVD (Ether Vibration Detector) had noted the disturbance in the recently traversed tunnel. EVD was not capable of radar or raserlike powers of location and dimension measurements, however. It could note only intrusions at a relatively near distance and those within a limited time period.

Warrant Officer Yazdi reported that the unidentified space object was 260 meters long and 210 meters wide and was oyster-shell-shaped. Ramstan did not listen intently; he could see the data and the object itself on a display screen.

"Looks like the *Popacapyu*," Tenno said.

10

RAMSTAN DID NOT reply to the obvious. It could be another Tolt ship, but he doubted that. As far as he knew, the Tenolt had only two alaraf-drive ships. This one must have followed them from Kalafala. Which meant that the Tenolt were more technologically advanced than the Terrans had supposed. Not until just before *al-Buraq*'s last jump had Earth's alaraf scientists developed a device to detect the vibrations of passage of ships in the "tunnels." This was in a primitive stage and capable only of sniffing out the tracks of vessels that had passed within a period of ten to twelve hours. The scientists had thought that, by the time *al-Buraq* returned to Earth, the EVD would be capable of a finer and more extended discrimination.

Tenno shook his head and said, "Perhaps it's only coincidence, and they didn't follow us here. It's difficult to believe that they have a better EVD than we. In fact, I can't believe they have any at all."

"You're showing your prejudice," Ramstan said. "Just because they worshiped—I mean, worship—an idol and have certain customs we regard as retarded, if not degenerate, doesn't mean that their science is on a low level.

"Anyway," he continued briskly, "they are here. And we can assume that they've followed us for some reason."

Tenno and Yazdi looked out of the corners of their eyes at each other. Were they both thinking of the object which their captain had brought into ship in a bag? If so, why didn't they have the courage to say what they thought? He would, if he were in their position. Were they really that afraid of him? Or was it that they were more afraid of being shown up as foolish if they were wrong?

"What we have to do first," Ramstan said, "is to attempt again to communicate with them. Maybe this time they'll respond. If they don't, then we'll do some backtracking. If it's not just coincidence, if they do have an EVD, they'll follow us."

Tenno's expression said, "And then what?" But he turned and spoke to the raser operator, who gave the second-level bridge raser operator an order. Presently the 2-L RO reported that he was getting no acknowledgments, even though he had transmitted in Tolt. The unknown (it was still classified as such) was, however, scanning *al-Buraq* with radar and raser.

"They wouldn't talk to us on Kalafala, and they won't talk to us here," Tenno said. "Why're they dogging us?"

"We have to make absolutely sure that they are," Ramstan said.

Reluctantly, he ordered that ship return to the Walisk window. This involved a 360-degree maneuver which required five hours. The stranger began to turn also a few minutes after *al-Buraq* did.

"That does it," Ramstan said. "There's no use in going into alaraf drive. Head her back toward Webn, Tenno."

The stars on the visual screen wheeled, and then *al-Buraq* was locked into the former course, guiding herself by the configuration of stars and the position of Webn's sun. When she had first arrived in this window, she had had no data about star fixes, of course. But once her navigators had figured out the correct course to Webn and had then fed in the data, she could navigate on her own. All she needed was the command, verbal or punched.

In the same way, she could backtrack to any other window, including Earth's, with only one short command.

Ramstan was relieved. He had not wanted to go back to

Walisk for fear of what might be lurking, if such a word was applicable, in the window. Or it could be in another window connected to a "tunnel" leading to the Waliskan window. Which meant that the thing could pop out and confront the Terrans with no warning.

Ship's rasers had not located any such massive object as Wassruss had reported. Therefore, the thing might have gone into alaraf-drive to another sector of space-time. But it could just as easily have returned to Waliskan space and be waiting. Or it could appear at any second in this sector.

Ramstan had already given ship her instructions on what to do if an object of the dimensions and shape of the thing described by Wassruss appeared. She was to go into alaraf-drive at once, even though this would probably mean she would come out into an unknown window. But this was nothing to worry about, since the ship could always backtrack.

What if the thing had an equivalent of EVD and could follow the "tracks" of *al-Buraq?*

Then she would have to either plunge into tunnel after tunnel, known or unknown, or stand and fight. Which action would be taken would depend upon how distant the thing was when it came out of the tunnel. If it were very close, say, within a hundred kilometers, then flight was the answer. If the thing (should he think of it as the *bolg?*) was far enough away so that its missiles would take more than three minutes to reach *al-Buraq*, then Ramstan would use lasers and rasers and torpedoes and, as a last resort, the ether-disruptor.

These might destroy the thing. But if it launched its missiles immediately on arrival in the window, *al-Buraq* might have to duck into another tunnel before the effect of its weapons could be observed. The *bolg* (there, he'd said it!) could spew out trillions of missiles, spread them out in a vast screen that *al-Buraq*, unless she happened to be at the top velocity attainable in m-g drive, could not escape.

And that depended upon the velocity of the missiles. How swiftly were they hurled from the *bolg?*

The *Popacapyu* maintained the same distance behind the Terran vessel. Ramstan would have liked to slow down and then speed up to determine if the Tolt vessel would match the deceleration and acceleration. But conservation of power was more important in this situation than satisfying his curiosity.

After ordering that he be notified immediately if anything demanded his presence, he went to his quarters. He removed the *glyfa* from the safe and placed it under the microscope on the table. He did not turn on the scope. Instead, he placed a hand on each end of the egg-shape, stroked the ends lightly, then gripped them tightly. It was as if he could force something from the *glyfa*, as if the intensity of his desire could be transmitted through his hands and choke words out of the thing.

"The *bolg* has come," he said softly. "I've seen a whole planet ravaged, all of its land life, plant and animal, killed. *Pegasus* is lost, and I fear that the *bolg* got her. I'm seeing ghosts from my childhood and hearing voices.

"Are the voices yours, are the ghosts images you've projected? If you can throw a voice as if you were a ventriloquist, why not an image? Speak! Speak, or in the name of Allah, I'll cast you out from the ship while it's in space and let you fall into a star!"

"Which would in no way harm me physically," the voice of his father said. *"I was forged in a star."*

The words sounded as if they came out of a mouth of flesh, one with teeth, gums, a tongue, a palate, one quite human. But they were not modulated vibrations of air striking his eardrum. They sprang without benefit of matter from the *glyfa* into his brain, where certain impulses evoked electrical configurations. And these seemed to sound in his ear and to originate from his long-dead father.

Now that he had gotten the thing to speak, he was speechless. His heart thudded, and there was a thunder in his ears as if he lay at the end of a giant's bowling alley and the ball would strike him soon and fatally.

The voice slashed through the roaring and seemed to sever it so that the ends dropped away. But his heart still beat faster than was good for it.

"You are not of much use while you are afraid of me," the *glyfa* said. "Afraid? No, in awe. That is the correct term. No. There is fear, though not of me so much as of yourself. You are afraid of what you might do. Which is wrong, since you have been doing what you fear you're going to do. Too late."

How could a nonvoice chuckle? Yet, it had done so.

"No, I don't really laugh. I just evoke laughter in you.

Laughter for me. Never mind. It's too complicated to explain. Tell me why you want to speak with me."

In one sense, the *glyfa* could read his mind. In another sense, it could not. It had told him that it had read his electrical matrix, the pulsing configuration of his neural system, when he had appeared at the Great Temple in Tolt's capital city. It had been able to "see" him as a skeleton of twisting lightning streaks, a storm of tiny stars and comets' tails. It had invaded his mind and triggered certain impulses in a configuration which had made Ramstan lust for the *glyfa* as he had never lusted for anyone or anything. It had enveloped him in a globe of light, a bomb-burst of energy which would have blinded those around him if they could have seen it. And perhaps Benagur had seen it, and Nuoli had been touched by it.

The *glyfa* had great powers, but these had certain limitations, and distance was one of the factors modifying them. Not until the three had entered the house of the *glyfa* had it been able to determine which of the three it wanted.

"I waited for eons for one, and then I got three," the *glyfa* had said. "Truly remarkable. Not at all probable. But there it was. As you Terrans say, 'Feast or famine.'"

The *glyfa* had been able to converse at once with Ramstan because it knew Urzint. But it had been compelled to "use" Ramstan's own voice. In the interval between the first time it had "spoken" and the second, it had learned much Terrish and Arabic. It was able to "see" the full referents of any word or image pulsing in Ramstan's mind.

At least, that was Ramstan's explanation for the *glyfa*'s quick learning of the two languages. The *glyfa* offered none of its own.

It was evoking the proper words in the proper order from Ramstan's own mind. In a sense, he was talking to himself. In another, he was conversing with the *glyfa*. If he had been asked to define the different senses, he would have failed.

Ramstan finally unclogged his mental throat. Subvocalizing, he said, "Here is what's happened since I last talked to you. Or do you already know it?"

"Tell me."

Ramstan did, finding that the *glyfa* seemed to leap ahead of his words, to pull out the word or the image by its roots, see the entire plant, the roots, stem, leaves, flowers, seeds, everything in one scan of unbelievable speed.

Strangely, the *glyfa* seemed more interested in the ghostly person in the hotel than in other events. At least, it spoke of this first.

"Do you think it is, indeed, al-Khidhr?"

"I don't know what to think," Ramstan said. "It could be an exteriorized projection of my concept of al-Khidhr. A subjective image seeming to be objective. Or it could be . . . I don't know what."

The *glyfa* chuckled. By now Ramstan found this sound sinister.

"No, not menacing or conspiratorial," the *glyfa* said. "Secretive, perhaps. But with good reason. In time all things that are capable of being revealed will be revealed. But I am making sure that you are not rushed too green into events which require for you a steady ripening, a slow and sure maturing.

"That is, if there's time. If not, then . . . Well, we'll see. This Webnite, Wassruss, is going to give you three gifts, and you have no idea what they are. But from your description of what happened before she told you this, I know. I am truly amazed, and, believe me, it takes much to amaze me. First, three of you come along after a wait so long that your mind couldn't grasp it. Three at once. Then the gifts of Wassruss. These could easily have been lost in space or have come to someone else.

"But there you were, Ali Baba-on-the-spot, as you say in New Babylon. Where, out of a vastness of cosmos, it was the only place I would have chosen you, if I had known there was a choice. I did not, of course, and yet, there you were."

"What are you talking about?"

"It's too early to tell you. Though, as I said, I may have to tell you anyway if events require it. But I was right when I picked you. Perhaps you are that exceedingly rare individual, one who is a magnet for unlikely events. One whose matrix overcomes the principles of probabilities.

"Such beings are possible, though I have never met one, until now, and I'm still not sure about you. Perhaps it is they who . . ."

"They?" Ramstan said.

"Never mind. Not now, anyway."

Ramstan exploded. "What about the Tolt ship, then? That captain is determined to get you back! And he's also, I'm sure, out to get revenge on me and perhaps the entire crew for the sacrilege! But he doesn't dare make a move which will imperil his chances of retrieving you! So he's taking it easy, shadowing, waiting for the first chance, and then . . . bang, boom, that's it! And I can't tell my crew why he's dogging us!"

"You'll find some way to handle it. It may be that you'll have to fight him. In which case, you'll have to convince your crew that the Tolt is a grave danger. And you'll have to antagonize him into attacking you."

"Do you know what you're saying?" Ramstan said.

"Calm down. Your agony is affecting me. Yes, I know. You don't realize as yet, unfortunately, that there is much more at stake than the fate of a few hundred Tenolt. Or a few hundred Terrans. Or even a few billion Waliskans."

"What is at stake then?" Ramstan cried. His voice rang back from the bulkheads, which shivered as *al-Buraq* caught a trace of Ramstan's pain and perplexity. If Chief Engineer Indra was hooked into ship's neural circuits at this moment, he would be alarmed.

"Your immortality, for one thing."

"I don't really care for that!" Ramstan bellowed.

"No, of course not. Not at the moment. However, I cannot tell you what the stakes are. Not as yet. You wouldn't believe me. Or, if you did, you might lose your reason. I am protecting you. Believe me. But then you have to believe me, don't you?"

"Damn you!" Ramstan shouted. "Why did you seduce me?"

"The unseduceable can't be seduced," the *glyfa* said. "You seduced yourself. When I made my offer, I did not force you to accept. There was no magic involved, no hypnotism. You had perfect free will or at least as near to perfect as is possible. It was your choice. You said yes. And your second thoughts are only that—second, that is, superficial. The first are the deepest."

Ramstan had no reply to this. There was silence. It was possible that the *glyfa* was overwhelmed by the emotional blaze from Ramstan.

The gap was suddenly closed again.

"This Branwen Davis, the woman you are so attracted to.

Haven't you wondered if there was a connection between her and the Tenolt?"

Ramstan was shocked.

"How could there be?"

He paused in his vocalization, but the *glyfa* was reading the images and emotions pouring out like the damned from the suddenly opened gates of Hell.

"I do not know. That is up to you to find out. Of course, I am only suggesting a possibility."

"And I thought I was paranoiac."

"Don't let your personal feelings for her interfere with good judgment. As for paranoia, anyone who has the imagination to postulate all possibilities is automatically a paranoiac."

"I don't see . . . well, of course, there could be a very slight possibility. But even so, she is, at this moment anyway, not important. What is vital is that monster that shoots meteorites, isn't it?"

"Obviously."

"And you won't tell me what it is?"

"When you get to a certain place and meet certain persons, if you ever do, that is, then I'll tell you. Though by then I may not have to."

Ramstan struck the top of the table with his fist.

"I am enjoying this splendid display of emotion, even if it hurts me somewhat," the *glyfa* said. "At the same time, I regret that you do not have better self-control."

Doctor Hu's voice came from the bulkhead.

"Captain! The Webnite wishes to speak to you. She says it's very urgent. It's my opinion, sir, that she hasn't long to live."

11

DAVIS STOOD BY WASSRUSS, holding one of the huge webbed hands with her two hands. Hu was looking at an oscilloscope screen on which a green horizontal line was displaying tiny sawteeth at irregular intervals. A medical technician was adjusting the dials on a panel.

Hu turned away from the screen and started when she saw Ramstan.

"You must have run."

Ramstan did not reply. He walked to the container in which Wassruss floated. She rolled her huge head toward him and fixed her great seal's eyes upon him. They were bright enough, but he thought he could see something like frosted glass deep within them.

She spoke for a long time. Branwen Davis finally said something, and the Webnite stopped.

"She's going too fast for me," Branwen said. "I asked her to start over again."

Wassruss opened her mouth and took in a great amount of air. Then, slowly, she repeated herself, pausing now and then to allow Davis to interpret.

"I, Wassruss of the Violet Isle, will soon be dead. I had hoped to live long enough to see my native sea, the deep blue waters around the rocky, pine-grown Violet Isle, before I died. But my life is draining away faster than I had thought. The *Tssokh'azgd* did that to me; it tore my soul to shreds. You do not see the creature that devours all life and remain the same being. You know then how insignificant and meaningless you are, what a cipher, what a tiny piece of meat. The you, that is, the *I* that thinks itself the center of the universe, the goal of the cosmos, the being from which all things spread out and return to, becomes suddenly and irrecoverably dwindled, cut off, alone. It is no longer the source and resource of the world. It is alone, unconnected, a nothing. Without a history, with no love from anyone and no love for itself.

"It suddenly realizes, not intellectually but in the deepest part of its cells, that it is without hope and always has been. That it doesn't deserve hope and should never have wished for it. That in the beginning was nothing, that there has always been, behind the appearance of something, nothing, that there will always be nothing.

"That we are masks with no faces behind them, *unless the void has a face*."

Wassruss stopped talking. The only sound was her heavy breathing. Branwen still held the Webnite's hand; her expression had become even more sad. Hu shook her head. The technician slipped out of the room. Ramstan saw that the frosted glass in Wassruss's eyes had floated up from the depths.

Presently, Wassruss withdrew her hand from Branwen's hands and reached with it into the belly pouch. It came out holding the three objects that Ramstan had seen on his first visit.

These were the gifts of which she had spoken.

Wassruss held all three in the palm of her hand, which was extended to Ramstan. But when he put his hand out to take them, she closed her fingers.

"I must tell you something about the gifts of the Vwoordha," she said. "The Vwoordha made these a long time ago. The Vwoordha were once a great people, very powerful. Now there are only three left, according to what I have been told. They have lost many of their powers, but not all, and the little they have left is more than that of many who boast of their greatness and riches.

"There are some who say that the Vwoordha are so ancient that they have survived the Death of All and Many Worlds."

Here Ramstan interrupted to ask Branwen if she was translating correctly. Wasn't the phrase "All and Many" a contradiction?

Branwen spoke to the Webnite, who gave a short answer. Branwen said, "No, that is what she said. It is an ancient phrase the exact meaning of which she doesn't know."

Wassruss began talking again.

"These gifts, these sigils, were once my grandmother's. She did not tell me the details of how they came into her hands. But she did say that she had once done a great favor for a queen of our nation, and the queen had given her these three objects. The queen herself had received them from her great-grandfather, who had gotten them from the captain of an Urzint spaceship. Neither she nor her great-grandfather ever used them. When she was about to die, she gave them to me. She told me what she knew about them, which was actually not much.

"But all you need to know is that each has a distinctive power. You must use one when you are in such a situation that there seems no other way out.

"Then you will place one in your mouth. Why there and not just in your hand, I do not know. That is all that is needed. The gift of the Vwoordha does the rest.

"But you must use, first, the *shengorth*, the triangle. After it has been used, it is of no more use to you. It can only be used once by one owner. If you use it, you should give it to someone you think worthy to have it, though that is not absolutely necessary. But not until after you have used the other two. Or, if you never use the other two, then, before you die, you must give all three to someone.

"Do not split up the three. Keep all three for yourself until the day comes when you give them away, and then give all three to one person."

Ramstan tried to keep his face expressionless. Did this creature really believe in magic, in this tale of three thaumaturgical objects?

As if Wassruss had read his mind, she said, "What I say of the gifts of the Vwoordha is no lie. Perhaps you are wondering why, if the gifts can take their owner from danger, I did not use one to save myself?"

Ramstan said, "Tell her I was wondering that."

Branwen spoke.

Wassruss coughed, and she said, "I did not wish to use the sigils unless I absolutely had to. I had no warning of the meteorite or missile or whatever it was. When it pierced my body, I went into shock. I didn't have enough of my wits left to place the *shengorth* in my mouth before I became unconscious."

She was dying, and if it made her feel better to give him the objects, then she should be able to do so. He'd be doing a kind deed. Allah saw every good deed and gave you credit for it.

That last was a stray thought that had no business in his mind. But, as Toyce had once said, "You can only wash off the dirt. The skin is still there."

Wassruss was saying, ". . . and so you must not forget to use the *shengorth* first. Next, the square, the *pengrathon*. Third, the disk, the *ph'rimon*. I do not know why, but to use one out of proper sequence nullifies the power."

She repeated, "And if you use all three, then you must pass them on as soon as possible to someone else. If, by the time you are ready to die, you have not used them, you must give them to someone who deserves them."

Ramstan could not help saying, "And what if I should die unexpectedly and have no chance to give them away?"

He was talking as if he believed that the things had power.

"Then someone will take them."

Ramstan was going to ask her how the taker would know how to use the objects. If he had no instructions and perhaps did not even know what they were supposed to be, how could the taker get any benefit from them? Or pass the knowledge along to someone else? And since this was likely to happen many times in a long period of time, and the three gifts were supposed to be very ancient, how had they escaped being lost or knowledge of their use lost? Why hadn't the chain been broken?

He had other questions, but why bother with them?

"Of course," Wassruss said, "like all gifts, they are not necessarily beneficial. If not used properly, they can harm or even kill their owner. And there may be situations where death will be preferable to using them. What these are I don't know."

"Perhaps it would be better if you gave them to someone else," Ramstan said.

Davis said, "She is honoring you in the highest way known to her people. You must not refuse! Uh, sir, that is, you *shouldn't*."

He shrugged. "Very well. But . . . why is she giving *me* the gifts?"

After listening to Wassruss, Branwen said, "The moment she saw you, she *knew* that you must be the one for whom the sigils have been waiting. Just as you will *know* the person to whom you are to give the three *ssuzz'akon*."

Wassruss spoke again.

"She said that there is a tradition that eventually the makers of the sigils will get them back."

"Sounds like a lot of ancient nonsense to me," Ramstan said.

Wassruss spoke weakly to Branwen.

"She says that she hasn't even told you what's most important. And she doesn't have much time left."

Doctor Hu said, "We can give her more time."

Branwen told Wassruss this.

The seal-centaur said, "*Tssisskooss*."

"She says, 'No.' "

Wassruss went into a long speech. When Branwen had heard her out, she frowned.

"She says the bearer of the gifts is also taught a mystery chant when she receives the gifts. She doesn't know what it means, but she thinks she could find out the meaning if her destiny depended upon it. *Destiny?* That may not be the correct translation. I just don't know her language well enough. Anyway, you must remember that the gifts may get you out of one danger but at the same time put you in another. She says that good has its evils and evils their good. The universe is tricky, the ultimate and the biggest trickster.

"Now she's going to recite the chant, the mystery. She thinks that you'll have to figure it out. The time for it is ready, and you are the one who has arrived at the time when it must be . . . uh . . . unspooled? . . . unraveled? . . . threaded through the Great Eye? What she said, literally, is that the spooling and the unspooling go through the eye of the same needle. You yourself are needle and eye and threader and unspooler and spooler. This is very strange, since the Webnites know very little about spinning or needles."

Wassruss said something.

Branwen said, "She says that the chant will be your property, yours, Captain, and *yours only*."

Ramstan said, "Property?"

"She doesn't use that word exactly as we do. Anyway, take the sigils now."

Ramstan held out his left hand. Wassruss said something weakly. Davis said, "No. Your right hand."

Ramstan obeyed. Wassruss extended her huge, brown-webbed hand and dropped the three objects into his palm. His fingers closed over them. They felt slimy.

12

WASSRUSS BEGAN CHANTING. It was obvious from the alternate deepening and raising of her voice, combined with significant pauses, that she was representing two speakers. Branwen translated after each phrase.

" 'What is the number of the worlds?'
" 'More than many.'
" 'What is the number of paths?'
" 'More than many. Yet they are one.'
" 'What is at the ends of the paths that are one?'
" 'Death or wisdom or both. *And one more thing.*'
" 'What is the way to the three?'
" 'There are many places to start. Webn is one.'
" 'And then?'
" 'Ring the bell at the first entrance past Webn.'
" 'And then?'
" 'Enter.'
" 'And then?'
" 'Ring the bell at the third entrance.'
" 'And then?'
" 'Enter.'
" 'And then?'
" 'Ring the bell at the fifth entrance.'

" 'And then?'

" 'Enter.'

" 'And then?'

" 'Ring the bell at the seventh entrance.'

" 'And then?'

" 'Enter.'

" 'And then?'

" 'Ring the bell at the ninth entrance.'

" 'And then?'

" 'Go to the only place to go.'

" 'And then?'

" 'To the tree which does not stand alone.'

" 'And then?'

" 'To the well.'

" 'What is in the well?'

" 'The wise one who swims,

" 'The laugher who hops,

" 'The cold-blood who drinks hot blood.'

" 'Is this the end?'

" 'Near the well is an old house. It is older than many stars.'

" 'And then?'

" 'Knock at the entrance.'

" 'Who shall open the door?'

" 'Three who should be dead.'

" 'And then?'

" 'Ask, but be willing to pay the price.' "

No one spoke for a moment. The only sound was Wassruss's whistling breath.

At last, Ramstan said hesitantly, "Do the Webnites have bells?"

Branwen said, "Yes. At the entrances to their underwater caverns and to their stone houses on the islands."

"So what you translate as *bells* isn't a mistranslation or a substitute translation? Tell me, are there puns in the Webnites' language?"

"Yes. Why do you ask?"

"I'll tell you later."

Wassruss's eyes became larger as if she had just seen something surprising. The frosted glass within them spread out. A sound as of mice feet scratching on a metal floor came from her mouth. Then she sighed.

The monitors emitted unmodulated *beeps*; the green lines on the 'scopes were like arrow shafts. Hu turned the machines off and did not think it worth the effort to apply the mentoscope to Wassruss.

Branwen held the big, brown hand for a minute, then gently lowered it.

"She was holding off until she had passed on the gifts and the mystery."

He looked at the triangle, square, and circle.

"I'll put these in my cabin-safe. Their status can be determined later."

"Status?" Hu said.

"Yes, whether they are my property or the government's. After all, they can't be said to be bribes."

"You don't know the twisted ingenuity of our bureaucrats," Toyce said.

The medical corps people came to take Wassruss's body away. Branwen seemed to be waiting for Ramstan to say something to her, but he walked out and went to his quarters. Instead of placing the gifts in the safe, he kept them in his pocket. He did not know why he had changed his mind. Then he tried to communicate with the *glyfa*. If it was receiving, it was not transmitting. He gave up after five minutes and went to mess. Hu came in late and sat down in the space reserved for her, the chair rising from the deck as she lowered her buttocks.

"Lieutenant Davis's fever—its cause—is as mysterious as ever. But I have a hunch . . . yes, smile, it's okay, a hunch. She is trying to tell us something. Or perhaps she is sick so that she won't have to do something she doesn't want to do."

Ramstan did not comment. When mess was over, he excused himself and went to the sickbay now formed to hold Davis alone. A marine stood guard at the entrance. Ramstan went in, the entrance closing behind him. Branwen was lying in bed staring up at the overhead. A large plate had been transformed into a screen on which an old 4-D movie was being shown. Her lackluster eyes did not brighten when he entered. She told ship to turn off the movie, and there was silence and less light.

"You look sick and are," Ramstan said. "Frankly, I think that Doctor Hu may be right. Your fever *is* psychosomatically engendered. Are you repressing something?"

She burst into tears and put her hands over her face.

Ramstan waited for a minute, then said, "What is it?"

She took her hands away. The eyes were brighter now because of the tears.

"You're wrong, sir," she said. "I'm hiding nothing. I don't know why I'm sick. I wept because it seemed so unjust to be accused of deliberately making myself sick. It's almost like being accused of malingering."

"There's nothing illegal about that type of goldbricking. But I get the feeling that you're . . . not quite truthful."

Indignation burned in her eyes. Or was it the fever?

"I'm not hiding anything," she said, and she began weeping again.

13

"THE TOLT SHIP is now in stationary orbit, sir," the petty officer said. "She's directly above the island. As you ordered, a message is being transmitted to her. But so far she hasn't responded."

Ramstan refrained from looking upward. He knew he could not see it, but he had an impulse to bend his neck back and gaze into the bright blue.

"Very well," he said. "Continue transmitting. If it does nothing else, it will annoy them. And it will serve notice that we're aware of them."

Al-Buraq, panting yellow, lay about fifty meters away. She was in starfish-shape now. Crewpeople were strolling around it, most of them nude, taking the opportunity to absorb some natural sunshine.

Another fifty meters in the opposite direction, the green-blue ocean lashed great white-capped waves at the yellow sands of the beach. The wind blew from the west, bringing with it a spicy odor from a large tree-capped island-peak 10 kilometers distant. The trees near Ramstan resembled Terran palms. Their fronds waved in the breeze. Yellow-and-scarlet birds with black toucanlike beaks and cartilaginous horns on top of their heads swooped over the crew. From the top of a double-

trunked baobablike plant an enormous green many-angled
insect dropped a sticky noose. Presently, along came a tiny
bird, and the noose jerked and ensnared the bird. Screaming, it
was drawn up toward the mouth into which the long gelatinous
rope was disappearing.

Branwen shuddered.

"Webn is beautiful, but it has its sinister features."

"Nonsense," Toyce said. "There is nothing evil about that
insect. It has to eat, doesn't it? And it really is beautiful.
Would you like to take a closer look?"

She held out an electron-telescope.

"No, thanks. I've seen them before at close range."

Branwen's fever was now very low; her body temperature
was only one-tenth of a degree above normal. Hu had given
her permission to go as interpreter with the burial party. It had
just come back from half a kilometer offshore where Wassruss,
weighted down with rocks tied to her, a wreath of flowers and
weeds attached to her chest, had been dropped into the sea.
There were thousands of dark-brown, flippered giants in the
water, floating in concentric circles around the corpse and
singing joyous songs.

There was no reason, now that Ramstan had carried out his
promise to Wassruss, for ship to stay here. Yet Ramstan did
not give the order to take off. No one seemed to have made any
criticism of this. The crew had been on extended shore leave,
but it did not object to going on another. Though *al-Buraq* was
not a cramped vessel, she could not offer open skies and
ground to run on and vegetation and a natural sun. Moreover,
there was fishing and swimming with the friendly seal-centaurs
and hiking through the woods and hills and much discreet
lovemaking behind trees or boulders.

The Tolt ship hanging above, invisible to the naked eye,
mute, sinister, could be forgotten easily enough by all but
Ramstan. He was aware of it in every waking moment and
sometimes in his dreams. It was an unseen shadow that
darkened the beauty and glory of island and sea.

Ramstan, thinking of this, walked through the woods on a
path which large beasts had made. The wild animals were so
unafraid of the strangers that they seemed almost domesti-
cated. When he reached the foot of the basalt mountain
dominating the island, he turned back. But he halted within a

few meters. Stocky, bull-necked, Assyrian-bearded Benagur blocked his way.

"I didn't know Hu had given you permission to leave ship," Ramstan said.

"I've been a good boy," Benagur said sarcastically. "And I've shown no signs of misintegration since my outburst. Which I don't think was a symptom of craziness. You don't believe in God, and you have stolen the *glyfa*. But . . ." he paused . . . "perhaps I was wrong in one thing. You do believe in a god, the Tenolt god."

"You'll only do yourself a disservice if you keep saying that," Ramstan said.

Benagur's bellow seemed to be the echo of the distant sea crashing against the base of the cliffs on the western shore. Like the sound of the ocean, it held a suggestion of danger.

"It's very frustrating for me! I know that you took the *glyfa*, yet I can't prove it! And if I accuse you officially, you will just have me locked up or sickbayed again! But you're the crazy man, Ramstan! You've put us all in the most extreme jeopardy, but you don't seem to care at all! You'll die for your sin, and so will we, the innocents!"

Ramstan felt sick with guilt and with hatred of Benagur. His hands curled into half-fists. He took one step forward. Benagur did not flinch. He crouched, and his left shoulder rose a trifle as if he was on the verge of adopting a boxer's stance. His hands, too, were partly clenched.

Ramstan felt like hurling himself at Benagur. But he saw something flicker at the base of a huge tree near the foot of the low hills beyond Benagur. The flicker became a figure in green. Its hood and robes were bright green; the face below the hood was featureless, shrouded in darkness. An arm rose, and its hand moved slowly back and forth at a 45-degree angle upward to the ground. The hood moved as if the turbaned head within it was moving to the right and then the left. It said as plainly as if it were speaking, "No!"

Al-Khidhr, the Green One, the Wanderer.

If he was indeed Elijah, the ancient Hebrew, he was watching over Ramstan, protecting the atheist ex-Muslim, not the devout Jew, Benagur.

But al-Khidhr was a Sufi, the pristine Sufi, and Sufis could be Jewish or Christian as well as Muslim.

Then Ramstan thought, I'm crazy. Benagur is right, I *am* crazy.

The green figure flickered and was gone.

Ramstan stepped back and straightened his fingers. His voice shook.

"You're the dangerous one, Benagur, the mad one. You almost provoked me into attacking you."

He took another step back.

"Is this a trap? Are you transmitting to my officers through the skinceiver?"

Benagur scowled.

He roared, "No! I came here to make a final appeal to your honor and your duty! To your reason or what's left of it! But I can see that it's useless!"

"And now what?"

"I will make official charges! You can do your best to get me locked up again, but the charges can't be ignored! They'll have to be investigated! Your quarters will be searched! And the *glyfa* will be found! Then . . ."

"Then . . . ?" Ramstan said softly. His voice was now as steady as a steel beam on bedrock.

"Perhaps they . . ." Benagur pointed up at the invisible Tolt vessel . . . "they will be satisfied with the return of their god! My God, Ramstan! Crazy as you are, surely you see what danger we're all in! We could all be killed, killed for no good reason! I don't know what impelled you to take the *glyfa*, what foul lust, what . . ."

"That's a strange word," Ramstan said, smiling slightly. "Lust! What made you say that?"

Despite his smile, he felt ice sinking through him from the top of his head toward his toes. It was, in a sense, lust. And he had no idea why he should have been seized with it. Nor how Benagur had stumbled over and on that description. Perhaps . . . Benagur himself had felt the lust.

Benagur said, "The *glyfa* must have made you lust for it!"

"It's just an artifact," Ramstan said. "Are you saying it's alive? A true god? A living idol? Who's crazy, Benagur? You or me?"

"I felt something there!" Benagur cried. "I felt a vast, an overwhelming evil! I knew where it came from! It came from the *glyfa*! And, yes, I'll admit it, Ramstan, since I am only human and so subject to temptation! I was tempted to succumb to the evil! But it was God who saved me, who showed me the ineffable Good, His true Nature! He stepped in, and He gave me a glimpse of Him, of His face, and so saved me!"

Perhaps we're both insane, Ramstan thought.

It was then that he got the first faint thought that he and Benagur might not be standing on the seashore of the world of Webn. Not in reality. They just thought they were there. They *seemed* to be there. Where were they, in actuality?

He got a flash of where they might be, and he just as quickly rejected the image.

He shook his head and then rolled it as if he were trying to dislodge some thing clinging to it, a giant louse, perhaps. Some filthy and blood-sucking thing.

"We have nothing more to say to each other," Ramstan said. "Not here, anyway."

He strode off though he was not sure that he should turn his back on Benagur. The man was no coward, far from it, but he might be overcome by his fury and jump on his captain from behind. Ramstan refused to look behind him. He did not wish Benagur to think that he feared him.

After cutting through a forest which covered the neck of the peninsula like a ruff, he came onto the seashore again. Half a kilometer inland, mighty *al-Buraq* stretched out across a clearing.

Chief Engineer Indra, nude, was sitting on a floating chair in the sun. On an extended arm of the chair was a half-full bottle of Kalafalan wine. In his hands was a book, a square plate half a meter wide and a centimeter thick. Ramstan paused behind Indra to read the phonemic-character words appearing and disappearing swiftly one by one. Indra did not have to move his eyes from side to side or down. It was *The Maltese Falcon*, a classical twentieth-century American novel translated into Terrish.

Indra felt Ramstan's body between him and the sun. He touched a control on the side of the book, and the text stopped moving. He twisted around; his teeth shone whitely in his dark face.

"Captain! I was hoping I'd catch you."

Ramstan came around the chair.

"Why?"

Indra stood up, the book held between two fingers.

"You'll remember that I told you some time ago that ship was growing a new circuit."

"Yes."

"I've just determined what it is."

Ramstan said, "I know what it is. It's an affection circuit. One that has an affection configuration, anyway."

"You know!"

"I'm not a bioengineer, but I know more about ship than anyone else."

Indra said, "How do you feel about it? I mean . . . do you respond to its affection with your affection? With love?"

"To be loved isn't always the same as to love," Ramstan said stonily. "We don't have time for experiments. There's that. . . ." He pointed at the sky. "I don't want to worry about ship getting hysterical or panicky if she thinks I'm in danger."

"She's not a dog," Indra said, "though she may have developed some doglike attitudes. I could find out just what effect the affection configuration has on her gestalt. But it'll take time."

Ramstan said, "Excise the circuit."

Indra frowned and bit his lip.

"That's an order, not a suggestion. Operate *now!*"

"Aye, aye, sir!" Indra said. He snapped a salute and stalked off. Ramstan watched him for a minute, then started toward the vessel. He stopped when he saw Branwen Davis. She was so beautiful that his heart seemed to ache.

He hailed her and then asked her about her health, though he'd seen the medical report on her that morning.

"I feel fine," she said. "The fever has gone as suddenly as it came, and the doctors don't know where it came from, what caused it, or where it went."

"Let's hope it doesn't return," he said. He paused, balled up what little courage he had, and used it all up in one sentence.

"Would you care to dine in my cabin tonight?"

She smiled, but she said, "No, but thank you for the honor, sir."

He was shocked. He had not really expected her to turn him down. No woman ever had.

Though he'd thought his face was expressionless, he must

have shown something somehow. She said, "I'm sorry. I don't mean to offend you, Captain. But I've talked to some women . . ."

"What does that matter? You're not one of them. You're different."

"They all said that they were in love with you and that you were in love with them. At least, you told them you were. But after a while, a short while, they said, you became very cold and then downright nasty."

"I was never nasty!" he said. "They lied!"

If she had been anyone else, he would not have deigned to discuss the matter. He despised himself for humbling himself like this.

"All of them?" she said. "Well, I won't argue. Anyway," she touched his arm with a finger and held it there, "I'm not rejecting you, you know. I'm just rejecting your invitation to dinner. I'm not ready to go to bed with you, and I may never be. But I don't dislike you."

"You don't like me, either," he said. He was astonished; someone else must have said that.

"Some people are very warm and, so, likeable," Branwen said. "You're not warm."

"I'm the captain of ship," he said.

"And so proud and lonely," she said, and she laughed. "No, you've got it the wrong way. You'd be aloof and lonely if you were the cabin boy. Captain Irion was a very good commander, but still there was something about her that made people love her." She paused.

"You're angry," she said. She withdrew her finger from his arm and he had a flash of image, a wound made by the finger, now closing up, the blood evaporating, and ice forming over the scar.

"Yes, I am," he said. "But not at you. Other things . . ."

He almost believed that he was not lying.

"I'll see you," he said, and strode away.

Ramstan went to his quarters and called the bridge. Over-lieutenant Ozma Garrick responded.

"I want Commodore Benagur arrested. He is to be put in his cabin, not the brig, and he is to stay there until Doctor Hu has examined him. Notify me as soon as he's quartered."

Garrick looked as if she'd like to ask him the reason for the order, but she didn't, of course. Ramstan then called Indra.

"Have you started yet on the circuit?"

"I haven't started operating."

"The order is canceled. Hold yourself ready to resume operating, though."

The Hindu smiled but said nothing.

Ramstan was glad that Indra had not questioned him. He himself didn't know why he'd put off the operation.

He sat down and drummed the fingers of his left hand on his thigh. Then he called the bridge.

"Garrick, resume signaling to the Tolt ship. If you get an answer, notify me at once."

Garrick's face faded from the octant. Ramstan sat motionless—even his fingers were unmoving—for a few minutes. Then, sighing, he heaved himself up and walked to the bulkhead. Shortly thereafter, he placed the *glyfa* on a table. He ran his fingers over the surface and marveled again at how some dead-for-eons artist had sculpted it so intricately and wonderfully and deep and yet it was so smooth.

He spoke to himself out loud. "If only I knew what the Tenolt were up to!"

The voice that answered him turned him around, his eyes wide, his skin paling, his heart threatening to burst. But he was the only human in the room.

"Allah!"

He spoke a few more words in Arabic, most of which were curses.

The voice had said or seemed to have said, "They know you stole me. But they don't want to attack while you're in ship. Above all, they want to get me back into their hands."

Now it said, "I should have warned you."

Ramstan leaned on the table while he gripped its edges. His heart began to slow down, but he could only speak in gasps at first.

"Why . . . do you use . . . Branwen Davis's voice?"

Only then did it strike him that the *glyfa* was reading his mind. He was outraged. No one or no thing should be permitted that violation.

"No, I don't read your mind, and I can't," the *glyfa* said in the voice of Khadija, his mother.

"If you can't . . . then . . . how did you know . . . what I was thinking?"

"I knew that you would have thought that I was," the voice said.

Ramstan had not wept for years. Now tears rolled down his cheeks.

"Please don't use her voice," he said.

"Very well. How's this?"

Benagur's voice boomed.

"No!"

"I'll speak to you as your mother, then."

"No!"

"You'll get used to it, and eventually you'll love it. I think you've been carrying your grief too long, even if you didn't know you had it buried so deeply."

"It makes me feel as if she's speaking from the grave," Ramstan said. "Or . . . as if you're her tomb, and she's talking to me from it."

"In a sense, she is," the *glyfa* said.

Ramstan asked it to explain the remark, but the *glyfa* ignored his question. It said, "You'll like to hear her. You've been using your quarters as a sort of womb in which you can take refuge. Now, hearing her here, you will be even more in the womb. That isn't a good thing, perhaps. But you seem to need it."

"If you can't read my mind, then how do you know so much about Davis and Benagur and only Allah knows who else?"

"I can detect vibrations and see objects at a distance," his mother's voice said. "I can detect electrical and electronic phenomena. I can detect other things, too."

"You can see and hear things outside this cabin?"

"Yes. Of course."

"How far?"

"Quite far."

"You won't tell me the exact distance?"

"I have my reasons not to."

"Could you tell the captain of the *Popacapyu* to go away and leave us alone?"

The *glyfa* did not answer.

Ramstan said, "It's obvious that you can't."

"Or that I may have some reason not to wish to."

"It's also obvious," Ramstan said, "that you can influence electricity at a distance. How do you do that?"

"The explanation would be meaningless to you."

"But you have to find the right words in my memory bank, put them together in Arabic or Terrish syntax, modulate them, get the right intonations, stresses, and so on. And when you use my mother's voice, evoke it. I mean, you use some words that my mother never heard nor read. Also, you must originate your transmissions of language in your own language. How do you manage the translation? I mean, even if you're transmitting your voice to me in some manner or some sort of coded signals or whatever, they wouldn't mean anything to me if I heard them directly. Via vibration of air through my eardrums, I mean. So . . ."

"It must be enough for you that I can do this," the *glyfa* said. "Now. To your original question to yourself. What are the Tenolt up to? They wish to get me back, and they're not going to use violence and so take a chance of losing me unless desperation drives them to it. Also, for all they know, you may have hidden me elsewhere than in *al-Buraq*. On Kalafala or Walisk, perhaps, or even on Webn. Though they would have seen you do that unless you somehow tricked them.

"Also, I am their god. It frightens and puzzles them that I permitted you to take me. Or, perhaps, and this must deeply disturb them, that perhaps you, Ramstan, were able to steal me because you might be more powerful than I. I doubt, though, that anyone on their vessel has dared voice that thought. It would go very hard with anyone who did, even their high priest."

A whistle shrilled. Ramstan was startled, but he spoke a few words to cut off video on his end of the line. Garrick's face appeared in an octant.

"Commodore Benagur has been arrested and confined to his quarters, sir. Doctor Hu is en route to examine the commodore, as you ordered."

"Thank you, Lieutenant," Ramstan said, and he cut off the transmission.

The *glyfa* said, "Poor Benagur. He's a mystic, and, in his search for the ineffable, he has caught a glimpse of it. Or is the rag of glory worn by something else? The Opponent, for instance? Would not the Opponent have a glory of his own, and would it not be difficult to distinguish his glory from the true glory?"

"You seem amused," Ramstan said.

Though he did not like Benagur, he felt sorry for him at this moment. Perhaps that was because he felt sorry for himself, too. Rather, he felt confused and, because of this confusion, helpless. He loathed that feeling and despised himself for it. He could make his way against all obstacles. At least, until recently, he had thought so. Now . . . he was not so sure.

He had to ask the *glyfa* some questions, yet he hated doing it. He should be able to find the answers by himself.

"What is the *bolg?*" he said.

There was a pause as if the *glyfa* had been taken by surprise. But Ramstan might be misinterpreting the silence.

"The *bolg?*" the *glyfa* said. "I haven't heard that name for a long time. A time so long you would be shattered just to contemplate the idea of it."

"Well?" Ramstan said.

"It's a name for a chaos-monster. The people who used it have perished long ago. In fact, several . . ."

Ramstan said, "Several what?"

"Never mind. Where did you hear it?"

Ramstan told it what had happened in the Kalafalan tavern. This gave him some satisfaction, despite the reawakening of the bad emotions connected with the incident. The *glyfa* had not been observing him when he was in the tavern. Was that because it was unable to do so or because it had preferred not to? Or was the *glyfa* lying for some reason and had known about the tavern incident all along?

"There are many in this war," the *glyfa* said. "I knew that long ago, but I still don't know who some of them are. But I have time enough. At least, I hope so."

"What does that mean?" Ramstan asked.

There was no answer.

It was evident that the *glyfa* must know about the destruction of Waliskan life. Ramstan asked it if that had had anything to do with the *bolg*.

"As of now, everything in the universes has to do with the *bolg*," the *glyfa* said.

"What do you mean by universes?"

"You shouldn't know everything at once. You couldn't handle all that."

Ramstan's anger flared up again.

"What am I? A mere pawn?"

"Pawns are not mere. Nothing that is necessary is mere. You are a focal point, perhaps *the* focus. And don't think I mean that you are a thing. A focus can be a person."

If the *glyfa* could reach inside him, activate memories and language units, it surely could trigger off emotions. How else explain why he had stolen the *glyfa?* That was an act that he would not even have thought of, not the captain responsible for the crew of ship and ship herself. He had put *al-Buraq* and her people in the most extreme danger, and he had never been sure just why.

Surely, the *glyfa* had wished him to take it, and it had moved him to the act as if he were a robot.

Hoarsely, he told the *glyfa* what he was thinking.

As usual, he got a half-answer from the thing.

"I am incapable of inserting desires in others. I can't operate on what doesn't exist."

"You must have monitored the dying of Wassruss," Ramstan said. "What are the three gifts? What does that question-and-answer chant mean?"

"There'll be a time and a time for those," the *glyfa* said.

Ramstan roared, "I'm fed up with your enigmas! Out you go! Out, I say! The Tenolt can have you back!"

Silence.

Ramstan yelled, "Talk, damn you! Unless I get complete and clear answers, I'm going to heave you out of here! I'll show you!"

Had the *glyfa* withdrawn, cut off detection? Or was it sitting in that impenetrable shell and smiling whatever kind of smile such a being could have?

He put his hands upon the egg-shape, lifted it a few centimeters from the table, then took his hands away. The *glyfa* dropped with a thud but did not roll.

If he took the thing out now, he would be observed. And the crew would know that he had taken it.

It would be better to remove it at night and carry it to some place out of sight, say, the top of a rocky ridge half a kilometer away. When the daylight came, or perhaps before that, the Tolt operator of the magniscope would see it. And the Tolt vessel would come down as swiftly as possible to retrieve the god.

Its descent would be detected, of course, and the crew of *al-Buraq* would have to be put on alert. Only he would know why the Tolt was moving toward them, and he could not tell anybody.

But what if the Tolt captain, having gotten the *glyfa*, decided to take revenge? Would he regard the theft as sacrilege? Would he then attack *al-Buraq?*

Or, if he contemplated such action, would he be stopped by the *glyfa?* Perhaps the *glyfa* would not want to stop the Tolt.

He paced back and forth, his head bent, his long chin almost touching his chest, his hands locked behind his back. Finally, he lifted the *glyfa*, put it back into the bag, and returned it to the bulkhead-safe. The deck trembled very slightly as if *al-Buraq* was aware of her captain's emotional turmoil and frustration and was shaking with sympathy. Which thought, of course, was ridiculous, Ramstan told himself. He was anthropomorphizing, no, theriomorphizing, too much.

A call came from the bridge. Doctor Hu wanted to speak to him about Benagur. Ramstan left his quarters almost at once. But as he strode down the passageways, he wondered what had made him keep the *glyfa*. Was it entirely his own decision? Or had the *glyfa* subtly steered him toward it?

14

Some mystics seek God by travel; others, by staying in one room.

Benagur had done both. Something had happened to cause him to venture forth from the little chamber in a house in Jerusalem near the Wailing Wall. No one but he knew what it was, but occasionally he had hinted at the event. When questioned by those eager to get the details, he had said that the event was indescribable.

He would seem to have been unfitted to be a crewmember of an alaraf ship. But he was known worldwide among theologists for his writings on Jewish and Muslim mysticism, and *al-Buraq* had several berths open for theologists. Benagur was accepted after, of course, the required physical and psychological tests. A deep psychic probe had not been needed to determine that he was eccentric, but it did indicate that he had the stability needed for alaraf-ship living. Besides, he was not the only eccentric aboard.

If he tended to keep to himself much of the time, he had a good excuse. Like many of the specialists, he was very busy with his professional duties. Unlike most of the others, he was given special privileges because of the rigors of his religion. Whenever possible, he ate by himself and only the foods his religion permitted. The other Jews aboard belonged to sects too liberal for him to regard them as genuine Jews. That was all right with the others; they thought he was a superfanatic. They had, however, a great respect for his knowledge.

Ramstan had had no trouble with Benagur until the night the *glyfa* was stolen. Though Benagur was very reserved, that had not bothered Ramstan, who was equally reserved.

Now, Ramstan felt some guilt. If he'd not done what he'd done, he would not have thrown Benagur into the strange frenzy possessing him.

Was Benagur crazy? Was he not, by all standards except Ramstan's, sane? Would not the others be acting much like him if they suspected what Benagur suspected?

On the other hand, none of them might have been affected as deeply. They did not have Benagur's psychic constitution; they were not near the edge of insanity and needing only a slight push to shove them over. After all, Maija Nuoli had been subjected to the same overpowering *light*, and she had not become psychotic. She had become more introspective than before, and she did not care to talk about her experience in the Tolt temple. But she had carried out her duties as a botanist as efficiently as before.

Ramstan wondered why the *glyfa* had asked for her to accompany him and Benagur. What part did she play in the drama the *glyfa* was undoubtedly writing? For that matter, what part did Benagur have? Perhaps he was no longer in the thing's designs. Whatever it was that had flooded the senses of the three, it had unbalanced Benagur and made him useless to the *glyfa*.

It was possible that the *glyfa* had summoned Nuoli and Benagur to come merely to ensure that Ramstan would not be singled out as the thief. They, too, would be suspects. If so, the *glyfa* had miscalculated. Suspicion had not fastened upon Benagur or Nuoli.

The *glyfa* might have some other reason, however, for inviting them.

Ramstan entered Doctor Hu's office. Hu rose from behind her desk as the captain entered.

"Sit down, Julia," Ramstan said. His use of Hu's first name indicated that no formalities were to be observed.

Ramstan made a sign, and a chair formed from the deck. He

sat down, and, after the silence lasted for several seconds, said, "Well?"

Hu did not look at Ramstan. "Commodore Benagur claims that you stole the *glyfa* from the Tenolt."

Now it was in the open, Ramstan thought. No, not really. It could perhaps be kept to Benagur and Hu.

"You gave him a lie-test?"

"Of course. It indicates that he *thinks* he's telling the truth."

"In which case, then, he's psychotic," Ramstan said.

Hu hesitated and then looked Ramstan in the eyes.

"That remains to be proved."

Ramstan reared up from the chair, bellowing, "What?"

Hu spread her hands out and shrugged.

"He's going to bring formal charges against you."

Ramstan sat down and bit his lips.

"I can't allow that. We're in a very grave and dangerous situation. The Tolt vessel . . . the terrible destruction of Walisk . . . no. All normal procedures will have to be suspended."

"You won't allow Benagur to make the charges?"

"I can't permit it now. After there's no more danger, I will, of course."

He leaned forward, his upper arms on his thighs, his hands clasped.

"Listen. If Benagur can be shown to be psychotic, then there's no need to log these ridiculous charges."

"He's certainly upset, which is not, however, the same as being unbalanced."

Ramstan leaned back and said, smiling slightly, "Has he also accused me of not believing in God?"

"No. He said nothing about that. Why?"

"A little while ago, near the seashore, he made that accusation. He seemed to think that it made me guilty, as criminal, as if I had stolen the *glyfa*. In fact, more so."

"He would be psychotic if he'd included that charge in the others," Hu said. "But he didn't."

"He came close to attacking me while we were on the beach."

Hu lifted her eyebrows. "Yes? Was his intention overt? Did he threaten you or make any obviously belligerent moves?"

Ramstan had done far worse than lie, but he just could not bring himself to lie about this.

"No. But it was evident that he would have liked to attack me."

Hu's grimace indicated that that was not enough justification to think Benagur psychotic. It also seemed to Ramstan that it said that Benagur wasn't the only crewmember who would like to assault him.

Ramstan stood up.

"Benagur will be kept in his cabin unless his condition gets worse and he has to be restrained. You or one of your colleagues will give him therapy."

Hu rose.

"There's nothing in the EEG readings or blood samples to indicate a psychotic condition."

"But those aren't sure methods of determining neurosis or psychosis, are they?"

"By no means. The psychosoma is vastly complex and often tricky. Centuries . . ."

"You have my orders," Ramstan said. He strode out. Hu could give the command for the chair to shrink back into the deck. It was protocol for the chair-riser to be the chair-ridder, but to hell with the doctor.

While walking back to his quarters, he used the skinceiver.

"Garrick, order all personnel to return to ship at once. We jump for Kalafala in an hour. I'll be on bridge in thirty minutes."

" 'What is the number of the worlds?'

" 'More than many.'

" 'What is the number of paths?'

" 'More than many. Yet they are one.'

" 'What is at the end of the paths that are one?'

" 'Death or wisdom or both. *And one more thing*.'

" 'What is the way to the three?'

" 'There are many places to start. Webn is one.'

" 'And then?'

" 'Ring the bell at the first entrance past Webn.'

" 'And then?'

" 'Enter.' "

The chant was obviously a navigational chart for the journey from the planet Webn to wherever and whatever the final destination was. Ramstan had seen that within ten minutes after hearing Davis's interpretation of Wassruss's ritual-song. He doubted that Wassruss knew what it meant; she had learned it by rote and given it as required, however meaningless it was to her. The Webnites had no means for space travel except as passengers on the alaraf ships of other sentients. Whoever had given the chant and the three gifts to Wassruss's ancestor had known what the chant meant but had not explained it to the donee. Or perhaps the donor had done so but the explanation had been forgotten.

The Webnites did have bells, and so the donor had been able to use "bell" when translating the chant from his or her language into Webnian. But the seal-centaurs did not have dumbbells, those muscle-building devices which consisted of two spherical objects connected by a shaft. It wouldn't have helped their understanding of the chant any if they had had them. It was extremely unlikely that their word for it would have been the transfer-meaning or pun used in Terrish.

Ramstan doubted that the originator of the chant had meant any connection between a "bell" and a "dumbbell." But the Terrans had made such a connection since there seemed to them to be a "shaft," sometimes called a "tunnel," between the "bell" of one star system and the next. It was possible and perhaps very probable that the originator of the chant had used a word meaning "bell" in his language. There had been no implication of "dumbbell" in the chant. The originator had just meant that when you entered a "bell," that roughly spherical shape with an opening or "mouth" through which you went to the next star system, you were "ringing" it.

Or it might be that the Raushghols had defined their terminology for alaraf travel to Wassruss when she was on their ship. Then, on *al-Buraq,* she had, Ramstan knew, been told briefly by Davis the Terran theory and terminology of alaraf travel. And she had substituted the word "bell" for whatever had been in the chant taught her.

The speculation about language did not matter. What did was that he believed that he had been given directions which were somewhat vague but still could get him to the destination

—whatever that was. He would try to get there because he might find an answer to the question of the *bolg*. And perhaps to other questions.

He went up to the bridge. He did not have to explain why they were going to Kalafala, but he said, "Lieutenant Davis was left there, and, if *Pegasus* has not been destroyed, she will come there to pick Davis up. We'll stay on Kalafala for a little while."

Al-Buraq had been in the Kalafalan bell only three minutes when the tec-op reported another spaceship a thousand kilometers distant. She was oyster-shell-shaped.

"*Popacapyu,*" the operator said.

Five hours after *al-Buraq* had landed on the Kalafalan port, the Tolt vessel set down. Ramstan wondered why she had landed here but not on Webn. And why had no Tolt left her yet, though it was protocol for her commander to report immediately to the control tower authority?

An hour passed. Then the ports of the Tolt ship opened, and about fifty Tenolt came out. The captain headed for the tower with some officers. The others went to the tavern. Ramstan waited until he saw the captain return to his ship. In the meantime, at least half of the original group had also come back to the *Popacapyu*. Another group then left the vessel for the tavern. Apparently, their captain was giving them a limited shore leave, time for just a few drinks.

Tenno said, "Sir, do you plan to give shore leave?"

"That depends," Ramstan said, and he did not say on what.

A half hour passed. Then two jeeps flew from the Tolt ship and headed toward the hotel. The commander sat in one.

Ramstan relaxed somewhat. He said, "It looks as if they're going to be here a while."

He told Tenno that there would be a limited and strictly regulated shore leave. Groups of forty could go out one at a time, the second group to leave after the first had returned at the end of thirty minutes and so on. They were not to go to the tavern or the hotel, but they could have a few drinks at the port bar. They should be ready to return to ship immediately if a recall occurred.

"Do you expect trouble?" Tenno said.

"Not really. But I want my crew closer to their ship than the Tenolt will be to theirs."

He left it up to Tenno to decide who would be among the shore-leave parties, and he went to his quarters. He took the *glyfa* from the safe, and, rubbing it as if he were Aladdin trying to summon the *djinn* from the lamp, asked it to talk to him.

Silence.

Ramstan bit his lower lip. Damn the thing!

He paced back and forth for an hour, stopping every fifteen minutes to call the bridge and get a report on the Tenolt. The captain of the *Popacapyu* was still at the hotel. The second Tenolt group had returned to their ship, and a third had gone out. The only ones armed were those in the jeeps accompanying the captain.

Ramstan paced again, then stopped. Frowning, he started toward the bulkhead area, holding the electron-microscope. Something had been bothering him, nibbling mice at the periphery of his mind. Only now did he realize what it was. The lighting was less bright than it should have been.

He called the bridge. "Tenno, is there anything wrong . . . ? I mean, any indications of a power malfunction, for instance?"

"Not that we've noticed here, sir. But I'll call the engineers. May I ask why you ask?"

"Just check."

He could not bring Indra to his quarters to look for a malfunction in the neural system. Troubleshooting might lead Indra to the safe. If Indra was then forbidden to open it, he would get suspicious.

He spoke to the *glyfa*. "For the sake of Allah, what happened here? Tell me! You must know if someone's been here!"

He could hear only his rasping breath.

There was one thing to check before he used the microscope. He told *al-Buraq* to run off the monitor. A screen glowed immediately, though not as brightly as it was supposed to be. He groaned. No video! Somebody had erased it! And he shouldn't have been able to do so!

He started again towards the bulkhead in which the microscope was. But he whirled, went to the table on which the *glyfa* was, and turned the a-g units on its ends to zero power. He gripped the egg and lifted it easily.

His cry rang out.

"It's a fake!"

15

THE LIGHTING DIMMED AND WAS GONE.

He called the bridge. No reply.

Feeling along the bulkhead, he located the slight protuberance that indicated the cabinet holding the flashlights. But his order to ship to open it up was not obeyed.

He swore again, and he called out the order to make an exit for him. Again, no response.

Someone had entered and then arranged for the malfunction, perhaps through an anesthetic or a controlled-rate drug. Or the drug might have been injected first and the person had entered. He or she . . . or it . . . might also have mixed a hypnotic with the anesthetic. Or perhaps there had been no drug, but the sabotager had somehow hypnotized *al-Buraq*.

No time for speculation now. He should get the pseudo-*glyfa* back into the safe. The bulkhead wouldn't close now, but he would have it ready to be closed.

He put the egg into the bag, and he groped to the opposite bulkhead and felt around until he located the hole. When the egg was in the hole, he walked slowly, his hands out, back to the table. He gripped its edges as if he could squeeze photons from it. The darkness seemed to have smothered all the light in the world. The air moved slowly over his sweating face and hands. He could hear only the blood rushing through him and the singing of silence.

If all of ship were drugged, obviously malfunctioning, Indra and his engineers would be troubleshooting furiously. It wouldn't take them long to find out what was wrong and to fix it.

Meanwhile, whoever had taken the *glyfa* would be long gone.

He sweated even more heavily.

If *al-Buraq* had been operating fully, the humidity in the quarters would have been dropped and the air would have gotten cooler.

"*Iblis* take this bio-ship!"

His voice sounded hollow and faraway to him.

There were many advantages to a biological spaceship, but now the disadvantages were too obvious. The designers had not thought of saboteurs or of a crewmember going mad.

He pounded the table top with his fists, allowing himself a lack of control he would never have shown anybody under any circumstances he could envision. Or to himself under different circumstances. But, here in this dark, silent hollow, he could behave like a baby.

As his fist struck, he caught a flash of green out of the corner of his left eye. He jumped back from the table, his hands still balled. Green? He could see color in this total darkness?

No. He hadn't really *seen* it. He couldn't have. Not his eyes but his mind had glimpsed the green.

Why?

He thought of the green-clothed man whom he'd identified as al-Khidhr or Luqman or Elijah or all three as the same, though there was no proof that the green man was any one of them.

It was his brain that had originated that slash of color in the blackness around him. Just as, if he were to bump his head, he might see white or colored "stars" for a second or two. Explosions of asterisks or comets caused by nerves firing impulses caused by a too-hard contact with real things. But he had not struck his head against anything. His fists had been beating the table, but that couldn't account for the parenthesis of green. A thin, curving zip of color . . . perhaps not so much a parenthesis as a scimitar.

Or the edge of a turban or cloak.

The edge of the green iris of an eye of a man wearing green?

He waited. He did not see the flash again. Nevertheless, he had an overpowering feeling that someone else was in his quarters.

He bellowed, "Who's there?"

Silence.

"Is it you?" he yelled, not knowing whom he meant by *you*.

He listened and looked, turning his head so he could sweep one hundred and eighty degrees and then turning his body to take in three hundred and sixty.

He thought, or thought he thought, that he saw something very pale green. But surely that was a ghost of a ghost, a reflection of an image of an image. Imagination supplying something to back up its reality.

Something spoke to him.

His mother's voice? The voice stimulated by the *glyfa?*

No. It had to be something he'd wished. It was so far-off, so thin, so . . .

The darkness began to pale. Then he could make out objects dimly as if he were deep under water and light was seeping through the surface of the ocean far above him.

Abruptly, full brightness swept through the chamber. Tenno's voice came. "Captain?"

"Here!" he shouted.

At the same time, he thought, Where is here?

The answer, of course, was, where I am.

"What happened?"

"We don't know yet, sir," Tenno said. "But Doctor Indra thinks that someone drugged ship."

Ramstan said, "Put out an ACRS. I want everybody back in ship in ten minutes. Check them out as they come in."

He paused. "Is Commodore Benagur in his quarters?"

He could have asked *al-Buraq* directly, but protocol demanded that he go through the executive officer.

Tenno must have checked quickly. He said, "Yes, sir, he is."

Ramstan called Indra. The dark hawkish face was distressed.

"Yes, it's a drug. It was carried through the circulatory

system, and its point of injection is the bulkhead outside your quarters. The traces of drug are being analyzed right now."

How had the drugger learned the code words?

Perhaps the drug had uninhibited *al-Buraq* so much that she revealed codes when the intruder had asked for them. Or perhaps she hadn't done that. Perhaps the intruder had just overriden the codes with a direct order to open.

He made up new code words and gave them to ship. The deck quivered under him as ship, in a manner of speaking, wagged her tail.

Ramstan stopped as he headed toward the exit.

"Allah!"

The *glyfa* knew the code words. It had "heard" him speak them many times. What if it had summoned one of the crew and made him carry it away? Or, now that he thought of how the Tenolt guards had not seemed to know he was in the temple, what if a non-Terran *had* entered and removed the *glyfa* with its help?

He would never know what happened unless he got the *glyfa* back. And perhaps not then.

Why should he worry about the *glyfa*? He was rid of it. He no longer had to carry the burden of its presence. As time passed, he would be able to shed his guilt. There would be times when he would burn with it, but the pain would lessen. From now on, he could act as the captain of *al-Buraq* should. Though he might never entirely forgive himself, he need not carry out every act with consideration of the *glyfa* darkening it.

"Let it go!" he said aloud.

He had the exit opened, and he stepped out into the passageway.

Down the right-hand bulkhead of the corridor raced a glowing circle. It stopped just ahead of him, then reversed its direction and matched his pace. Tenno's face was solemn as he said, "The ten minutes are up, sir. Everybody's reported in . . . except one."

"Who's that?"

"Lieutenant Branwen Davis, sir."

Ramstan entered the lift, the circle following him into it and stopping on the door before him.

"Have you called her?"

"Yes, sir. She doesn't answer."

"Just a moment."

Ramstan spoke the necessary order, and the circle was bisected, half of it showing a reduced image of Tenno and the other the face of Indra.

"Is ship fully recovered?"

The engineer lifted his right wrist to one ear. Perhaps he was listening to the time through his skinceiver.

"My people say she'll be fully operational in ten more minutes, sir. There's still a residue of drug not flushed out yet. It takes time . . ."

"Notify me the second she's ready."

Indra's face disappeared. Tenno's swelled to fill the circle. But the lift door opened, and he was in the bridge. He at once asked the exec if he had questioned the crew on Davis's whereabouts.

"Yes, sir. Everybody's been contacted. Three say they saw her in the port main building for a few minutes."

Ramstan had to force himself to ask the next question.

"Did they say she was carrying a large bag? Or a box? Anything bulky?"

Tenno looked startled. Those on the bridge who had overheard gave him expressionless glances but some looked at others as if to transmit a silent message.

"I don't know, sir. I just asked if she'd been seen."

"Ask them if she was carrying a bag or a box!"

Tenno put ship on all-phone and did as ordered. Ramstan ordered several search squads out. They were to cover the port and also to question Kalafalans about Davis. Within forty seconds, Tenno made his report.

"Lieutenant Davis *was* carrying a box, sir."

"Al-Khidhr, Isa, and Muhammad!"

The exclamation was subvocalized; he had enough control not to show his panic.

If Davis was the one who'd taken the *glyfa*, why hadn't she accepted his invitation to bed? She could have seen his quarters in order to better her plans. She could have tried to get the code words out of him. She'd have failed, but surely she would have made the attempt.

But then she probably thought that getting into his cabin wasn't necessary. Nor had it been.

Who had put her up to this?

He mastered his rage, sickness, and fear. He said, "Send out two more search parties. Post two people where they can observe the Tolt ship."

A minute later, a CPO reported from the port tavern.

"Sir, a Kalafalan says she saw an Earthwoman who was carrying a box go into the hotel."

Ramstan ordered Tenno to have two jeeps with marines armed with olsons only ready to go within two minutes.

"I'll be in command. We're going to the hotel. Call in the search parties. Put ship on emergency take-off status, alaraf drive. As soon as I get back, we'll depart."

Tenno swallowed and said, "May I ask what this is all about?"

"I don't have time for explanations now," Ramstan said. "Be ready!"

He strode to the lift. If he caught Davis and brought the *glyfa* back with her, what then? She would reveal what she had done and why, and he could not deny that he had taken the *glyfa* from the Tolt temple. He'd be arrested.

He stepped out of ship. The bright sun was sliding down the final quarter of unclouded, pinkish sky. The air was delightfully fresh even though strained through his mask. Far to the west, black was building up on the horizon, a storm charging in from the ocean. It was a beautiful serene view with a hint of something sinister coming—typically Kalafalan in scenery and psychology.

The marine sergeant in command saluted. Ramstan looked briefly at the armed and masked men, got into the back seat of the front jeep, strapped himself in, and said, "To the hotel." The jeep rose to an altitude of 12 meters and began accelerating.

As yet, Ramstan had not ordered that any Tolt accompanied by Davis or any with a large box be intercepted. He was certain that an attempt to stop them would meet with vigorous resistance. There would be shooting. Then what? Would the Tolt ship attack *al-Buraq?* Probably. He would have put ship and crew in unnecessary danger. He'd be responsible for the deaths of many and for the wipeout, perhaps, of *al-Buraq*.

Why did he not just call off the search? He'd told himself that he was fortunate to be rid of the *glyfa*. He should have thought of some excuse to leave Kalafala. Branwen Davis would be marked down as a deserter.

He sighed deeply. Despite his original intentions, he was lusting for the *glyfa*. He had to have it back. Yet, he couldn't explain to himself why he must.

Perhaps, somehow, he could get the *glyfa* without altercation and could get rid of Branwen. He didn't have the slightest idea how this could be arranged nor did he genuinely believe it could be. Nevertheless, he would try.

Then he reared up against the restraining magnetic field, his hands pressed to his ears. The hands did not diminish the noise or his pain.

He screamed and he could hear his cry, though he should not have been able to do so.

The vast whistling sounded as if the very fabric of spacematter was being ripped apart.

As if the universe was crying out in a death agony.

16

THE JEEP DRIVER'S HANDS were pressed to her ears; her eyes were puddled with agony, and the face under the mask must be contorted. The jeep, its controls released, automatically slowed down and stopped.

Ramstan strove to overcome the pain from the whistling. He looked around for its origin but saw only that the other marines were also trying to block out the whistling with their palms. Their efforts were as useless as his. All around and below him, the Kalafalans on the street and the hotel steps were clamping their hands against their own ears, their mouths wide open as if they could ease their agony by letting the sound out from their mouths, their eyes also wide open, and their faces twisted, as if the whistling was a wringer through which their faces were being run.

Many were running headlong, stumbling, bumping into others, knocking them down or themselves falling. Others stood motionless as if turned into pillars of salt.

Some of the marines were screaming and so were many of the Kalafalans. He could hear them clearly through the whistling. Yet that awful noise should have overridden any other sound. That it did not meant that the whistling came from within himself. No! He was not originating it! That noise came from somewhere, but it was not transmissible in air or flesh; it came from something other than vibrations in the atmosphere.

"Run, Ramstan, run!"

The words were those of the voice in the tavern, but the voice was not the same. He did not recognize it.

He fought down the impulse to leap out of the jeep and run at top speed to . . . where? . . . anywhere to get away from the horror and the pain.

The driver shouted, "For God's sake, what is it? I can't stand it! I'm going crazy!"

Ramstan had no need to shout to be heard, but he roared with panic and desperation. "I don't know! Control yourself! Drive on! Drive on, I say!"

She took her hands away from her ears, said, shakily, "Yes, sir," and grabbed the wheel and put her feet on the pedals. She was quivering, and she looked as if she were about to scream back at the screaming in her head.

"There! There!" Ramstan said, pointing. Just beyond the hotel steps were two teardrop-shaped Tolt jeeps poised a half-meter above the sidewalk. Six armored and armed Tenolt sat in the first, the lower part of the prognathous faces masked, the woolly upper part between mask and helmet exposed. Five were in the second vehicle, two in the front seat and two in the back with Branwen Davis seated between them. Though she was masked, she was easily recognizable. All were holding their ears, and the jeeps had automatically stopped.

Ramstan shouted at the driver, "Get down there before they recover!" He pointed at the Tenolt.

He turned and bellowed at the marines. "It's no use holding your ears! Get ready to attack! Fire when I give the order! Shoot to kill!"

They might not have been able to hear him above the screams and yells of the frantic crowd below them, but they understood his gestures. Their hands came down, and they unholstered their olsons.

As suddenly as it had arrived, the whistling was gone.

The pain dwindled away swiftly, leaving in its wake a relief almost as pleasurable as the pain had been agonizing. But there was no time for Ramstan to savor it. The Tenolt drivers had resumed control; the jeeps were moving up and towards the spaceport, though slowly. And, as was evident from the gestures of the Tenolt, they had seen the approaching Terrans.

A marine behind him screamed, "Oh, God! Oh, God!"

Most of the Kalafalans had ceased shrieking, though their babbling was loud. But now they started screaming again, and many were pointing upwards and past Ramstan.

He turned and looked westward. The whistling had given him a sense of the unreality of the world which he had not yet overcome. Now the numbness and the feeling of being unmoored from the solidity of matter and time made a quantum jump. He could not understand, could not accept, what he was seeing. The thing in the sky should not exist. It was monstrous, unnatural, and yet there it was in Nature. Vaguely, he felt betrayed.

From the valley far away drifted the bonging of thousands of gongs.

There, surely, was the thing that had caused the whistling. The *bolg*. It was a sphere hanging over the planet, blotting out most of the sky, a frightening body that looked close, close, another planet just about to fall and crush all life, smash the earth, rip it apart, make it reel with the inconceivable mass, melt earth and the rock beneath the earth with the force of the collision.

But it was not falling. It was moving swiftly eastwards, though not nearly quickly enough, if it had the mass evidenced by its size, to stay in orbit. It should have fallen by now. It was not falling. It was moving above the planet's atmosphere, perhaps just beyond the outer boundary, seemingly held there by its power.

It was as round as a baseball, dark except for some paler markings which made it look like the face of a Halloween jack-o'-lantern carved by a palsied hand. A tiny horn, a truncated cone, projected from the bottom. Another horn, glittering in the light of the westering sun, stuck out from the center of the "face" like a parody of a nose. And there was another on the near side of the equatorial line.

Ramstan clung to the back of his seat and stared as the ground westwards raised itself and curved, undulating, towards him. The distant mountain range shimmied. The back of the earth curved up and down like the swellings of a heavy sea.

Forests lifted up and fell. Buildings rose and exploded and hurtled to the ground in fragments.

At the same time, a wind from the east began keening past him. The air struck him like a fist.

There was a cracking noise like a Brobdingnagian whip snapping. The ground waves passed beneath the two jeeps, the crest of one almost touching the bottom of the vehicles. Roaring, the hotel collapsed. In the distance, the spaceport control tower leaned over and then broke in half. Tiny figures spilled out of it.

He fought against withdrawing into himself and cutting off all the world outside his mind.

The rumble caught up with the snapping, then. The entire planet was growling and shaking—or so it seemed to him.

The people on the ground had been hurled down. Some were trying to stand up again but could not do it because the earth was rocking like slush in a bowl in the hand of a terrified person.

There were more cracks and rumbles. The earth split open in a great zigzag extending as far as he could see from the west. It sped like a crazed snake past him, people toppling into the suddenly opened crevasse, others, just on its edge, trying to crawl away or motionless with their faces pressed against the ground.

The wind became stronger. Hats, pieces of clothing, branches, leaves, and dust flew by him.

A voice was yammering from his skinceiver. Even though he held it close to his ear, he could not understand it. There was far too much noise from wind, screams, rumbles, and crackings. But he thought that he knew what the voice was warning him of.

The western sky between the horizon and that sphere was on fire.

At first, there seemed to be many, thousands, perhaps, of thin, blazing lines. They originated from above the atmosphere, no doubt, from the truncated cone which stuck out from the bottom of the gigantic thing. Meteorites. Missiles. Such as had swept fierily over Walisk. They were few, comparatively few, in the beginning. But now the curving lines from the upper air to the earth had become more numerous, seeming to expand, and now the sky between the vast bulge overhead and the ground was a solid curtain of fire.

The *bolg* was moving east, towards the Kalafalan capital, towards him, towards *al-Buraq*.

The ground undulated again.

The crust of Kalafala was tortured by the gravitational pull of the *bolg*. It was rising, was being ripped upwards, shaking, falling apart.

The air of Kalafala was being pulled upwards, also.

So was the oceanic area. Colossal tides would follow the path of the *bolg*.

Vomit threatened to spew out of him. But he looked at it again and saw that a shimmering corona, white shot with blue, surrounded it. Was that an energy discharge?

The world was literally falling down around him, and he had to get his marines back to the ship before that onrushing metal storm caught them. Or before a chasm opened up beneath *al-Buraq* and swallowed her. Yet . . . he could not leave Branwen or the *glyfa* here.

The two Tolt jeeps were moving towards the spaceport now. Their passengers were bent over, their faces turned away from the wind smiting them. Below them, the natives were rolling over and over, pushed by the wind though their fingers dug into earth or they clung to pieces of rocks or fragments of buildings blown their way. Some of the natives spun into the first crevasse opened or into new ones which had formed afterwards.

Ramstan looked away and saw that the Tolt jeeps were accelerating.

He bellowed, "After them! Shoot them! But don't hit Lieutenant Davis!"

Even if the situation had been that expected, he would not have been sure that they would immediately obey his orders. There had been no war on Earth for one hundred and thirty-five years, and these marines had not experienced even simulated combat. They had probably not expected to fight.

And now they were close to complete shock and panic. They would want to get back to ship as swiftly as possible. He did, too, but he would not permit himself to be diverted from his original mission.

Ramstan's skinceiver quit yammering. The voice was replaced by a shrill and loud series of dots and dashes. Code:

RETURN TO SHIP AT ONCE. RETURN TO SHIP AT ONCE. MISSILES FROM USO [Unidentified Space Object] APPROACHING AT RATE OF 1999 KILOMETERS PER HOUR. ARRIVAL HERE ETA TEN MINUTES. REPEAT. RETURN TO SHIP AT ONCE. ALARAF IN NINE MINUTES. REPEAT. RETURN TO SHIP AT ONCE. ALARAF IN NINE MINUTES. REPEAT . . .

Tenno was doing what he would have done. Regardless of who was or was not within ship, she would go into alaraf drive in nine minutes.

His mother's voice spoke. "Get back to ship! Now! Don't waste a second! Now! If you don't, you'll die! All will be lost!"

Ramstan forgot to subvocalize. He said, "I can't leave you here! And what about Davis?"

"Get back to *al-Buraq!*" the *glyfa* said, now switching to the voice of his commandant at the space academy. "Now! Now! It's the *bolg,* you fool! The *bolg!*"

Light flashed in the rear Tolt jeep, the one in which Branwen was. Three short, bright, thin beams. Allah! Branwen had pulled her olson from its holster or snatched one from a marine by her. She had shot the two beside her. Another flash. She had shot the fourth.

The jeep dived, struck the ground, bounced up, half-rolled, tossing the box out—the box which held the *glyfa*, surely —crashed on its side, and rolled completely over, sliding until its side rammed into a tree.

The other Tolt jeep stopped, swiveled, and started back. The ship's captain was in it, and he had great coolness and courage. He had ordered the jeep to come back and pick up the *glyfa*. And perhaps to kill Davis. Or pick her up. After all, he would probably not have seen that she had beamed her escort. The *glyfa*, however, would be his overriding concern.

Ramstan yelled. His driver had slumped over. Her face was slack. The jeep had stopped. Out of the corner of his eye he saw, but did not fully register, that the other jeep with his marines had pulled up alongside. He raised the driver and saw the holes, cauterized, in the front and back of her head.

A Tolt had shot her.

A hole appeared in the windshield by him. A marine in the back seat bent over. His helmet had a very thin hole in its back.

The marines in his jeep did not seem to know what was happening. But those in the jeep by his were firing their olsons at the Tolt jeep.

The box was a meter or so near the edge of a ragged crack in the earth. Branwen had gotten free of the vehicle—its security magnetic field must have gone off when the jeep was wrecked —and she was crawling away from it. The ground was swelling beneath her, she was on top of a wave, and then the torn earth collapsed beneath her. Her legs and buttocks were buried beneath dirt.

The wave had shifted the box nearer to the crevasse.

"You damn fool!" the space academy commandant's voice said. "Get back to ship! Leave me here! Come back and get me later! After the *bolg* is gone!"

"I might never find you!" Ramstan shrieked.

Something streaked fierily from the Tolt jeep. The jeep beside him exploded, and Ramstan felt heat and some stings on his side.

He did not remember how he had done it. But the body of the jeep driver was in the back seat and he was at the controls. His jeep shot by the Tolt jeep. A marine fell on him. He had been hit and had fallen on top of his captain. Ramstan ignored the corpse and directed the jeep towards *al-Buraq*, which was panting a yellowish-red light. A port opened in her, Ramstan drove the jeep into it, and slammed on the brakes. Energy shot red-bluishly from its vents. The magnetic field cushioned him and prevented him from dashing out his brains against the control panel. The shock emptied him of action for a moment.

The port crew had scattered when they had seen the speeding jeep. Now they ran out and gathered around him. The entrance closed up like a healing wound; the illumination within the port became brighter.

"Take care of them!" Ramstan said, waving his hand to indicate the dead or wounded in the jeep. He ran through the corridors, speaking into his skinceiver while he did so.

"Is everybody in?"

"Everybody except your marines," Tenno said. "I mean those in the other jeep."

"They're dead," Ramstan said. "Put ship in alaraf! Now! Destination: the Tolt bell!"

"Aye, aye, sir," Tenno said. His face, on the screen moving along the bulkhead to Ramstan's right, was fixed, seemingly emotionless except for intensity on the next order.

"That's the thing that destroyed Walisk!" Ramstan said. Tenno did not reply, but he paled.

A few minutes later, Ramstan was on the bridge.

All there were pale, and their faces were strained. A few were calling on God under their breaths. They all stank of deep fright. Ramstan was not sure that he had not wet his own shorts.

"We can write off Kalafala," Ramstan said. "We weren't able to get to Davis. I'll have a report from personnel later. Did the Tenolt send any messages?"

"No, sir."

"We're going back to Kalafala. We have to check it out. But not for some time."

"What could that thing be?" Tenno said. His voice was low and trembling. His head shook.

"I don't know. But I think that it can detect our trail and follow us."

"Follow us?" Tenno said. "Why? How?"

"I don't know."

Ramstan called Hu.

"We all need some antishock, Doctor."

"I have it ready, Captain. I was just about to call you."

A few minutes later, Hu, followed by two corpsratings, entered. They scanned every person to determine the amount each needed, and then applied the flat ends of their osmosers to the skins of the "patients." Ramstan immediately felt better; the sense of unreality and the numbness of perception faded.

Ramstan thought that it would be best if he told his officers why he was going to Tolt.

"I want to determine whether or not that monster has attacked Tolt."

His thoughts kept slipping back to the *glyfa*. And near it would be what was left—not much—of Branwen Davis.

Unless the Tolt officer in the jeep had rescued the *glyfa* and, perhaps, Davis.

He wondered if the *Popacapyu* had alarafed before the storm had swept over it. Or had it waited too long for its marines to return with the *glyfa?*

Six days later, the pear-shaped planet of Tolt filled the viewscreens. Clouds covered three-fourths of it, but the heat detectors and the analyzers showed that great fires were still raging in many areas. *Al-Buraq* curved around to the nightside; here, the large areas of heat were visible to the eye through the clouds.

"There's no use going down there," Ramstan said. "What happened is evident."

Though he had no evidence at all that he was responsible for the destruction of so much life, for the slaying of billions of sentients, he did feel guilty.

Tenno motioned with his finger for Ramstan to join him in a privacy field.

"I don't think we should be overheard, Captain. I'm worried, justifiably so. It seems that the Tenolt were able to track us through alarafian space. If they can do that, why not someone—or something—else? That monster that's been destroying planets, for instance?"

Tenno paused, looking as if he did not want to say what he must say.

"What is it?"

Tenno swallowed, and he said, "If it can track us, it could follow the path we've made from Earth back to Earth. Follow the space traces, I mean."

"We don't know that," Ramstan said, grabbing Tenno's arm. Tenno's pained expression made him release his grip.

"We don't know that it can't," Tenno said. "And that is what counts!"

"All right," Ramstan said. "One thing at a time. What concerns me most just now is the thing seemingly appearing from nowhere. I realize that anyone seeing us just come into a bell would think that we, too, popped out of nowhere. But this thing doesn't enter a bell at its edge. I'm not sure that it can't appear anywhere it wants to."

"If that's true, it doesn't use alaraf drive. Not the kind we know."

Tenno paused, then continued. "Also, it seems to me that that horrible whistling might be caused by a . . . a disrupting of normal space-matter structure. As soon as the thing is fully in normal space-matter and space-matter has resumed its normal structure—whatever that is—the whistling stops. I don't know. I'm just speculating. Whatever the thing is . . . it's unheard of . . . horrible . . . horrible . . . whoever would have thought . . . ?"

The vast, dark shape hovered in their minds, blotting out almost all thought except of it.

As soon as he could, Ramstan got rid of the pseudo-*glyfa* by sending it via ship's peristalsis to the trash disintegrator.

While *al-Buraq* circled Tolt, Ramstan paced in his quarters. During mess, he did his best to keep the conversation going and on light topics, but he failed miserably. After the third mess, when the drinks were brought in, he made an announcement.

"We're going to return to Kalafala."

There was silence.

"By the time we get there, that thing should be through with its . . . work. And it should be gone on its next hellish assignment. It may be tracking us down, though there's no proof that it is doing that. Anyway, if we do find it, or if it finds us, we'll not run away unless we have to."

He paused and looked around at the pale faces.

"We'll test its attack capabilities. And if it looks as if we'll have a chance, we'll attack it!"

17

HIS PLAN WAS COURAGEOUS but also probably foolish. However, the prospect of facing the enemy instead of running away seemed to raise the spirits of the crew.

Al-Buraq's probers searched for the *bolg* but could not detect it. There was no doubt that it was gone, its work done. An object of its size and mass could not have hidden. It could, however, and no one forgot it for a moment, appear seemingly from out of nowhere.

There was smoke covering Kalafala, but it was much less dense than that over Walisk and Tolt. Except for some small islands, the planet had only one continent, which had only the surface area of Greenland, and half of it was empty of people and vegetation. It should not have taken long for the Destroyer to ravage all land life, but it may have been acting automatically, a mindless thing that carried out its work according to the surface available, not the location of life.

Ramstan ordered *al-Buraq* to the capital. Since it had been the most heavily populated area, he said, it was the best place to make a detailed record of the effects of the cataclysm. Ship came down and poised twenty meters above the still-fissuring surface of the spaceport. He requisitioned for himself a small excavator craft. He did not explain why he was working with the other members of the survey, nor why his search plan placed them for several hours at a considerable distance from him.

Ramstan flew through the smoke at five meters above the surface while he watched the screens in front of him. When the probers indicated that he was in the same area as that in which the *glyfa* had fallen, he put the machine into a decreasing horizontal spiral. The hotel was gone except for some shattered pillars and some dented steel beams. The sidewalk was gone. The grass and the bushes and trees were gone. Much of the fertile earth had been washed or blown away, revealing a clay. Ramstan could not directly see this, but his probers indicated what was left. There were also the expected missiles, some on top of the clay, some wholly buried, some half exposed.

A half hour passed, and he was beginning to think that the *glyfa* had been gulped into a fissure and was beyond the range of his ground-sonar. And then, as desperation mingled with fury slid through him, he saw the egg-shape on a screen. It was a meter and a half under the clay.

The box around it had been scattered in shreds by the missiles and the a-g units knocked off. The *glyfa* itself must have been pounded into the ground by several larger missiles and perhaps had fallen into a shallow fissure which had then closed up.

It did not take Ramstan long to direct the machine to cut a wide cylindrical hole around the *glyfa* with lasers and to pulverize the clay and suck it out. It took him more time to direct a robot arm down to put new a-g units on the ends of the *glyfa* and then to fit a unit over each end of the egg. The preset units made the *glyfa* weigh little enough for it to be sucked up through a pipe into the body of the machine.

Ramstan opened a cover behind the seat and pulled the egg loose from the clay sticking to it.

"You didn't think I could do it, did you?" Ramstan said.

Silence.

Shrugging, he put the egg in a case supposed to be used for specimens. He drove the machine back into *al-Buraq* and took the case to his quarters. There he washed the smoke and clay from it and placed it under the electron microscope. As he had expected, its sculpturing was undamaged by the missiles.

Again, he tried.

"It's I, Ramstan!"

"That makes two I's," his mother's voice said in Terrish. "I wasn't sure that you'd return. Which meant that if you didn't, I . . ."

"Yes?"

"It doesn't matter now."

"It does to me," Ramstan said. "I must know certain things. Otherwise . . ."

"Otherwise, what?"

"I may leave you here after all. Drop you to the bottom of the sea."

"Of course you will. What is it you want to know? Aside from the questions you've asked so far."

"At least tell me why you allowed Branwen Davis to steal you. You must have been aware that she was doing so. You may have known some time ago that she planned on doing it. Tell me why you permitted her to take you and why she did it. And if she was killed or went with the Tenolt."

His mother's voice said, "From your viewpoint, my powers are almost semidivine. Though I suspect you'd say semidemonic. But I lack what even the lowliest of most animal life has."

It paused. Was it considering if it should reveal something that might make it vulnerable?

"That is mobility. The power to move on my own. If I'm placed on a hillside, then I must roll down it as helplessly as a stone or an egg. I must go where anybody who has the energy to move me wills that I go."

It did not sound bitter. It was just stating a fact.

"You're evading my questions!" Ramstan said. "What about Davis?"

"The Tolt captain picked her up. Perhaps he didn't kill her because he didn't know that she had shot the men with her. Or perhaps he wanted to torture her. In either event, she is useless to him now that he does not have me. But I suppose he'll be back soon to look for me."

"I know," Ramstan said. "We're leaving soon. But tell me why Davis stole you? I think that the Tenolt abducted her from the experimental station on the north coast and forced her, somehow, to steal you and leave a fake in the safe. Why didn't you summon me when she came for you?"

"I didn't have my detectors on. I was . . . voyaging . . . and thus unaware of what was happening just then."

Ramstan did not believe him. Even if it was quiescent then, it must have probed Davis's mind just as it had undoubtedly probed every mind within its range of detection.

"Why," he said slowly, "didn't the Tenolt take you? If they had time to get Davis, they had time to get you."

"I have the power to confuse minds with certain electrical means. It's limited in range and time. But I made them forget me for the moment. And the Tolt in command while the captain was gone was screaming at him to get back. By the time the captain returned, he would have recovered from his mindstorm, but it was too late to try to get me again. The missiles were approaching too swiftly."

"You still haven't told me why you didn't warn me about Davis."

Silence.

"You won't answer that. Very well. What is the *bolg?*"

Silence.

Ramstan put it in the bulkhead-safe and went up to the bridge.

"It's possible, if not highly probable, that the Tenolt will be coming back," he said to Tenno. "We don't want to be here when they come. I don't know why Davis disobeyed my orders to stay within the port limits or why the Tenolt had her. We may never know. In any case, they attacked us, and we had to shoot back. We can assume that the next time they show, they'll attack us."

Tenno asked no questions about Davis. Ramstan ordered that the survey parties return to *al-Buraq*. Within ten minutes, ship was sealed up and ready to go.

Ramstan felt in his jacket pocket. The three gifts of Wassruss nestled there. Why had the dying Webnite given them to him? Was the *glyfa* responsible in some circuitous fashion for that? Or was someone else moving pieces on this cosmic chessboard? He thought of the warning voice in the tavern and the flash of the figure in green and the figure that had seemed to him to be al-Khidhr.

"Set course for the Webn bell," Ramstan said.

"Aye, aye, sir. The Webn bell it is."

Ramstan called in the navigation chief, Suzuki.

"I'm just checking, Suzuki. The other bell in the Webn system is in the area of the first planet of Webn's sun, isn't it?"

Suzuki's brown face and slanting eyelids expressed curiosity. But she only said, "Yes, sir."

"Put in a course in NS drive for the first bell. I'll want it as soon as possible."

"Just ask ship for it," Suzuki said somewhat smugly. "I laid it out long ago just in case we might need it."

"Thank you for your zeal and foresight," Ramstan said. "But the next time you do something like that, tell me about it."

He told himself that he need not have sounded as if he were rebuking her.

Fifty hours passed. Ramstan, when not in his quarters trying to get a response from the *glyfa*, roamed *al-Buraq*. He checked everything he could think of, mostly to keep himself occupied. Then Tenno called him just as he was about to take a nap.

"Ship will be in the first bell within two hours, sir."

"Call me back in sixty minutes."

After a few seconds of concentrated imagining of a black spot a few centimeters from his eyes and within his head, he fell asleep. A whistle from a screen woke him just as he was crawling through thick impeding brush from something dark and shapeless. He was whimpering.

He took a shower and dressed in a jumpsuit. Then he spoke to the *glyfa*, but he got no reply. After eating a sandwich, he went up to the bridge.

"Did you check out the bell?" Ramstan said to Tenno.

"Yes, sir. It seems to be virgin. At least, the instruments indicate it is."

Ramstan thanked him, and he ordered that *al-Buraq* go into alaraf. Two minutes later, they were within 500,000 kilometers of a planet. The star was GO-type, and the planet was T-type. *Al-Buraq* filmed the constellations. Ramstan particularly admired a giant blue star. Celestial inhabitants were staggeringly beautiful, and even long acquaintance with them had not staled their awesomeness.

"It won't be virgin territory any more," Ramstan said. "We're going to alaraf. Pioneer."

Tenno seemed to be surprised. Not far off was a planet like Earth's, and he had expected that *al-Buraq* would survey it from orbit and perhaps descend to it.

Two minutes later, they were in what Ramstan knew to be another universe, if he had interpreted Wassruss's phrase correctly.

" 'Ring the bell at the first entrance.'

" 'And then?'

" 'Enter.'

" 'And then?'

" 'Ring the bell at the third entrance.'

" 'And then?'

" 'Ring the bell at the fifth entrance.' "

Each bell was "connected" to another bell. There were only two bells or windows, as they were sometimes called, in each area within the planetary system. Therefore, so Ramstan had reasoned, the third and fifth bells in Wassruss's chant were the third and fifth planets respectively in the systems of the universes alarafed into from Webn's universe.

Al-Buraq scanned the new system. It had ten planets.

Ramstan ordered that *al-Buraq* go to the neighborhood of the fifth planet. An hour after the entrance, Ramstan ordered that ship alaraf again.

Tenno obviously wondered why his captain was choosing different planets. Why didn't he just jump where he came out?

Ramstan could not tell him at this time the reason. He was not sure that he was on the right "path." He might be making a fool of himself by following what he believed to be instructions in the ancient chant. If so, only he would know it.

A planet distorted space-matter fabric in the area of its gravitational influence, the influence varying in accordance to its mass and its relation to other large relatively nearby masses and the square of the distance from the planet and its neighbors. It seemed to him that he may have discovered a principle hitherto unknown to Terran science by his following the directions in the chant. But it also seemed to him that the location and the mass of a planet did determine the "direction" of the opening the alaraf ship took.

One of the theories about alaraf drive was that it was a form of time travel. When a ship jumped, it went into time. Backward while on the "outward" journey, forward while on the "return" journey. A ship leaving Earth in alaraf drive went back to a time when the Earth was elsewhere on her journey through space. That explained why the ship found herself in unknown space, the Earth and its sun nowhere visible.

But, if the *glyfa* had told him the truth, there were many universes. And each time a ship alarafed, it plunged through the "wall" between two universes.

Ramstan ordered that ship alaraf again. And again they were in an area never seen before.

Ramstan ordered that *al-Buraq* proceed to the neighborhood of the seventh planet of the new system. It was done, but the bridge personnel were silent and tight-lipped.

"The Tenolt may have trouble finding us," he said loudly. Let them chew on that for a while, he thought as he went to his quarters.

This time, the *glyfa* answered. Ramstan wondered if it had some deep reasons for its silences. Or was it double-minded, and did one mind take over the other now and then? No. That was a fantastic and incredible explanation. He was projecting onto it his own doubts about his own double-naturedness.

The *glyfa* asked him what he had been doing. As soon as it was fully informed, it said, "You are doing well. But before you get to the only place to go beyond the ninth entrance, come to me."

"Why?" Ramstan said.

"Whatever you do, don't tell them that I am on ship."

"Them? Who's them?"

Silence.

18

ON THE RIGHT were three great stars, one red, one green, one
yellow, each forming the point of a triangle. Making up the
lines of the triangle were seven stars between each point, small
and white.

Far "below" these was a dark mass reminding Ramstan of
the Horsehead Nebula of Earth's universe. But the head
formed by a vast "dustcloud" profiled by blazing gases behind
it looked like that of a troll. At least, that was what Nuoli said
it resembled. To Ramstan it seemed more of an ifrit's head.
The features were humanoid but bestial. Bestial humanoid. Yet
beautiful and awesome.

The third planet of the system beyond the ninth entrance was
T-type, and its sun was GO. It had been 707,000 kilometers
from *al-Buraq* when she had burst from the other universe.
Ramstan had at once ordered her to proceed at top speed in NS
drive to the planet.

" 'Go to the only place to go.' "

Ramstan thought that, if Wassruss's chant was not nonsense, that phrase indicated that the inhabitable planet was his
goal. Fortunately, he did not have to choose between two
planets. He had not expected to. No solar-type system so far
found had more than one inhabitable planet. There was a

narrow range of distance from the sun which determined whether or not life could originate and thrive on a planet. And sometimes even then the planet in that range was biohostile.

Life was rare and fragile. Yet it was also frequent and tough. Give it a foothold, and it fought to hold on, to flourish, to evolve into forms impossible to imagine until seen.

Al-Buraq's probes reported that this world was slightly smaller than Earth but had slightly more mass. She went into orbit just above the atmosphere and over the only continent. This was much longer than it was wide and stretched around the southern hemisphere in the temperate zone. Its two extremities were separated by 3,000 kilometers of islandless ocean.

" 'To the tree which does not stand alone.' "

How in the seven hells was he to find that one? Except for freshwater bodies and the upper slopes of the highest mountains, the continent was covered with thick trees. There were no meadows or open spaces of any consequence.

Ramstan sent ship down into the atmosphere about twenty kilometers above land-level. He ordered her to follow a path which would eventually cover every hectare. They soon determined that there was much bird and insect life in the upper reaches of the forest and many species of animal. Among these were monkey- and apelike creatures.

The biodetectors showed that each tree was attached to its immediate neighbors by four to six thin, leafless, glossy-black branches extending horizontally in a circle from the upper middle part of the trunk. These formed an interconnecting and supporting system extending continent-wide. The trees on the edges of the beaches and seacliffs only grew the connectors inward to their neighbors.

Though approximately one out of a hundred trees was dead, they did not seem to fall until completely rotted and eaten by the insects. Where this had happened, treelets were growing up from the mounds of the dead predecessors.

" 'To the tree which does not stand alone.' "

Allah! How could he make any sense out of that?

He began pacing back and forth but stopped after a minute. It was not good for the bridge people to see him so obviously worried. He ordered Toyce to call him if any sentient life was detected.

"Yes, sir. But sentiency may not be obvious."

"Do the best you can."

He went to his quarters and there resumed pacing. Once, he stopped to take the *glyfa* out, but it did not respond.

"I need you now!" he cried, and he struck it a glancing blow with his fist. The round a-g units attached to it did not prevent it from rolling over and dropping off the table onto the deck. The deck quivered, not from the impact itself but from *al-Buraq*'s reflex to what it considered might be Ramstan's fall. Or was it due to ship's monitoring of his emotional state? She was always sensing him, the play of electrical fields on his skin, his body temperature, the tone of his voice.

He turned, jumped, and gasped. The green man was standing by the far bulkhead. His arm was outstretched, and a fingertip was on the center of a seven-sided screen.

The vision lasted no longer than two eyeblinks.

The green-shrouded man had indicated the empty screen. What did that have to do with the tree that does not stand alone? Perhaps nothing. Something else might have been meant by that fingertip on the center of a blank field.

Did al-Khidr really exist? Or was the thing that he, Ramstan, had seen just a form beamed by someone? Had al-Khidr been shot forth like a three-dimensional hologram from Ramstan's four-dimensioned brain, self-awareness being the extra dimension?

Something, objective or subjective, nonhuman or human, was trying to *tell* him something.

He began pacing again but halted after twelve steps. Perhaps the vision was not referring to the screen as a whole but to its center. *Look for the center* was the message. The center of what? His own center, the inmost recess of his being?

No.

Look in the center, the middle, of the forest.

That could be it.

At one time there may have been only one tree on this continent, an Urgenitor, the hermaphroditic Adam-Eve of all these now existing. Possibly, it had stood or was still standing in the geographical center of the land-mass, and where it was was his goal.

He called the bridge. The scanners having fed the data into *al-Buraq*'s brain, the geographical center and the middle point of the land-mass were located. The latter was that point halfway between the two extremities of the continent and halfway between the north and south coasts. Since the two centers did not coincide, Ramstan ordered that ship go to the latter first.

Her central part contracted into a rocket-shape, her lower outer part shaped like the wings of antique airplanes, *al-Buraq* sped above the surface of the green arboreal-ocean. At 300 kilometers from her destination, she began descending and decelerating and within ten minutes was poised over it. Ten meters below the bottom of her hull, the tip of the highest tree rocked in the wind. Ramstan did not think that it was a coincidence that the tallest and most massive tree grew from the continental center.

The sun had almost zenithed. The sky was cloudless. The only life visible to the unaided eye was aerial, large insects, primitive birds, and some small and some large mammals. At least, the latter were assumed to be mammals since they were furred. The biggest had wingspreads of eight meters, batlike bodies and wings, and bloodhoundish faces, but their cries were monkeylike. They were too heavy to take off from the tree branches, and their webbed feet suggested that they used water as their landing fields. The nearest large lake was 50 kilometers away, so the dogbats must have an amazingly extended range of flight. They dived down and caught the smaller birds and mammals and ate them while flying.

Though the tossing green surface looked lifeless from a distance, it was, when seen closely, surging with vitality. In addition to the winged things skimming it, insects and some unclassifiable creatures crawled, ran, or hopped on the broad, dark-green, leathery-looking, cupped, and immense leaves of the Brobdingnagian tree just below them. The foliage did not swarm with the creatures, but it was well-populated.

This was where the top branches met the open air. What about below that level?

The viewbeams could not penetrate the density more than a few meters.

Nuoli, looking at the magnification on the screens, said, 'You'd think that the leaves below, all growth below the upper leaves, would die from lack of sunlight. Surely . . .''

Ramstan said, "Yes?"

"Surely, it can't be as thick as it seems. At least, elsewhere, the sun must be able to penetrate here and there."

What could live down there besides pale things of low or no intelligence, blind, moving slowly in the darkness?

But if "the tree which does not stand alone," meant anything, it must apply to the prodigious plant below him. It stood higher than the others by a thousand meters. Its circumference, the circle formed by the tips of the branches at a level with the tops of the surrounding trees, was 10,000 meters. Outside the edge of the circle, through small breaks here and there in the foliage of the smaller parts of trees, the connecting branches could be seen.

"The mothertree?" Ramstan muttered to himself.

The sunlight glanced from some of the tossing leaves, which seemed to contain mica. There was nothing visible to suggest anything sinister. Yet, he felt that there was danger under those leaves. Not the expected peril of feral animals or poisonous reptiles. Something or some things which he could not possibly anticipate, entities which had been beyond the ken, and still might be, of humankind.

The unknown had always held fear. The human mind was constructed to project fear into the nonexplored whether or not there were reasons to be afraid. On the other hand, the unknown also enticed. Humans could not resist its allure and had to plunge into whatever dangers might exist there. Also, there was a fascination about fear itself that had its allure. Humans, some humans, anyway, liked to be afraid—to a certain degree. Perhaps the basic drive here was the desire to test their courage. No, that was not the only basic. Curiosity, monkey curiosity, also pulled them into the unknown.

This situation, however, differed from any which Ramstan had been in. He had always felt confident that he could handle any predicament. But this one . . . there was something about it . . . something so vast and powerful that it made him feel very small and weak . . . no . . . he must not think like that. Even smallness and weakness had their powers, their advantages.

"Besides," he said aloud, "I am Ramstan!"

Nuoli, who was standing near him, jumped. She said, "What?"

Suzuki was also looking strangely at him.

"Nothing," Ramstan said. "Nothing."

So . . . he was Ramstan? So what? He was unique, but so was every sentient being. So, for that matter, was every one of the millions of seemingly alike trees on this land. The difference was that he was sentient, self-conscious, and he had a self or a series of selves called Ramstan, and that Ramstan had a body-mind and a development through a unique environment that no one else had. No one, not even God. God might *know* every sentient, might even participate in the full consciousness and unconsciousness of every unique sentient. But not even He could *be* that person. There were limits even to God's powers. Which, since God was by definition all-powerful, meant that God was not God. Which meant that the definition should be restated.

He had no time to think of the implications of that. He ordered that a launch be readied for take-off in ten minutes. He also told Tenno that he, Ramstan, would be on it.

"We're going down to the surface," he said.

Tenno had obviously been speculating on his captain's reasons for coming here. He said, "You're following the directions in Wassruss's chant?"

"Yes."

Ramstan hesitated, then said, "It may be in vain. But, after all, our mission is scientific, and anthropology, I mean, sentientology, is one of our main studies. This chant . . . it's so curious . . . it intimates that there have been alaraf drives in the very distant past . . . perhaps before humanity was quite evolved from the ape. Anyway, I have more than one motive for traveling through the walls of the universes . . ."

Tenno interrupted. *"Walls?"*

That slip checked Ramstan for an instant. He opened his mouth, could not get the words out, glared, shut his mouth, briefly closed his eyes, then spoke.

"Yes, walls. I'm not at all certain that we are, per theory, traveling from one galaxy to another either by time travel or by tunnel-bell. You know that it's been suggested, though, I'll admit, not seriously, that when a ship jumps it penetrates the 'wall' between one universe and the next."

He paused and Tenno said, "The multiverse hypothesis. Though, really, it's not even a hypothesis. It's a wild speculation, and . . ."

"I tend to think that it's more than that. But what's the difference what the truth is? In this situation, anyway. You're in charge of ship now, Tenno. You have your orders on what to do if the Tenolt or that monster appears."

Tenno said, "Aye, aye, sir," and saluted.

Five minutes later, Ramstan was seated in the launch. It left its port and nosed down toward the tree. Seen from ship with the naked eyes, the plant seemed a solid monolith. As the launch neared it, however, its occupants saw vast openings, the entrances to the emptinesses between the levels of branches. The branches were gigantic, ranging from 50 to 70 meters in radius near the trunk, and were supported about a third of their length from the trunk by arboreal flying buttresses, branches growing at a 45-degree angle upward from the trunk and merging into the lower part of the branches they upheld. In the outer part of the vertical aisles formed by the branches was a space about 100 meters high. The launch moved into the aisle formed by the seventh and eighth branches from the tip of the tree.

They went abruptly from brightness and a not-quite-comfortable warmth into an illumination like that just before dusk. The temperature was another degree lower.

The animal, bird, and insect population here was more numerous and much noisier than the aerial life above the tree. The creatures did not have to go down to the ground to drink water. It oozed from the branches where the thick bark formed shallow crevices and collected into little pools and springs.

Here and there, the sunlight broke through and fell on hairy, scaled, feathered, or chitinous things. It also was reflected from the huge leaves, some of which curled upward and contained rainwater.

Ramstan ordered the launch to stop long enough for a *yeoshet* to pull loose three leaves for specimens.

"The glittering stuff can't be mica," he said. "It would make the leaves too heavy."

The upper transparent part of the rowboat-shaped launch closed down, and it went on with its passengers protected from attack by the sometimes aggressive actions of the citizens of the tree. Most of these consisted of fruit hurled or excrement dropped by monkeyish creatures or kamikaze-divebombings by squadrons of insects. Several times, Ramstan had to order the de-icing liquid released over the upper-sheet shell to kill the cloud of insects obscuring the pilot's vision.

When the launch dropped 600 meters, it was no longer among such thick masses of insects. There were plenty at this level, but they did not gather on the upper part very heavily.

Though the buzz and screech were less, the darkness and cold increased. On reaching the twentieth branch-level down, Ramstan had the lights turned on. It was still possible to see objects without them but easier with them.

At ten more levels down, the air temperature stabilized. The launch people were quite comfortable, since the vehicle was air-conditioned, but the exterior heat was not quite enough to be comfortable. It was at this level that Ramstan noticed that many of the leaves were turned at different angles. And as the launch sank, the illumination became more, not less.

Nuoli said, "It's a system to reflect sunlight down."

Here they first saw the seemingly parasitic plants sprouting from the trunk and branches. These were of three kinds: toadstool-shaped, cone-shaped, and seven-pointed star-shaped on long drooping stalks. All glowed with a light, each having a will-o'-the-wisp brightness, but the total illumination was that of just-after-dusk. The eyes of some animal, bird, and insect life glowed as if reflecting light from a campfire. Since there was not enough light for this, Nuoli speculated that the eyes had their own source of illumination. The winking of these, she said, reminded her of the glowings from Terran fireflies.

"Some sort of cold light activated by electrochemical means."

Though he'd seen many strange things since his first landing on a non-Terran planet, Ramstan thought that this phenomenon was among the strangest. It also seemed unexplainable—at least, for the moment. Fireflies excited their photonic-emitting tails as sexual signals. Did these creatures flash their eyes off and on for the same reason? If they did, the flashing must leave them temporarily blinded.

He thought, Perhaps the light shed by so many of the things and events I've encountered recently, especially the *glyfa*, should be illuminating. But it's blinded me.

Another curious thought strayed or swooped across the field of his mind.

What if these creatures were in league with, or controlled

by, the entities he guessed were at the base of this tree? What if their eye-flashings were signals, biological Morse, to the entities that his imagination had visioned as waiting for him; the signals telling the shadowy things at the base that an object bearing passengers from a far distance and time was approaching and what the passengers looked like?

He failed to discern a pattern in the flashings. They seemed to be just so much "noise." What seemed to him randomness might, however, be intelligence to someone else.

The launch dropped down at the rate of ten kilometers an hour in a vertical zigzag around the branches. The photonemitting growths increased until branch and trunk seemed to be encrusted with strangely cut jewels. Unlike Terran trees, the horizontal branches at the lower levels became shorter and more slender. Nevertheless, the flying-buttress supports were thicker and extended further out. This, Ramstan supposed, was because the luciferian plants were so many that they heavily weighed down the branches.

The birds and beasts became less numerous with every lower level, but the insects were larger. Some rather huge species, rat-sized, had transparent flesh through which glowed the plants they had eaten. Their thumbnail-sized droppings also shone, though with a lesser light. These monsters were not true insects. Terran insects could not grow so large. Being lungless and depending on spiracles as air-inlets, their size was limited. A mutant Terran insect as large as a rat would die because oxygen would not flow into the inner parts of its body.

One species of the larger insects had a long slightly downward-curved proboscis and a rod growing from the back of the head. The length of this was equal to the length of the creature's body, and at its end was a ball which glowed. This reminded Ramstan of certain fish of the Earth's oceanic abysses. They used the light at the ends of their rods to lure other fish close enough to be caught and eaten.

Another creature was a basketball-sized, balloon-shaped arachnid which floated in the air and traveled from place to place, usually branch to leaf or vice versa, by shooting out a sticky thread for anchor and then pulling itself in by the thread. It also jetted out the thread to entangle smaller insects and so draw the prey to its mouth, which was surrounded by six tiny, clawed arms which unceasingly moved except when they seized the living food.

The launch sank deeper. It passed a snakelike thing which was at least 12 meters long. Its six-sided head bore four long curving horns; its eyes were huge and four-sided; its tongue was froglike, speeding out to catch insects or the very small, emerald-green lizardoids and, once, a tiny snake.

"The zoologists would go ape here," Nuoli said.

Ramstan did not comment. He was wondering what kind of sentients would choose to live here. Wassruss's chant had implied that at least three made this continent their dwelling place. But the chant was very old, and those mentioned in it might have moved away or died. For no rational reason, he believed that this was not true, that the three would be here. Which could mean that they had an incredibly long lifespan. Incredibly? Yes, to someone who did not know the *glyfa*.

Abruptly, the launch entered a zone which seemed to be lifeless. Of course, there was life; the tree was not dead. But there were no insects, birds, or animals. And a sense of timelessness stole through Ramstan. There *was* time—as measured by the launch's chronometer, by the beatings of his heart, by the motion of machine and people. Nevertheless, Ramstan felt that time had died or at least had slowed down so much that it was in suspended motion or was sleeping. He felt somewhat disorientated, slightly dizzy, and vaguely and weakly panicky.

He ordered that the upper covering be opened and that no one speak or make any noise. For some reason, he was strongly compelled to *listen*.

Listen to what? For what?

Not knowing made him crackle with the static electricity of panic as if giant but impalpable fingers were rubbing his dry nerves.

The others, though they said nothing, rolled their eyes as if they, too, sniffed danger in the wind. But there was no wind except for the almost imperceptible movement of air made by the passage of the launch.

Ramstan looked upward, though he did not think that there was any peril—at this moment—from above. The sun and sky were blocked out by the branches and the leaves. They were dead, buried under vegetation. A strange thought.

As dead as time itself.

Yet, if the chant told of true things and beings, the death of time or of its near-dead heartbeat meant life for those who waited for him.

Waited? How could they know that he was coming?

Perhaps the *glyfa* had told them.

But the *glyfa* was silent and would not speak to him now.

When the upper part of the launch had been opened the first time, Ramstan had smelled a faint stench, not altogether unpleasant, of decaying plants and animal excrement. Something in it reminded him of rotting toadstools, though he did not think that he had ever smelled these before. The air had also been very dry or had seemed to be so. He was not certain, since he was beginning to distrust his senses. Now the odors were gone, though the lack did not make the air seem healthy. Indeed, it was like that of a tomb in which only the dust of corpses remained and all corruption was over. But the tomb should have been as dry as the mouth of a man lost in a desert and without water for three days. Yet, the humidity had suddenly risen. As the launch plunged soundlessly into the timeless zone, the water content increased. Ramstan suddenly felt that the moisture was stealthily increasing and, without warning, they would pass from a watery air into airless water. His throat closed up.

It was as if the planet itself had begun sweating. Drops rolled down his forehead and into his eyes, saltless water which, when licked, gave him the sensation that his tongue was betraying him. Despite the wetness, however, he smelled nothing dank or rotting. The crowded growths on the tree shone even more brightly; their cold illumination seemed to have stopped death and decay. Or to have slowed it, since there was no stopping these universal basics. Another strange thought.

He started, and he hated himself for this unwilling signal of his nervousness. He glared at Nuoli for having put her hand on his arm.

Was that touch the intimation of death? Touch. Death. Another strange thought. Strange? No thoughts were strange, but the unfamiliar or not easily available to his conscious would seem so.

Touching.

"There's something down there. It looks like a big hole," the tec-op said. "It's between two roots. Roots of this tree, I mean."

Ramstan checked on the report. The screen showed a shadowy equilateral triangle, and the readout indicated that it was 64 meters long on each side. Another readout showed that it contained a clear liquid. The bottom of the well, probably stone, was 64 meters from the surface.

The launch sank unchecked by any order from Ramstan, passed tremendous wrinkled treetrunk bark almost covered by the glowing growths, and, after what seemed like a long time, though Ramstan still was seized by a sense of timelessness —curious paradox, but were not all paradoxes curious?—the launch was at the edge of the well nearest the tree.

There was no lining of the well, no coping, only bare earth around the air and the water. The three sides plunged straight down and were smooth as mud pressed by a trowel.

The launch moved out, its undersurface lights filling the well like honey.

There were three creatures moving through or on the surface of the well.

19

"IT ISN'T WATER," the tec-op said. He pointed at the column of numbers by the side of the screen. He said, "See, sir. It's a liquid, but it's heavier than water. Specific gravity is 1.6. Just a second, sir. There. The spectrographic analysis. *Jesús!* Nothing like it in the comparison bank!"

Nuoli, who'd been looking over the side of the launch, spoke. "One of them is hopping over the surface of . . . whatever it is."

Ramstan told the pilot to take the vehicle down to ten meters above the well. Meanwhile, the tec-op had been scanning on all sides for the "old house" which Wassruss had mentioned. He could not find it, but the building might be on the other side of one of the immense swellings at the base of the trunk. These, which plunged into the ground to become roots, were wider in diameter than ten subway tunnels put together.

The face looking up at him, the grinning face of the hopper, startled and repulsed him. It was humanoid but far more triangular than any *Homo sapiens'*. The hairless, deeply seamed, and leathery upper part of the skull projected so far over the face that it could have been substituted for an umbrella. A wide, blue vein passed over the central part; it pulsed sluggishly as if it were filled not with blood but with a growing colony of microbes or some yeasty organisms.

The overhanging forehead ended abruptly; the division between it and the face was right-angled. The face seemed to be something attached with adhesive to the bottom of the dome. The two eyes were deep, deep and dark blue. They were also huge, apparently one and a half times the size of Ramstan's, though he could not be sure. The tec-op's screen indicated that the creature was three meters tall.

Just below the eyes was not a nose but a large round appendage of leathery flesh darker than the face, the color of which was a pale red. There did not seem to be any nostrils or openings of any kind in the projection. It pulsed like the vein on top of its skull.

The mouth was much more like a human's; the lips were very everted. The jaw was thick, and the chin was a ball with a deeply punched-in, six-pointed star.

"Some dimple," Nuoli muttered.

The ears were very small, flat, close to the face, and their convolutions were nonhuman alto-relief arabesques.

Ramstan ordered the magnifying power to be increased so he could look directly into the wide-open mouth. The teeth were like a pig's; the purplish tongue was warted.

The red leathery body reminded Ramstan of a kangaroo's, but its tail ended in a wide fan and its feet were wide, splayed, and webbed, a frog's. It used the feet and the tail to propel itself over the surface of the strange liquid.

Its upper limbs, however, were quite human and so were its hands.

The "wise one who swims" was slowly circling the well near its wall. It looked like an extinct salmon, though it was at least twelve meters long, six times the length of the average man laid out for his funeral. Another strange thought. Why had he used that comparison?

Ramstan was flabbergasted. He'd assumed that the three spoken of in the chant would be sentient. It was possible though not probable that the hopper was. But a fish could not be sentient.

Looking directly at the "cold-blood who drinks hot blood" hurt his eyes and made him feel even more disorientated. It was a shimmer of pale-reddish light fringed by purplish light.

The glowing body expanded and contracted; its major length was ten meters, its minor, nine, and its major height was three meters and its minor, two. Now and then, in no regular pattern that the scan-computer could determine, the shimmering was cut off, and Ramstan got a flash of the thing behind the light. It seemed to him at first that it looked like a mixture of bat and octopus. It had a head, but it was on top of the central part of an oblong body, not at one end. The features and the teeth, if they were teeth, were like a South American vampire bat's. He had no sooner fixed that in his mind than the next glimpse showed him a broad face, half lion, half human, and a hint of something else. He did not know what the something else was.

Nuoli said, *"Jumala!"* and spoke then in Terrish. "I saw into its eyes. They looked black, genuinely black. And . . . I must have been seeing things . . . my imagination . . . I thought I saw stars deep within them. Constellations . . . a gas cloud . . . shining . . . white."

Ramstan did not reply. He ordered the launch taken to a meter above the head of the hopper. It had sunk to its waist, but now it began thrusting its webbed and splayed hands and feet against the liquid. It rose swiftly, spread out flat on the surface, then reared upright. And it began hopping.

Ramstan told the com-op to put some Urzint phrases into the translator. He did not believe that these would be understood, but Urzint was the interplanetary language in the areas where he'd been, and he had to try something.

The hopper stopped, began sinking, and also began laughing. At least, the hooting sounded somewhat like laughter.

The huge fish rolled so that its right eye was above the surface, and this regarded the launch steadily.

The shimmering thing did not move.

Ramstan was not the only person startled when the hopper gabbled in an unfamiliar language full of throaty and hissing sounds, then switched to Urzint.

"Go to the house! Go to the house! Go to the house!"

Nuoli was the first to break the silence in the launch. "What I tell you three times is true," she murmured.

"It's not indicative but imperative," Ramstan said. "Nothing to do with validity."

"Well, at least we know it's sentient."

"Not necessarily," he said. "It may be like a parrot. Trained to utter the directions when it's spoken to by strangers. Or . . ."

"But in Urzint?"

Ramstan did not comment. Obviously, the Urzint people must have been here at one time. Or perhaps the hopper had met the legended pachydermoids on some other planet.

He ordered the launch to rise to the left. That seemed as good a direction as the right, though he may have had psychological reasons for choosing it.

The house, if it could be called such, was located three root-swellings over from that by the well. The distance from the well was 300 meters, which Ramstan would not have said was "nearby." It was three structures arranged vertically or perhaps was one structure with three stories which only looked like separate ones stacked. If it, or they, were a habitation, it was certainly one he had never before encountered.

The main body of each was an oblate sphere from the equator of which extended a long tapering body toward the tree. He at first thought that each looked like a round birdhead with a long bill. Then he perceived it as a spermatozoon with its thick head and long thin tail, except that the tail was straight, not curving. His third impression was of a mace, a staff at the end of which was a big ball for bludgeoning. The spheres were, according to the scanner, 50 meters in diameter and the extensions were 100 meters long.

The bottom structure was green; the middle one, blue; the top one, black. Over each a rusty-red lichenous growth formed circles and near-squares and rough triangles but with enough of the metallic-looking surface exposed to reveal its color. The growth was thick enough to provide nesting places for the archeopteryxlike birds and various species of lizardoids and insects. Also, and this surprised the Terrans because they had by now assumed that this planet's birds were in a primitive stage of evolution, there was an owl, or what looked like one, and a storkish avian. The "owl" cachinnated at them, its cry sounding like the hopper's laughter, and flew off on snowy black-barred wings. The "stork" looked once at the launch and then began jabbing itself in the breast plumage, apparently in search of parasites.

"They may not be indigenous," Nuoli said.

Ramstan thought that she could be right, but he did not say

so. Her comment annoyed him; she had always been too given to talking when it would have been better to be silent or to confine herself to elemental moans and sighs and screams.

Moreover, except for the owl's cry, which had broken the glassy silence or—strange thought—blasphemed it, there was a lack of sound even deeper than that in the levels where life had ceased to be evident. Ramstan suddenly realized that this silence had existed since he had entered the seemingly nonzoic area.

Whatever his misgivings, starts, and too-late perceptions, the air was heavy, motionless, and dark. The light-shedding plants were less numerous than above. Around him was a twilight, brooding in between day and night. Brooding.

Something, or some things, sat and waited for him, but their thoughts were not entirely on him.

"It's spooky," Nuoli said.

As the launch settled like a sinking canoe in the deeps, Ramstan told the marines and sailors to have their weapons ready. But they were not to hold them. The holsters for the olsons should be unsealed and the larger arms should be on the deck out of sight of anyone in the house.

"We don't want to appear belligerent," he said.

They looked as if they'd like to have much more information than this. For instance, why were they here and what was in the house?

The launch settled on the thick lichenish growth which spread from the building and covered the earth between the two colossal root-swellings. Nobody spoke for a moment; the silence was as if sound itself had died.

After a long look at the "house," Ramstan said, softly, "I'll go alone."

A section of the lower hull slid open as the covering was lifted. Ramstan walked through the opening onto a collapsible ladder, a series of seven steps, which slid out from the hull. He sank in the growth up to his calves, smelling for the first time a faint odor from it. It reminded him of fermenting grass in a compost heap. He walked through the impeding stuff and up a gentle slope to the house. It seemed to stare back at him without eyes.

He paused before and below the outward curve of the first story.

" 'Knock at the entrance,' " Wassruss had said.

What entrance? The house had neither door nor window.

He did the only thing he could do. He raised his fist and beat on what looked like metal but was warmer than metal would have been in this cold air and felt springy. He could hear no sound from inside the sphere. He had expected a reverberating echo, a booming.

After striking three times, he waited, his fist upraised for more hammering. Within a few seconds, the seamless wall showed a faint line, round and with a diameter wide enough to easily admit him. He wondered if the door was regulated for the occasion. If he had been much shorter or much taller, would the seam have accommodated his height?

Instead of a section withdrawing or coming out, a panel swinging one way or the other, the area within the seam became wavy, then misty, then disappeared. He was confronted by a circular hole.

If there was a pressure differential, he could hear or feel no air blowing out or in. Beyond the hole was darkness. The light from the plants did not penetrate it. Ramstan shouted in Urzint instead of speaking softly as he had planned to.

"I am Captain Ramstan of the Terran exploratory interstellar ship, *al-Buraq!* I come in peace! And I have questions."

He felt foolish saying this, but what else could he say?

Immediately following his declaration, he saw, or thought he saw, a dim flash of green in the darkness.

His heart had been pounding hard before this. Now it accelerated.

Al-Khidhr?

Slowly, the darkness faded as light built up, seeming to leak out from every square centimeter of the walls, ceiling, and floor of the huge room. At first, he could not distinguish among the furniture and the three beings standing in the middle of the room. The room was round, and the doorways were seven-sided. The ceiling was a pale white; the walls, pale red; the floor, where not covered by a very thick, white, furry rug, was pale green. There were about a dozen mirrors against the walls or forming part of them. Their bases were set on the floor, and their sides tapered up, making long triangles, curving with the walls, their apexes meeting in the center of the domed ceiling. From this point hung a chain made of thin golden links and ending in an emerald the size of Ramstan's head.

A little red-furred animal with a long thin snout and great tarsierlike eyes was curled around the jewel. The one red eye that Ramstan could see was directed at him. Ramstan wondered how the creature had gotten to the emerald; it was so high above the floor that the beast could not possibly have jumped to it.

The furniture was sparse and consisted of fragile-looking chairs and sofas and tables of ornately carved black-and-white striped wood. The legs were very short. Here and there were enormous pillows piled around rugs folded over three times.

Omitting the front "door," there were three oval entrances to the great chamber, one in front of him and two on each side.

One of the three beings, the one in green robes, stepped forward. She spoke in Urzint. "Greetings, Ramstan. You've taken a long time getting here."

The one clad in blue said, "You should have been here much sooner. That is the fault of the *glyfa*."

The one in black said, "Ask, but be willing to pay the price."

20

RAMSTAN FELT AS IF his blood had become mercury and was heavily draining into his feet.

The voice of the green-robed one was the voice he had heard in the Kalafalan tavern.

"The *bolg* kills all but one! . . . God is sick. . . ."

She? He? It? Whatever sex the green one was or was not, the voice was hers.

In that moment, he knew, though he could not rationally justify his knowledge, that the green one was female. And it seemed to him that the others were also female.

Moreover, he believed that she was the shadowy, briefly seen figure in the hotel and the being who had appeared on Webn while he and Benagur were quarreling.

Was she also the old person he had seen when he was entering his parents' apartment in New Babylon?

Encountering these three had been like a tremor before a great earthquake. Hearing her voice was the great earthquake itself. Now, he was seized with aftershocks. He could not stop trembling, and he was afraid that he was going to vomit.

"You should sit down," the one in green said. Her eyes were large and as green as her robe. Deep wrinkles radiated from them; her face was that of a ten-thousand-year-old mummy.

The teeth in the seamed lips were black, though he did not think that they were rotten. She was ugly, yet the hideousness went beyond ugliness. She was also very beautiful, not as a young woman was beautiful but as an ancient star was beautiful. Something radiated from her, and her eyes seemed to shed kindness. Or compassion.

Certainly, he had wrongly conceived the green one. Whatever she was, she was not al-Khidr. His childhood religion had made a certain mold in his mind, a preconception, and her image had been fitted into that mold.

Again, the green one said, "You should sit down."

Ramstan looked around. If he did sit, and he needed to do so before he collapsed, he'd have to look up at them. He'd be at a psychological disadvantage. Allah knew that he was weak enough now, that he needed every advantage and strength he could get.

"No, thank you," he said. Surprisingly, his voice was firm.

"As you will," the green one said.

She sat down on a pile of rugs and leaned back against some giant pillows. The others also seated themselves, their legs crossed under their robes. They did not have to care that they must look up at him. Or perhaps they were giving him a chance to rest and to be on the same level at the same time.

He lowered himself on a pile of rugs and crossed his legs. He said, "Pardon me. I must tell my crew what's happening."

After speaking briefly into his skinceiver and telling Nuoli that no one must follow him as yet, he waited for a few seconds for his "hosts" to speak. When they did not, he said, "You know who I am. But I don't know . . ."

"At present," the green-robed one said, "I am called Shiyai."

The black-robed one cackled, and she said, "At present! She has been Shiyai for a billion of your years, Ramstan!"

The others broke into high-pitched laughter. When that died, the black-robed one said, "I am called Wopolsa."

"And I," the blue-robed one said, "am called Grrindah."

"What we are called and who we are are not the same," Wopolsa said.

"These are my sisters," Shiyai said, waving a withered, blue-veined, dark-spotted hand. "Sisters in name only, since we do not belong to the same species and were born more years apart than you can imagine, even if you can encompass the time in a phrase."

"Language is cheap," Wopolsa said. "Time is dear."

"Yet, waste time as much as you wish, there is always as much as before," Shiyai said.

"If you are like us," Grrindah said.

"And one other," Wopolsa said.

"Or perhaps two others," Shiyai said.

The three looked at each other and burst into their nerve-rubbing laughter again.

If they were trying to put him at his ease, they were failing. His stomach was folding in on itself like a flower at nightfall.

"What is this planet called?" he said.

"Grrymguurdha," Shiyai said.

"At least, that is what it sounds like to us," Wopolsa said. "That is what the tree calls it."

"The tree?" he said, feeling foolish. Were they playing with him? What would they gain by it?

"Yes, the tree," Grrindah said. She waved a hand. It was webbed between the first joints of the fingers.

"It need be no riddle or mystery," Wopolsa said. "The trees are one tree, and it is this planet's sole native sentient. We three planted its seed, and we helped it to evolve into sapiency."

Her face was more deeply hooded than the others. Her eyes were black, and Ramstan could not look long into them, though he tried. He shivered. They reminded him of the eyes of the shimmering thing in the well.

"We three calls ourselves the Vwoordha," Shiyai said. "Though not very often."

She laughed again. The others smiled, their faces cracking open like defective eggs in boiling water.

"You have some rather strange pets," he said.

"Pets?" Grrindah said. The blue eyes regarded him steadily, and, though she had been blinking before, now her eyelids did not move. There was something about those eyes . . . where had he seen them before?

"In the well."

"He calls it a well," she said, and all three cackled.

Ramstan became angry.

"You're very rude!"

That made them laugh again. When the shrilling died, Wopolsa said, "We are beyond politeness or rudeness."

Shiyai said, "You are sweating, but your voice sounds as if your mouth and throat are very dry. I think we could all do with some refreshment before we get away from the small talk. Would you care for some?"

Ramstan nodded, and he said, "A cool drink would be nice."

Shiyai clapped her brittle-looking hands, making a brittle noise. The creature coiled around the jewel hanging from the chain straightened out and dropped to the floor. Ramstan started. He had forgotten about it.

Though it had fallen from a height of at least 20 meters, the animal landed without seeming to hurt itself and ran out of the room through the door on the right. Ramstan was surprised at its size; he had thought it was only a meter long. He was also surprised that it ran on its back legs. He'd assumed from its long body that it was four-footed.

"I don't know how much I have to explain," Ramstan said. "I mean, who I am and why I'm here. You seem to know . . . I mean, my experiences . . . you've talked to me . . . I've seen you, you, at least . . ." He pointed a finger at Shiyai, then raised his hands, palms upward.

There was a silence for a few seconds. Then Grrindah said, "We'll wait until Duurowms serves us."

Ramstan held the skinceiver area close to his mouth and asked in a soft voice for the time. His eyes on the three if they should object to his reporting, he told Nuoli what had happened so far. Her only reaction was to ask if he thought that he was in any danger.

"I don't think so," he said. "I may be here for a long time. I'll report every fifteen minutes or so. Relay this to ship."

Nuoli must be wondering why he just did not keep his skinceiver on so that she could listen in. He could not tell her that he could not because the *glyfa* would probably, no, undoubtedly, be mentioned sooner or later.

He waited. The three were motionless, free of the fidgeting and eye-rolling, sighing and coughing, twitching and turning that possessed most sentients in similar situations. They looked withdrawn, but he felt that each was not just communing with herself. They could be holding a lively conversation among themselves. Telepathy? The scientists still had neither proved or disproved its existence.

Presently, and it seemed to be a long time, the creature called Duurowms entered. It carried in its two front paws a large tray with four silvery-looking goblets and a plate with tiny squares of some food. It came to Ramstan first and extended the tray, bowing at the same time. Ramstan looked into its large eyes. The eyeballs were entirely dark-brown, soft, liquidish—animal eyes. But sentients were animals. And the paws were not paws; they were hands, four humanoid fingers and an opposable thumb.

The goblets bore figures in both alto- and bas-relief, figures he could identify as animal, bird, fish, reptile, and bipedal and quadrupedal sentients, and things he'd never seen before. But they lasted only a flash to be replaced by other figures, which in turn were replaced. Alto-relief became bas-relief and vice versa.

Three of them held a blue liquid with a pleasant odor. Odors, rather. They seemed to change as swiftly as the figures on the goblet sides. Perhaps they coincided with the changing figures. He could not say that they did, since the transmutation was confusingly swift. Each odor evoked memories in him, all pleasing. None were ecstatic, just highly gratifying.

He was a baby, and his mother was nursing him. He was a baby, and his father was bathing him. He was a child in a boat on the *Shatt-al-Arab*, and his mother and father were teaching him how to fish. He had just mastered the Terrish alphabet; he had just mastered the Arabic alphabet. He had just been informed that he had been accepted as a cadet in the Terran space navy. His uncle had taught him the signals of the squirrels in the great forest just outside New Babylon, and he was "talking" to them. His father and mother were showing him, for the first time, the family genealogy book, and they were telling him the origin of the family name. Originally, it had been Ramstam, brought to the newly built city of New Babylon by a Scot transported to this area by the "hostage" system of the world government. Ramstam, in Scots Gaelic, meant "reckless or stubborn." During the generations after his coming to this land, the Arabic language of New Babylon had changed Ramstam to Ramstan.

It had also been a pleasure, which his parents for some

reason found ecstatic, to discover that he was a descendant of the prophet Muhammad. Certainly, his parents were in a state exceeding pleasure because of this. But he could not attain their emotional heights at the news. Why should he? There were millions all over the world who could claim the same lineage.

Ramstan tried to ignore the pleasant memories. He looked at the goblet containing a different liquid. This was reddish-brown, and its odor made his nose wrinkle and evoked unpleasant memories. It looked like rapidly oxidizing blood, and its smell verified that impression.

"Take whichever one you like," Wopolsa said.

Ramstan looked up from lowered lids at her. She seemed to be smiling, her mouth just a larger wrinkle in a mass of smaller ones. The teeth, unlike Shiyai's black ones, looked red.

A tremor passed through him, and his stomach, which had been expanding at the pleasing memories, shot back into a contracting ball. And someone was kicking that ball down . . . what field?

"Take one," Shiyai and Grrindah said at the same time.

"Only one?" Ramstan said, and he enjoyed the change of expression in the three. He did not know why. Perhaps because he had surprised them, and they were supposed to do the surprising.

Wopolsa, however, said, "All, if you wish."

"No, thank you," he said. He gripped the goblet nearest him. He came close to dropping it because the seeming metal gave way under his fingers. If anything, it felt as if it were made of something that was part mercury. It held together, but it yielded. It was part rigid substance, part liquid. When he released two fingers, the indentations filled out.

This goblet, for some reason, terrified him more than anything that he'd experienced in this house. It told him that he was in the presence of a science far advanced beyond any he had so far met.

He lifted the goblet but did not drink.

"After you," he said.

Duurowms carried the tray to Wopolsa first. Ramstan wondered if this meant that Wopolsa was the leader of the trio? He also noticed for the first time, though he should have seen it before, that the liquid in her goblet gave off a thin steam.

" 'The cold-blood who drinks hot blood.' "

It was Shiyai, the green-eyed and green-robed, however, who first lifted a cup.

"To the other," she said.

"To the other," Grrindah and Wopolsa said.

Ramstan raised his goblet. "To the other."

After a brief pause, he said, "And to the one who is not the other. To both."

He did not know why he said that or what it meant. But some sort of defiance was called for.

The three looked at him over their goblets. Then they said, "To both," and they drank.

Ramstan, flicking his gaze from the one on his left to the one on his right, sipped. The liquid was heavy but cool and delicious, though he could not quite identify its contents. He knew that he could not taste anything which his tongue buds were not receptive to. But it was also possible that these were genetically receptive to this liquid yet had not experienced on Earth, or anywhere until now, this particular taste.

Lowering the goblet, Ramstan said, "I have many questions. I hope you don't mind answering them."

"We have questions which have gone unanswered for eons," Grrindah said. "I hope you aren't going to ask us any of those."

She broke into laughter again.

He looked with some disgust at Wopolsa. Unlike the others, she was still drinking.

"The cold-blood who drinks hot blood." Cold-blooded? She looked as human as the others; she was no more batrachian or reptilian than they. Or did something other than blood flow in her?

Ramstan sketched the story of Wassruss, though he felt that they knew it. Then he said, "I followed the directions in the chant. Now, if you please, tell me the origin and reason for the chant."

"You could find that chant in many millions of societies," Shiyai said. "We originated and instituted it on thousands of planets and it has spread over millions of years. But, more often than not, it has become distorted and so useless. However, it has served its purpose. You are here."

This confused Ramstan and made him more uncertain than before.

"The same chant existed on Kalafala. But you were not there long enough to encounter it."

"You mean," he said, "that this chant was made long ago and far away just so that I might hear it?"

"In a sense, yes," Grrindah said. "But there were and are millions who might have heard it before you did. They would have served us as well."

"I don't understand."

"You and those like you, male and female adults, even some precocious children, were and are of a type inclined to follow the directions and to bring with them what we need. Also, because of their peculiar temperament and magnetism, they cause a focus of certain forces about them."

"I still don't understand."

"There is physical and psychic magnetism, though the two spring from the same source. Perhaps it would be a better analogy to say that there is physical and psychic gravitation. Just as a certain mass bends space around it, no matter what the quality or composition of the mass, so does psychic gravity bend events toward itself. But psychic magnetism differs from physical magnetism in that it is not the mass but the quality and proportion of qualities that determine the psychic gravitational attraction and the kind and quality of events it draws to itself. Perhaps someday we'll show you the mathematics of this. I doubt it, though. None of us has time for that."

Ramstan bit his lip, then said, "Shiyai, it was your voice I heard in the tavern. And it was surely you whom I glimpsed outside my hotel door and on the beach on Webn. I . . ."

"It was also I whom you saw on the tape in your quarters," the green-robed one said.

"How? Why is that?" Ramstan said.

"She rides the thoughts of God," Grrindah said. "Or something like It."

Grrindah laughed.

Ramstan was irritated by her cachinnations. How, he wondered, could the others have endured this rasping habit for so long?

"Not she but her projected image, though it's not really an image as you think of such," Shiyai said. "It's a method of

mental transportation in one sense. In another, it's something
else. A plucking of certain strings in the harp of spacetime
fabric. A music which you hear with certain of your mental
senses, which *hearing* is transmuted into physical sight and
sound, sometimes, smell and taste and feel, too."

"Just as an electron may be described as both a wave and a
particle," Wopolsa said.

"And something else too," Grrindah said, and she cackled.

"I would say that Shiyai rides, not the thoughts of God or
Whatever, but Its voice. The vibrations of Its voice, rather,"
Grrindah said.

Ramstan was thankful that she did not laugh this time.

"We are using poetry to try to tell you what happens
scientifically," Shiyai said.

"Poetry and science. Never the twain shall meet," Wopolsa
said.

"Not in the Pluriverse we know," Grrindah said. "But there
is a realm where they do."

She laughed.

Ramstan thought of when the *glyfa* had mentioned the
Pluriverse. And that made him wish that the *glyfa* would speak
up within him now. He needed counsel desperately.

The animal, Duurowms, had taken the tray out of the
chamber. Now he returned and leaped upward, catching the
giant jewel in his hands, drawing himself up, and coiling
himself around the top of the glittering gem. One dark eye
fixed upon Ramstan. Sometime later, glancing up, Ramstan
saw that the eye had closed and that the animal seemed asleep.

"It takes immense energy and artistry to ride the voice of
God without falling off," Shiyai said. "It is also very dangerous, which is why I do the riding or the plucking of the harp,
and not my sisters. I am the most energetic and artistic. And,
since it is so demanding and perilous, I seldom ride. That is
why you did not hear or see me more often."

"Besides," Grrindah said, "the other was also enticing you
here. Though the other is working against us, it is also working
for us. It can't help it any more than we can help working for
and against it."

Shiyai said, "It's time to quit being coy, sisters. We should
tell him everything."

"Everything?" Grrindah said, and she laughed.

"All he should know and a little more."

Ramstan boiled with eagerness to hear this, but there was also something he must say.

"Your pets in the well?" he said.

The three looked at each other, two smiling widely, Grrindah laughing.

"He's very perceptive," Shiyai said.

Then their flesh began melting or seemed to do so. A shimmering wrapped around them, reddish, blue-streaked waves which hurt his eyes, though not so much that he could not look directly into them.

Suddenly, the light and the melting had ceased. Now Shiyai was a beautiful young woman. Grrindah was a handsome middle-aged woman. Wopolsa had seemed to be so old that she could not possibly look more ancient. But she did, and her eyes seemed to have expanded, and Ramstan saw stars in the abysmal black emptiness. Only for an instant. They made him cold and frightened.

Shiyai said, "Now you see us in another form. Not because we have changed form, but because we have allowed other constructs, molds in your mind, to be filled with us. Yet, in a sense, you are seeing us as we are. Especially, Wopolsa."

Ramstan ignored her remarks.

"The pets?" he said. "Are they really pets? Or are they . . . really you? And you are the projections? Are they the sentients, the masters?"

All three laughed uproariously.

When the last of the echoes had bounced from the far walls, Grrindah said, "Perhaps the beings in the well are only projections. Which would, of course, also make us projections of projections. Or perhaps the citizens of the well have been projections so long that they have become realized as solid beings, actualizations of the potentialities of matter, fantasies of light that have transmuted into reality. Though, of course, fantasy is as real as reality, being engendered by reality and maintained by it. Without matter, there is no fantasy, though there may be matter without fantasy. Or is it the other way around or both at the same time?"

"That's enough," Wopolsa said. "Ask, and you must pay the price. But, first, we will tell you what the price is. Your questions so far have been for free."

"I have many questions," Ramstan said.

"The price from now on is the same for one or many," Wopolsa said. "However, first . . ."

And the three told him much, though not all he needed to know. What he did hear, however, was more than he liked to hear.

21

IF A TACK COULD have feelings and it had been hit directly with a sledgehammer, it would have felt as Ramstan did. If a rabbit had been seized by a tiger, it would have felt as Ramstan did.

Even so, he thought, and the thought was fire though a flicker, even so there was a difference between him and the tack, between him and the rabbit. He was a man and, thus, not helpless. He had not been utterly crushed and ruined by the hammerblows of the revelations. He was not paralyzed with fear forever. He could still fight; the flicker would become a roaring flame.

Was that just bravado? No sooner had he told himself that than he had been hit with another great shock. No. Two more.

While he was still sitting in the trio's chambers, reeling though sitting, Nuoli had called through the skinceiver.

"Captain! You must return to ship! At once!"

Her voice seemed to come through many layers of wool, to be so muffled and distant that it was like a voice in a dream.

"What's the emergency?"

"I don't know, Captain. Commodore Benagur has ordered it."

"Benagur?"

He found it difficult to concentrate upon what she'd said.

There was nothing important outside this room. But he forced himself to give at least part of his mind to Nuoli.

"Benagur? He's still in sickbay. What's he doing . . . issuing orders? Where is . . . what's happened to Tenno?"

There was a silence. Nuoli must be using a different frequency to talk to ship. Why?

She spoke again, her voice tense.

"Neither Benagur nor Tenno will tell me, sir. They just repeat that you must return at once."

The Vwoordha had been silent for some time awaiting his answer.

He said, "Pardon me. I must call my ship."

They said nothing.

He spoke into his skinceiver, but there was no response from *al-Buraq*.

He then called Nuoli. "What frequency are you using when you talk to Benagur?"

"I'm sorry, sir," she said, "but Commodore Benagur has ordered me not to divulge that to you."

The rage thrust deep under the iciness volcanoed out. He shouted, "Who's in command? Benagur or me?"

Even the Vwoordha started, and the animal opened its eye.

Nuoli hesitated, then said, "I'm sorry, Captain. You've been relieved of your command."

"How in Satan's name could that be?"

"I don't know, sir. Just a minute."

Ramstan rose unsteadily, his legs numb from sitting cross-legged for so long.

"I must go now," he said in Urzint.

Shiyai raised beautiful black eyebrows and said, "Your answer?"

"That will have to wait."

Grrindah said, "Someone on your vessel has found the *glyfa*."

Ramstan felt the blood drain from him again.

"How . . . how do you know?"

"I don't know. But I suspect that that would be the only reason you'd be deprived of your command. Perhaps the *glyfa* has guided someone to it so that it could be found. I do not know why it should, but it plays a deep game."

"No!" Ramstan cried. "It would have told me that it had been found!"

"Not if it had a reason not to."

"Benagur! He must have gotten into my quarters somehow and found it! But if he did it was with the connivance of someone else! Indra! Only Indra could have done it!"

He stopped. He was breathing heavily. Then, almost irrelevantly, it struck him that the three understood Terrish. Until now, he had assumed that they did not. But if one of them could ride the thoughts or the voice of God or whatever it was through the Pluriverse, then one could also eavesdrop anywhere.

Wopolsa said, "If you no longer have the *glyfa*, then you cannot help us. But the price is still the same."

He turned and strode out the front door. Down the slope was the launch, its entire crew looking up at him. Even at this distance, he could see the strain on their faces. He spoke into the skinceiver. "Bring the launch here."

The vessel had just landed by him, and he was taking the first step up, when the com-set blared. Benagur was speaking.

"Nuoli! Return to ship immediately! The Tolt ship has just been detected in orbit above us! I repeat, return at once! If Ramstan is not aboard, return anyway! I repeat, return at once at full speed within the limits of prudence!"

Nuoli said, "Commodore, Captain Ramstan is aboard. Will leave at once as ordered!"

Ramstan thought of jumping off the launch and taking refuge in the house of the Vwoordha. He could only face disgrace in *al-Buraq*, and the *glyfa* was lost to him. Though the urge was strong, it did not overcome him. Whatever wrong he had done, he had acted with full knowledge of the possible consequences and full, though not ready, acceptance of the punishment if he were caught. Whatever he was, he was not a coward. If he had been one, he would no longer be.

In other circumstances, the affirmation might have been a temporary relief. Not now. The Tolt ship was a menace, and his ship was commanded by a madman. How had Benagur been able to assume command? Why had not Tenno taken over? Surely, he must know that the commodore was not fit for the post of captain. Perhaps, the discovery of the *glyfa* by Benagur had vindicated him, had convinced Tenno that Ramstan had falsely accused Benagur of insanity for his own perverted reasons. But Doctor Hu surely had her doubts about Benagur, and she would not have been hesitant to voice them.

There was nothing to do but wait until he returned to *al-Buraq*. This was done swiftly, the pilot having set the launch to return on the plotted course, the computer slowing the velocity only when turn and obstacle demanded it.

Sitting in the rear, the only one watching him a marine guard, Ramstan moved his lips, subvocalizing. He called to the *glyfa,* but he got no reply. Ramstan cursed and struck his thigh with his fist, causing the marine to jump back, his hand moving toward his holstered olson.

"Don't worry, lad," Ramstan said. "I'm just angry at myself."

The launch shot into the port in the midst of shrill alarms and glowing orange orders on moving screens. Ship was being readied for standby before alaraf drive.

The deck and bulkheads quivered, *al-Buraq*'s welcome home to him, a tail-wagging, as it were. He wondered how ship would react when she found out that he was no longer the master. Would she shift loyalty to Benagur? The commodore probably was not aware of the affection circuit in her system, but Indra was. Would he recommend its excision if Benagur had trouble with her?

In the long history of sea navies, many crews had mutinied. But, so far, there was no record of a rebellion in a spaceship.

A squad of marines was waiting for him. If the marine lieutenant felt any emotion at arresting her captain, she did not betray it. Her face was expressionless, and her voice was steady. She told him that he would be conducted straight to the brig. He was outraged.

"Benagur is trying to humiliate me! He could at least let me be in my own quarters!"

"Sorry, sir," she said. "Orders."

He was marched through the passageways and up a lift and was put in a spherical room with a diameter of four meters. Unlike the ancient cells, this had no bars. He could close the iris-door if he or his jailors wished. But if he tried to pass through the opening without authorization, he would be stunned with a beam.

An armed marine stationed himself on each side of the

entrance. Ramstan wanted privacy, so he told ship to close the door. Meanwhile, the cell had been enlarging. Evidently, *al-Buraq* did not think that he had enough room. Ramstan at once told her to contract it to regulation size. Otherwise, an engineer might notice that she was ignoring the order to obey the new master.

He tried to call the bridge, but the transmission was now one-way.

He called to the *glyfa*. No response. Why was it not telling him what was going on? It could not be refusing to communicate because it was afraid that the Vwoordha would detect it. It must know that they were aware of its presence in *al-Buraq*. It had curiosity, the characteristic of all sentients; it could not have resisted listening in. It would have to know what was going on.

"The *glyfa* plays a deep game," Grrindah had said.

Ramstan paced back and forth while he tried to imagine what was going on. Benagur had the *glyfa,* but what was he going to do with it? Would he allow it to attract and persuade him as it had his captain? Or would he. . . ? No, surely he would not! Would he give the *glyfa* back to the Tenolt?

A luminous circle on the bulkhead showed Benagur's head and shoulders.

"Hûd Ramstan!" the bull-like head bellowed.

Ramstan stopped, unclasped his hands from behind his back, raised them toward the image, and said, "You see me." He was acutely aware that the commodore had not addressed him as "Captain."

Benagur did not look triumphant or as if he regarded Ramstan as contemptible or repulsive. Though his voice was that of a judge sentencing a criminal, his expression was the mask of one who was attempting to show supreme indifference. No, not indifference. Aloofness.

"You will be tried at court-martial in due time. Meanwhile, you'll have benefit of counsel. You can name any of the crew you wish to defend you, with the exception of those charging you. I recommend Lieutenant Enver, our lexologist. She is on duty now, however, and won't be available until the current crisis is over. No one will be until it's over."

"Thank you," Ramstan said.

"When there's time," Benagur said, "I'd like a complete

report on your mission. Nuoli is giving hers, but I want to know what happened in that . . . habitation."

"I'll record it as soon as possible."

"I want to know every little detail!" Benagur bellowed.

"Where is the *glyfa*?"

"It's not necessary that you know."

Benagur paused, smiled, and said, "We've been in communication with the *Popacapyu*. Her captain has been told that we have the *glyfa*, and we're negotiating for its return to their ship."

Ramstan kept his face rigid to conceal his dismay.

"One of the items in the negotiations is the return to us of Lieutenant Branwen Davis. We haven't heard her story yet, so we don't know if she'll be subject to a court-martial. The Tolt captain, however, has told us that she was forced by them to steal the *glyfa* from you."

Ramstan thought, How did they make her betray me? I mean, us.

He said, "Commodore . . ."

"Captain, not commodore!" Benagur said loudly. "I am the captain now!"

Ramstan swallowed his rage. "Captain Benagur, please think about this. The Tenolt will never forgive the theft of their god. They will arrange for its return, but, once they have the *glyfa*, they'll do their best to destroy ship and all in it. Their religion demands that they do that. They won't rest until the thieving blasphemers who stole the *glyfa* are destroyed. So . . ."

"I know that!" Benagur shouted, raising a finger as if he were a teacher admonishing a pupil. "I know that! Your crime has put all of us in peril! Believe me, that will be marked against you when you stand trial! I've told the Tenolt captain that you and you alone are responsible, that we were not in the plot to steal the *glyfa*, that we knew nothing about it until just now, that we share no culpability, that we are eager to make amends by returning the *glyfa* at once! But their captain has told us that if that is true, then we must surrender you to them!"

There was a slience. At last, Ramstan said, "I'm not pleading for myself, not asking for mercy. The Tenolt will torture me until I die. They have to do that, since their law exacts that as punishment for blasphemy."

"Their captain has told me that," Benagur said. He paused, then said, "Their captain has informed me that we will not share the blame, that he will not attack us if we deliver you to him."

"You can't trust his promise," Ramstan said. "According to what I know of Tenolt law, you, everybody in the crew, is guilty by association. He'll get the *glyfa* back and then attack."

"I don't think so," Benagur said. "His first duty is to get his false god back to its temple. If he attacks us, he risks being destroyed and so committing an unforgivable sin by not returning the *glyfa* to the temple. He'll take it back and then come looking for us. He must. That's his inescapable first priority."

"That may be," Ramstan said. "Are you going to give me up?"

Benagur reddened.

"Believe me, I'd like to! I'd do it if I could! You deserve such a fate!"

He bit his upper lip, then said, "But I'd take no pleasure in that. I despise you, but I would not wish you to suffer what the Tenolt would inflict on you. I am not vindictive! I weep for you, believe it or not, I weep for you because you are what you are! But . . ." he drew in and expelled a deep breath . . . "my first concern is ship and her crew! What am I to do with you? *About* you, I mean? Captain Tkashikl demands that you be given to him. But you are under Terran law, not Tenolt. I'm required to keep you under arrest and bring you to trial. I know what the trial will result in. There's not the slightest doubt that you are guilty."

He blew out another deep breath, his lips forming an *O* as if he were expelling smoke from a fire in his own body. "You are guilty, aren't you? Admit it, Ramstan, and save us!"

"Save you?" Ramstan said.

"Yes, save us. At least, redeem yourself somewhat, Ramstan. Admit your guilt. If you do, then you'll make the way clearer . . ."

"For deciding whether or not you'll turn me over to the Tenolt?"

"No!" Benagur said. His fist flashed across the screen and struck something beyond its field of vision.

Somebody—he sounded like Tenno—said, feebly, *"Captain!"*

"No! Terran government law and naval regulations forbid me to turn you over to any extraterrestrial authority, regardless of what you've done! But . . . this . . . case . . . wasn't anticipated by either. I have to make a decision on an unprecedented situation. I have to bear all the responsibility!"

"You're the captain now," Ramstan said. At the same time that he relished Benagur's plight, he sympathized with him. But he somehow had to make the commodore understand that this particular predicament was unimportant, of no real significance. Vital as it was for himself, it was as nothing compared to the larger event.

Then he thought, No, this situation is very important. Not just because my honor and life are at stake. I, and I alone, as far as I know, can tell Benagur, tell the crew, what is involved.

The commodore, however, gave him no chance. He shut off the channel, and, though Ramstan tried to get him to reopen it, he either was not hearing him or was ignoring him.

He had no idea at what stage the negotiations were. If they were in the final phase, then they would be only a few hours, as long as it took a launch from the *Popacapyu* to get to *al-Buraq* or vice versa.

He opened the door and called to one of the marines.

"I want a messenger to take a recording at once to . . ."

He swallowed; it was difficult to use the title.

". . . Captain Benagur. It's extremely urgent, a matter of life and death for everybody."

"I'm sorry, sir," the marine said. "I have no authorization for that."

"You must! To hell with authorization! If you don't, we'll be attacked by the Tenolt!"

"Sorry, sir, I can't do it."

"Listen! There's one possibility Benagur and I overlooked! The Tenolt are not going to insist that Benagur turn me over to them! Once they have the *glyfa,* they'll get me by destroying *al-Buraq* and everybody in it!

"Also . . ."

"Sorry, sir."

Ramstan closed the door. He took the three gifts of Wassruss from his jacket pocket and looked at them. The triangle, the square, the circle. He did not know if they could do what Wassruss claimed, but the Vwoordha had said that they could. They had certainly been eager to get their hands on them. He could escape now. Flight, however, was the last resort. Allah alone knew where he might end up; wherever it was, he could be stranded there until he died.

"Glyfa!" he cried. "I must talk to you! You must know what the situation is! Are you going to allow everything to go to hell?"

Silence.

22

IN ONE ASPECT, that lack of response was encouraging. It might mean that the *glyfa* knew that he could do what was required by himself.

On the other hand, the *glyfa* may have abandoned him. Perhaps it had decided that Benagur was now to be its means for getting whatever it was that it wanted.

Ramstan stood before a glowing but empty screen and spoke a code word. It overrode all other commands or at least was supposed to do so. When he had given it to *al-Buraq* in secret, he had been empowered by all the laws governing ship to do so. Now, he was acting against regulations. What about it? He had been doing that for some time.

At once, the screen displayed words in the Arabic alphabet of the twenty-third century.

"Acknowledged, Captain!"

Al-Buraq's brain was supposed to be no more self-conscious than a dog's, but there was considerable debate about the degree of that. It was, however, agreed that a dog had far more self-awareness than a parrot. What mattered now was that ship would obey his orders whether or not she comprehended human language.

Ramstan spoke, and a darkness appeared on the screen. Of

course. The *glyfa* was locked up in a safe. He gave another order, and now the view was from a screen in Benagur's quarters. The bulkhead opposite the one on which it was placed was that containing the safe.

He gave another order. If *al-Buraq* responded, and there was no reason to think she would not, the *glyfa* would be passing through an opening in the back of the safe. Moved along by osmosis, the *glyfa* would head for Ramstan's cabin.

While waiting for the too-slow process, Ramstan activated a screen in the bridge. It was placed high but was tilted so that he could see the central part of the control room. Benagur was pacing back and forth much as Ramstan did when he was there. Nuoli stood by a bank of screens. Tenno, by the com-op, said, "The Tolt launch is one hundred kilometers distant, sir, slowing down now."

"Very well," Benagur said. He did not look pleased, though. His enormous black eyebrows were bent downward below a wrinkled forehead; his mouth, when closed, was tight.

"The *Popacapyu* hasn't changed position?"

"No, sir."

Toyce came within range of the screen. Benagur said, "Doctor, bring the *glyfa* up now."

"Yes, sir." She hesitated, then said, "Captain, I'll get a container for it. The Tenolt won't like the idea that we've been handling it with bare hands. They'd regard that as sacrilegious. In fact, even after the *glyfa* is boxed, whoever carries the box should wear gloves."

Benagur stopped, grimaced, and said, "Sacrilegious! That idol! Very well, Toyce. We have to respect exotic mores. You're the sentientologist. Do what you think is best."

Toyce walked out of view of Ramstan's screen. It would take her perhaps five minutes to get a container unless she had one prepared. She probably did have one. Give her two minutes to get it and five to get into Benagur's quarters and discover that the *glyfa* was gone. No. He could gain more time. He gave *al-Buraq* an order to refuse to open the bulkhead-safe for her. Toyce would be irritated and would think that there was a malfunction. She would call one of the bioengineers, perhaps the chief, Indra. It might take him five minutes to get to the cabin or he might do his troubleshooting from the main engine room. Probably, the latter.

Ramstan had ship show him that room. Indra was sitting cross-legged on the deck, his eyes on some screens, the mentoscope attached to a band around his head, its detection-end, looking much like the end of a plumber's helper, against an indicator-bossing. His eyes, their epicanthic folds reflecting his Chinese ancestors, were slitted even more in deep thought. His large hawk's nose was moving, his nostrils flaring out.

Indra already knew that something was wrong. But he did not know what that was. Otherwise, he would have been reporting to Benagur.

Ramstan checked with *al-Buraq* on the progress of the *glyfa*. It would take ten more minutes before it reached his cabin.

The chief engineer's eyes snapped wide open, and he muttered something in Bengali, his natal tongue. Then he rose swiftly to his feet.

Ramstan shot orders at *al-Buraq*. Immediately thereafter, a similitude of Carmen Mljako, the subcommander engineer, appeared on a screen in the main engine room. It was Ramstan who spoke, but his voice was reproduced as Mljako's.

"Sir, I need your assistance in supply room 3-A at once. It's an emergency!"

"In a supply room?" Indra said. "Take care of it yourself, Mljako. I have a greater emergency to handle."

"I've found something you should look at at once, sir," her image said. "A bulkhead section fell out, why I don't know. But the nerve cables behind are damaged. I can't figure it out."

Indra grimaced. "Just a minute."

"No, sir, the cables look diseased."

"Diseased?"

"Rotting. Pustulent."

"Impossible!"

"I don't think so, sir."

"Maybe that's the trouble, though I don't see how it could be," Indra muttered. He strode swiftly down the corridor, the screen which showed Mljako's image preceding him. He turned into the supply room. As soon as he had stepped through it, the iris closed behind him, and the bulkheads moved in. Indra yelled, but he was squeezed between the four bulkheads and unable to move. Though he shouted for help and gave *al-Buraq* orders, he was not heard. All communication to the room had been cut off.

Ramstan watched Toyce as she walked down a corridor holding the handle of a large plastic box. Benagur had told ship to open the iris to his quarters; Ramstan had told *al-Buraq* to obey this order. Toyce went into the big chamber and spoke the code word given her by Benagur. She put the box on the deck while the bulkhead iris was opening. Straightening, seeing that the safe was empty, she said, "What the. . . ?"

Behind her, the entrance iris closed. She did not notice it because she had thrust her head into the safe and was feeling around it. The walls of the safe closed down; the iris extended lips and closed like a mouth over her head and shoulders. Though she screamed and struggled furiously, she was held tight.

Benagur, on the bridge, was speaking through the translator hanging by a cord from his neck. The machine spoke Tolt in answer to the commander of the launch from the *Popacapyu*. This was stopped a few meters from a port on the starboard side. Ramstan, looking at a bridge screen, could see the white set face of Branwen Davis through the transparent upper part of the hull. There were also twelve Tenolt there, heavily armed and looking grim.

"Your god will be here within a minute or two," Benagur said. "I assure you that you have no reason to fear treachery. I regret deeply that our former commander stole the *glyfa*, and I will see to it that he gets maximum punishment."

The launch commander had identified his rank as *'sakikl*, equivalent to commodore, and his surname as Khekhani'l. His deep harsh voice, speaking Terrish through the translator, said, "The fate of the blasphemer thief is up to you. Our only concern is to get our god back."

And then? Ramstan thought.

He gave another order to *al-Buraq*, following it with the code word to put the order into action.

Benagur looked at the bridge chronometer. He momentarily turned the translator off and said, "Tenno, open the channel to my quarters."

It was obvious that he meant to find out if Toyce had left the cabin yet.

Tenno did as ordered.

"The screen is blank, sir," Tenno said.

"I can see that," Benagur said. "Try voice."

Tenno spoke into the screen. Then, "No response, sir."

He opened a channel to the main engine room. It was empty, so he used the all-ship channels to call for an engineer.

Benagur scowled and said, "I don't like this, Tenno. Get Indra on it. Put me through to Ramstan."

The *glyfa* would arrive in another five minutes. Ramstan began pacing back and forth as if he were thinking deeply about something, which he was. Benagur's face appeared on a screen, and he bellowed, "Ramstan!"

It might have been better to seem to be startled, but Ramstan would not give Benagur that satisfaction. He stopped and turned slowly. "Yes?"

Benagur looked the brig over, but he would see nothing out of the way. Nevertheless, he was suspicious. His expression said that his prisoner had to be up to something and that he was probably responsible for Toyce's being late and for the malfunction in his cabin channels. Still, he could do nothing about it.

Benagur did not even give Ramstan the courtesy of answering him. The screen went blank.

The cell screen showed Ramstan the bridge. Benagur said, "Tenno, send someone after Toyce and scan ship for her."

He looked at the chronometer again and then at the screen showing the Tolt launch. "Where's Indra?"

"Can't find him as yet, sir," Tenno said.

"Can't *find* him?" Benagur's voice lost some of its deepness. "What do you mean, you can't find him? What's going on?"

Tenno called Mljako. "Do you have any idea where Commodore Indra is?"

Mljako shook her blonde head. "No, sir. Just a minute ago he was in the main engine room, testing."

"For what?"

"He said he suspected some sort of malfunction."

"He was right!" Benagur said. "We're up to our ass in malfunctions!"

That was the first time Ramstan had heard the commodore use any phrase even hinting at vulgarity. Ramstan smiled. Benagur was very nervous.

The Tolt commodore spoke again, asking what was causing the delay. Benagur replied that Toyce would be on the bridge within a minute with the *glyfa*. He asked the commodore if he would enter ship now. It would expedite matters. The Tolt refused, and, a minute later, called Benagur.

"My captain gives you ten more minutes to surrender our god. If I don't report that the *glyfa* is in the launch by then, I am to proceed back to my ship."

That meant that the *Popacapyu* might attack as soon as the launch returned. Branwen Davis would still be a prisoner.

Ramstan thought briefly about her. She was very attractive, and he was very fond of her. But he was not in love with her. He could not, would not, permit himself to be. All the women he had fallen in love with and who had fallen in love with him had left him. Those who had told him why they had left had said that he was missing something vital. He was flawed. Not that they could not tolerate certain flaws in their men. As the saying went, nobody was perfect. But he was always thinking of something other than them, even at the times when he should have been entirely with them. One with them, as Nuoli had once said. He did not satisfy them. They did not use that phrase in the sexual sense; he was far from wanting in bed. Physically, that is. But he was searching for something, and when he drove hard into their bodies, it was as if he was trying to clutch that something inside them.

They did not have it, of course, and they hated him for using their bodies as a channel for it.

Ramstan had denied their accusations at first, but eventually he had admitted to himself that they were right. He did not want things to be that way. But he could not help himself.

What was he looking for?

Immortality? He could have had that from the *glyfa*, though it was in a form that he would take only as a last resort. Perhaps not then.

Despite this, he grieved about Branwen Davis, though only for a short time. Allah alone knew what she faced if she remained the captive of the Tenolt. Even though they had forced her to be their tool, they would regard her as a blasphemer. She had touched the *glyfa*.

Until now, the Tenolt had never been absolutely sure where their god was. They had preferred a waiting game; using cunning and guile and patience. Now, they knew that the *glyfa* was in *al-Buraq*. They were getting very impatient and very desperate. They could attack and destroy *al-Buraq* and not harm the *glyfa*. Its hard surface would defy even a laser or an atom bomb, if what the *glyfa* had told him was true. It had been forged in a star, had burned up the star as fuel. It could fall into a white dwarf and not be damaged or affected in any way.

For all Ramstan knew, the Tolt launch was armed with a neutron bomb. Its commodore might be under orders to set it off if he had to. He would not hesitate to do so. His act would ensure his soul eternal delight within the *glyfa*.

The more Ramstan considered this possibility, the more he was sure that the Tenolt would be prepared for such an act.

In any event, he did not plan that they would get the *glyfa*.

If he gave the code word now, *al-Buraq* would go into alaraf drive. She would vanish from the sight of the Tenolt. If they indeed did have the ability to trace the passage of *al-Buraq*, they would still have to chase her, and Ramstan thought he might lose them. Even if he could not, he could get ship to a more defensive or offensive situation.

Going into alaraf drive, however, would leave Branwen Davis in Tenolt hands.

He thought furiously for a moment and then decided to take a chance. The weapons in the launch might be set to operate automatically if *al-Buraq* or her crew made a sudden offensive move. And even if that was not the situation and if the launch crew was not overcome swiftly enough, its commodore might trigger a bomb—if it had a bomb.

He gave another order to ship. Her deck and bulkhead quivered. He had ship fold a shock-cushion of flesh around him, a formation from the deck. Partially enclosed in this, he said, "Now!"

The swift movement of *al-Buraq* thrust him sideways into the yielding but still-holding flesh. Anyone else in ship who was unsecured would be hurled from the deck or pressed against a chair or bulkhead or whatever. There would be injuries, but he could not help that. He must do what he was doing if Branwen was to be saved from torture and death.

Al-Buraq shot toward the launch, swallowed it in the port, and deck and bulkheads and overhead squeezed down. The launch was being pressed down—if things were going as Ramstan planned—until there would be only room enough within the launch for its occupants to lie on the deck. The hull would be a mangled can squeezing them, keeping them from moving enough to get to the controls. And the control machinery should be compressed and out of operation.

That was what he hoped would happen.

A bulkhead screen flashed out in code, "Order carried out. Awaiting next phase."

Ramstan could not keep from crying out triumphantly. Then he said, swiftly, in code, "Next phase."

The shock-cushion spread out from him, and he arose. The lessened weight told him that *al-Buraq* had gone into alaraf drive.

23

A BULKHEAD SCREEN showed that the two marines had regained their guard posts. Ramstan gave an order. The brig shrank to compensate for the widening of the bulkheads directly behind the marines, their hollowing-in in the central portion, and their lipping-out at the edges. The pliable bulkheads then swiftly straitjacketed the two guards except for their heads. They were helpless to do anything but yell.

The iris could not fully open because of the bulging out of the bulkheads, but Ramstan squeezed through it. He had the marines released one by one, took their olsons, and put one in his jacket pocket. He ordered them to enter the brig. There he gave another order to *al-Buraq*. The deck flowed up and around them until it covered their lips. Though no one but he could hear them, he did not want to be distracted by their voices.

An olson in one hand, he left the brig, ran down the passageways to a lift, and took it down two decks to the port which had swallowed the Tolt launch. At his order, ship opened up enough to let him in. The distorted bulkheads parted for him as the Red Sea had for Moses. The port crew was enfolded in the reddish substance of deck and bulkhead. Their protruding heads reminded him of a scene from Dante's

Inferno. Ignoring their cries for help, he walked on, the bulkheads dividing for him, and he came to what was left of the launch. *Al-Buraq* had crushed it, trapping Branwen Davis and the Tenolt crew inside it.

Branwen was the only one alive. The others, unable to get free and doubtless acting on orders given before they had left the *Popacapyu,* had committed suicide. They had probably done it by code words which had released poison from minute containers in their bodies.

Ramstan cut with his olson the hull sections which trapped Branwen, put the weapon in his jacket pocket, and helped her to her feet. She was very pale and covered with vomit. Her hand shaking, she pointed at the forward part of the launch.

"I think there's a bomb there," she said.

She staggered toward him, and he held her up. The stench sickened him.

"The commodore couldn't get his hands free to pull a button from his uniform," she said. "He kept screaming at the others to get loose and tear the red button off."

"Button?" Ramstan said. "Are you all right?"

"Yes. I think that tearing the button off would activate the bomb."

"I'll tell the crew to take care of it," Ramstan said. He half-lifted her and urged her out of the port. The heads yelled at him, asking questions, begging to be released. He ignored them.

As they went down the passageway, he said, "The Tolt captain admitted that he'd forced you to steal the *glyfa* and leave a fake in its place. How'd he manage to do that? I mean . . . once you were in *al-Buraq,* you should have been safe. You could have told us . . ." He stopped. Obviously, she had had a good reason to keep quiet.

"The fever?" he said. "That have anything to do with what the Tenolt did to you?"

"Yes," she said huskily. "The fever was a temporary reaction to the artificial protein-explosive mix implanted in me. They took . . . they took . . ."

She choked, then said, "They took out a section of my vaginal wall and replaced it with the mixture. It's undetectable from natural flesh unless a piece of it is removed and subjected to a laboratory test. The explosive could be set off with a certain radio frequency. I was told that if I didn't cooperate with them, I'd be blown up."

"But you could have told us. The surgeons would've removed the section."

"With what? Steel or plastic tools would set off the explosive. I was told that the explosive radiated a field that would cause an explosion when there was direct contact of any hard substance with the artificial flesh. Laser beams would also trigger it. I don't know . . ."

"That what they told you was true?"

"Yes, but I couldn't . . . wouldn't . . . take the chance."

"There were plenty of times when we were far away from the Tolt ship. They couldn't send a triggering frequency then, and I'm sure that Doctor Hu would've figured out something. At the least, you could have told us what the situation was. Maybe we couldn't remove the section, but we wouldn't have been ignorant . . . blind . . ."

"Look who's telling me what a cowardly traitor I am."

"You were afraid, and you kept silent," he said. "I have no love for the Tenolt. But they can't be blamed too much. I did steal their god, and they believe that without their god they are nothing. Nothing! By the way, how did they know that I did it? What about Benagur and Nuoli?"

"They figured that you were the only one with enough authority to keep the officers and crew from asking questions. But I suppose they didn't really know who'd taken it. Their speculations were right, though. You did steal it!"

They entered his quarters. She went to the bulkhead where a symbol, three wavy black horizontal lines, was at her eye-level. She pointed at her open mouth, and the bulkhead bulged out, became a down-curving pipe, and a section formed a cup which fell off. She held the cup until it was almost full of water, signaled for the outpour to stop, drank, and then slapped the cup against the bulkhead. It seemed to melt and shortly was part of the bulkhead again. The pipe-form remained in case ship's captain might wish a drink also. The affection circuit was responsible for this. Without it, ship would have automatically retracted the pipe.

Ramstan drank also. Branwen came up to him. Her green eyes, reminding him of the surface of the Persian Gulf, seemed to expand, to grow like balloons in his mind, to crowd out all else that was vital at that moment.

"Can you really blame me?" she cried. "What was I to do? Ethically . . ."

He said, "Yes, ethically?"

"Right or wrong? That's what I mean! Weren't the Tenolt basically right, justified? Weren't you the criminal, the unjustifiable? What was I to do? I believed, half-believed, anyway, that they had the right!"

"There's no time for this kind of talk," he said. "Any kind of talk. I'm here, not on the bridge, and . . ."

"I don't know what kind of hold the *glyfa* has on you," she said. "But you betrayed . . ."

"Be quiet!" he yelled.

She quivered, reminding him for some reason of the shaking of the deck when *al-Buraq* was excited or anxious about him.

"Why should I?" she said. "What can you do to me? Or for me? You're nothing. I know that you're not the captain, you're in disgrace, you've been brigged. Benagur told the Tolt captain, and he told me. Only . . ."

She waved a hand to indicate that she did not understand what was going on. Even in her shock, she must comprehend that the situation was not what had been described to her. Otherwise, how would Ramstan have been able to leave the brig, rescue her, and come to his quarters?

"Take your seat, and stay there," he growled.

"I'll take it. I may not stay."

By then the bulkhead was glowing with forty-nine screens, each showing a key-point in ship. By now, some crewpeople were trying, without using lasers or other violent means, to get Indra out of the grip of the storeroom. They were failing, of course. Other screens showed faces with many differing expressions or without expression, which was as indicative of emotions as the liveliest masks. Most displayed various kinds of anxiety or fear or panic or stunned incomprehension which concealed a comprehension their owners did not want to admit.

Ramstan now concentrated his thoughts on Benagur. What he ordered was what the crew would do. Unless he, Ramstan, snatched the leadership from Benagur.

He paced back and forth, knowing that he had to act very soon. Branwen, smiling strangely, spoke.

"I'm very passionate, but I've been without sex since I was first captured by the Tenolt. The friction of anything in my vagina would set off the explosive. That's why I turned you down when . . ."

He whirled and said, savagely, "This is no time to talk about such trivialities!"

"Trivial! I can't ever go to bed with a man again! There's no way the section can be removed!"

"There are other forms of sexual intercourse."

"Spontaneous sex means spontaneous combustion," she said, and she giggled.

"For the sake of Allah!" he roared in Arabic. Then, in Terrish, "Must I throw you out? Be quiet! Let me think!"

"I've been through a lot," she said. "But I'm not cracking up . . . I don't think."

He and Indra could not be the only ones who knew about the affection circuit. One of the bioengineers would think of it soon, if he or she had not already done so, and he would notify Benagur. The engineers would cut the circuit off from the rest of the neural system. How long would they take? They could not go in ripping and tearing; brutal surgery might damage *al-Buraq*'s brain.

A bulkhead screen pulsated orange, then showed the *glyfa* momentarily bathed in light. It was in the safe now.

Ramstan removed it and placed it on a table formed by ship. Branwen's eyes became large, and she left her chair to walk to a bulkhead which was as far as she could get from the *glyfa*.

"Speak!" Ramstan cried. "I need you!"

Silence.

"Damn you!"

His fist struck the table top. *Al-Buraq* quivered.

Ramstan shouted out orders to ship. Immediately, every screen throughout it, except those connected to the exterior-detection system and those in Ramstan's quarters, showed him throughout the vessel. He saw Benagur start when most of the screens on the bridge displayed the prisoner's face and shoulders. Benagur's face paled as if touched with frost when he realized that the room behind Ramstan was not the brig but the captain's quarters. Then Ramstan stepped aside briefly so that the *glyfa* was visible. He could almost hear Benagur's blood draining from his head.

"Yes, I have complete control of ship," Ramstan said. "And you, all of you, are going to listen to me whether you want to or not. I don't know if you'll believe what I have to say. I hope you will. If you don't, if you reject my testimony, then you will put Earth in even graver peril than she is in now. You'll put the universe, all of the universes, in . . . you'll doom them!"

"He's insane!" Benagur shouted. "Don't listen to him! Tenno, get marines down to the prisoner's quarters and blast through the iris! If Ramstan resists, kill him!"

"They won't get near me," Ramstan said. "Ship will capture them. And if they do get off some shots, they're likely to injure ship. You can't take that chance, Benagur. Not when the Tenolt may show up any moment now."

"Tenno, you have your orders!"

Ramstan bellowed, "Tenno, don't carry them out! Don't even try to! Anyone who makes a hostile move will be enfolded! And you, Benagur, if you don't stop talking and start listening, you'll be wrapped up in a deck-extension, wrapped like a mummy."

Benagur took a deep breath and shut his eyes. When he opened his eyes, he said, quietly, "Very well, traitor. We'll listen because we have to."

"There's no need for insults, even if they should be justified," Ramstan said. "First, though, you have to know about Lieutenant Branwen Davis, formerly of *Pegasus*. That violent sidewise movement of ship was ordered by me so that she could capture the Tenolt launch and rescue Davis."

He described how Davis had been forced by the Tenolt to steal the *glyfa*. And he explained what might happen if the *Popacapyu* got close enough to transmit a radio signal to the artificial flesh-explosive mixture in her.

"She has no idea what the energy potential in the explosive is. If set off, it might blow her to pieces and those very near her. Or it might destroy ship and all in her, of course. That's one more reason why we must play hide-and-seek with the *Popacapyu* or find some means of destroying her before the signal is used."

He paused and then said, "I hope no one will be cowardly enough to suggest that Davis be gotten off ship at the first opportunity."

Tenno said, "But . . . but all we have to do is to put her in a room with radiation shielding."

Ramstan smiled grimly. "That's an obvious idea. I told Davis the same thing, though I suspected that there had to be a reason why she hadn't confessed everything and then taken refuge behind shielding. It's because . . . or at least the Tenolt told her this and it may not be true . . . the transplanted section contains more than explosive. It also has a time bomb, a biological fuse, a fleshly clock, which is set to go off at a certain time and trigger the explosive.

"Davis wasn't told when the clock would strike. All she knew was that the Tenolt had allowed her an unspecified time. If she did not have the *glyfa* back in their hands by then, she would blow up. The biological clock, however, could be forever stopped by a certain frequency transmitted by the Tenolt. That would be done as soon as she got the *glyfa* in their hands. By that, I suppose that they meant inside their ship."

Benagur opened his mouth, then closed it. Nuoli said, "Either way, she'll be killed!"

"Perhaps," Ramstan said. "We don't know if the Tenolt were lying about that. But we can't take a chance."

"Poor Branwen," Nuoli said softly.

"She wouldn't be in this horrible situation if you hadn't stolen the *glyfa!*" Benagur bellowed. "None of us would be!"

"True," Ramstan said coolly. He gave the order, and the deck swelled up all around Benagur and enfolded him tightly. Only his head from the nose up was visible. That was very red, and his eyes were rolling like ball bearings about to tear loose.

"Tenno, I'm going to let a marine come down here," Ramstan said. "But only if the marine is unarmed. The marine will escort Lieutenant Davis to a launch. A technical force will prepare shielding for the launch. The launch will be the one that has alaraf drive. When this is completed, by that I mean so that no radio signal can penetrate it, Lieutenant Davis will be put in it. The launch will be programmed to accompany *al-Buraq* at a distance of two kilometers. No, make that three. I don't know how powerful the explosive is. The program will automatically direct the launch to keep pace with ship at this distance. When we go to another bell, the launch will go also. Lieutenant Davis will be given enough life support for four weeks of ship's time. Is that clear?"

Ramstan's words had been recorded, and, if Tenno was uncertain about their meaning, he could play back the recording. He said, "Aye, aye, sir. Clear."

Ramstan felt relief. One more crisis gotten through. He had not known if Tenno would disobey him because he thought that Benagur had to be, according to regulations, still in command. But Tenno could not be trusted. He might be going along with his former captain because there was nothing else he could do at the moment. For the moment, he was obeying, and that was what Ramstan wanted.

Davis said, "You're really doing this to me?"

He turned. "Listen, Branwen, I don't like it. But it's absolutely necessary. I'd be justified if I had you ejected into space. You're a very real danger, and there are events . . . things . . . which you don't know about. These make your situation very insignificant . . . unimportant . . . comparatively speaking. I'm extending myself . . . I shouldn't even be doing this for you. . . ."

"They're right!" she cried. "They're right!"

He did not ask her what she meant by that. He supposed that she was referring to what the other women had told her about him. She was wrong, though, in assuming that this situation had anything to do with his relations with the crewwomen. If she were not so frightened, she would understand that he had to do this for the preservation of ship and her crew. And for even larger matters. Much much larger.

He told her that she should leave his quarters now and go to meet the marine.

"I can't wait until he gets here. There may be little time left. But you can hear what I have to say in ship and the launch. It'll clarify this business for you."

Or perhaps make her even more confused, he thought.

She turned her head to glare as she walked by him toward the iris.

He said, "After all, I did save your life, and I'm doing all I can to keep you safe. It's much better to be by yourself, no matter how lonely you are for a while, than to be blown up. And I do have to consider the safety of ship first."

"*Now* you do," she said. "What about *then?*"

He did not reply. He assured the tec-op and com-op that the order for silence while he talked did not apply to them if the detectors picked up anything that might be dangerous.

24

"FIRST, I MUST TELL you what happened when Commodore Benagur, Lieutenant Nuoli, and I went to the temple of the *glyfa*. I must because you cannot understand the events following unless you know what impact this had on us three. Especially, on me."

He paused. And the *glyfa* spoke.

"Ramstan, tell me what's been happening since I last talked to you and what is happening now."

This time it was using his father's voice.

He started, and he came close to choking.

"Officers and crew! Just a minute!"

He turned, though it was not necessary to do so, to speak to the *glyfa*. Human beings, all sentients he'd met, felt that looking at the face of the one they were talking to ensured a fuller communication and a deeper trust in whatever that one was saying. The face expressed the soul, the consciousness, the sincerity. The speaker could be judged by his, her, or its expression. But the egg-shape was unchangeably fixed; no play of emotions crossed its surface, no ripple of face, no bodily movements, only the voice itself was the index of truth or falsehood. And that voice was changing and could be his mother's or father's or anyone he knew. It was like talking over an ancient telephone or radio transceiver which lacked the image of the one you were talking to.

Also, what the Vwoordha had told him about it when he was in their house weighed heavily on him. The atmosphere seemed to thicken, to become layers on layers of glue-impregnated paper, layers rising to unimaginable heights, a crushing weight. He was pressed down as if a building had fallen down on him, and he felt as if the building was something unknown before. One which towered up, up, up past the boundaries of air and Space.

Boundaries.

The word flashed like a meteorite over the fields of his mind.

"*Glyfa!* I've been trying for a long time to get you to talk to me. But you didn't reply."

"I was thinking."

"You may have been," Ramstan said. "But you were also not receptive to anything outside yourself. You were recharging your . . . battery? . . . fuel? . . . self? You didn't answer me because you couldn't hear me."

"The Vwoordha told you this."

"Yes. They told me that you had periods of unwilling withdrawal. That you have to depend upon a fuel source, like all life, to keep alive, if alive is the correct term. When your source of energy is not equal to your demands on it, you must rest and draw in the energy before you. . . ."

"So. They told you. I expected that they would. I have a very small surface area. Though I operate on a 67-percent economy, which is more efficient than anything or anyone else in this cosmos, excluding one, I have to go through periods of . . . hibernation . . . suspended animation . . . no, you'd understand the analogy to a recharging battery best."

"But you have a wide range of energy sources," Ramstan said. "Electricity, X-rays, gravitons, even antigravitons, photons, antiphotons. There's no reason why you should recharge so often. Especially when there's an energy source on ship and I could connect you to it."

He paused, then said, "No. I'm wrong. The bioengineers would note any unexplainable consumption of power. They'd track it down."

He still did not believe that a forced quiescence during recharging accounted for all or even half of the *glyfa*'s silence.

Most, if not all, of the time it had failed to respond to him, it had done so for reasons only it knew.

It was trying to nudge him here and there with both its silences and its enigmatic revelations.

The Vwoordha were pushing him towards their goal, too. When the *glyfa* nudged, they counternudged. And vice versa. Or were the Vwoordha and the *glyfa* just pretending to be opponents?

"You know two of my limitations," the *glyfa* said. "Did the Vwoordha tell you about the third?"

"Yes."

"I know when you're lying. You're lying now."

"Then I won't lie to you from now on," Ramstan said. "Maybe. I don't know that you can tell when I'm lying. My truth may not be yours."

"Sly, sly. Always considering all the variables—as you can see them. *See*. Why must you sentients use this term? There are so many things that you can't *see* but can still sense otherwise. Even without light, you can see. Within limits."

"All senses have limits," Ramstan said. "Except one. And even that . . ."

"You must have had a long talk with the Vwoordha. But it could not have been long enough. However, they did tell you of my restrictions. I am dependent on other sentients for mobility, and I am dependent on my energy source, like all of my kind. Though it may surprise and even repulse you, I am of your kind, though I am artificial."

"What . . . who . . . was your model?"

"None! Or perhaps a thousand were my model. Whatever the sources of my creators . . . the models . . . the end result was unique. Just as you, the result of a hundred million models . . . are unique."

"Uniqueness does not necessarily mean anything more than mediocrity . . . even idiocy . . . a pale similitude of humanity," Ramstan said. "Listen! This is getting us nowhere. Let me tell you what I've been doing since you withdrew to . . . recharge. I'll have to go fast. The crew is waiting for me. They must be wondering what the hell's going on, why I should have started to tell them everything."

"Everything?"

Ramstan felt his skin warming. He realized that the *glyfa*

was, in some ways, just like him. It questioned the inexact use of a word or term; it liked to demonstrate that the other did not know exactly what he, she, or it was saying. Was this characteristic a means for putting down the other and so showing his own superiority? Or was it his personal requirement, quite justified, for the precise use of a word? Or both?

It might even be that the *glyfa* was not like him. It might be subtly mocking him. It might be that it knew that no sentient could ever use a word in the dictionary sense, the objective sense, that every sentient had his own personal, unique language.

Ancient as it was, the *glyfa* could not use language as he, Ramstan, so impermanent, so time-bound, so mayflyish, used it.

"Within your limits . . . and mine . . . even mine . . . everything," the *glyfa* said.

"I haven't time," Ramstan said.

"Tiiiiimmmme." The word murmured, swelled, leaped up, like a surf wave striking a cliff, and receded. Now the speaker was Ramstan's uncle, the one who'd taught him "squirrel talk," the queerly inconsistent philosophical and humorous uncle. The uncle long-dead who still lived in his mind and had been resurrected by the *glyfa*.

"No, I don't have time!" Ramstan shouted. "Listen while I tell the others!"

"Others! Others! Others!" echoed and then faded away.

Ramstan turned from the *glyfa* and spoke again to the crew.

"When I went into the Tolt temple with Benagur and Nuoli, I, too, experienced something phenomenal. Numinous. The very nature of the experience, if reported, would have made you doubt my sanity. I was flooded with light, just as Benagur and Nuoli were. Not photonic light. It was a light such as few have ever seen."

Suddenly Ramstan had been Muhammad the prophet, yet at the same time was also himself. He was sleeping in a house near the sacred Kaaba in Mecca. He had gone to bed weary and sad because he had gained so few disciples after the angel Gabriel had appeared to him in a grotto, had shown him a scroll, and said, "Recite!" That is, read and then reveal the divine contents to mankind.

The fatigue, disappointment, and discouragement lasted

only for a few seconds. He was awakened when Gabriel entered the house, the archangel Gabriel with his many-colored wings and the glorious light streaming from his face.

Ramstan described the events following very rapidly. He would have liked to dwell with great detail on them, but he did not want to weary his audience, and time was vital.

"After Gabriel had purified my heart by washing my breast with water from the sacred well of Zamzam and poured over me the *hikma*, which is symbolic of faith and wisdom, he took my hand. And *al-Buraq* appeared, *al-Buraq*, the Lightning, the fabulous unique animal. It had the face of a young woman and wore a golden crown. Its body was a mule's, its hoofs and tail were a camel's, its harness was of pearls, its saddle was a single carved emerald, and its stirrups were turquoise."

Before helping Muhammad-Ramstan onto *al-Buraq*, the archangel told him that Allah had decreed that this night he would travel through the seven heavens and would be allowed to worship the face of the Truth, the Everlasting, the Father of All.

"No language is anywhere adequate to describe my ecstasy," Ramstan said. "There are no words which can communicate to you more than a very slight fraction of the power and intensity of my feeling. The mystical experience has always been indescribable. How can I describe how many-colored light bathed every cell of my body and how every cell throbbed with ecstasy and how I *saw* every cell and knew its *name?* Or how I felt, like a giant glowing shadow behind me, behind my soul, a being that was only a reflection of the glorious face of the Ineffable yet would have blinded me if I could have turned when I felt Its hand on my shoulder and looked upon Its face?

"I did not wish to turn because I knew that even the shattering light would not blind me to Its shattering beauty. And Its ugliness. At the same time, I felt that I might turn and, horrifying thought, see nothing there."

Ramstan skipped through the journey on *al-Buraq*'s back from Mecca to Jerusalem, ancient Jerusalem, the holy city of the prophet's time. He passed briefly over his entering the sacred mosque and meeting the prophets of God who had come before him. He did mention that he was greeted by Ibrahim, Musa, and Isa, that is, Abraham, Moses, and Jesus.

Then he rode *al-Buraq* to the first heaven, a sphere the color of turquoise, while Gabriel, carrying a standard, preceded him.

Heaven after heaven, rank upon rank of angels, greatest of the great men, Adam in the first heaven, John and Jesus in the second, Joseph in the next highest, Idris in the fourth, Aaron in the next, Moses in the one above Aaron's, and Abraham in the last and highest of the heavens. Though he had to be sketchy, he could not stop himself from giving some details of the White Cock in the first heaven, the angel which looks like a bird and whose comb touches the bottom of Allah's Throne and whose feet rest on Earth. Nor could he keep himself from telling some of the terror and awe he felt on seeing the angel, half snow, half fire, who held in his left hand a rosary of snow and in his right hand a rosary of fire and who recited the rosary, telling the one hundred beads, making a sound like thunder as he moved the beads.

He also could not help revealing some of the terror he felt in the second heaven when he encountered the Angel of Death, Azrael, the decider of lots, who rests one foot on a chair of light and the other on *al-Sirat*, the razor-thin bridge between Heaven and Hell.

"And then I heard the voice of the All-Abiding, and I worshiped Him," Ramstan said. "Truly, at that time, I felt that I was indeed Muhammad and myself, two yet one, and that I was experiencing the glory, the unutterable ecstasy, that comes from hearing the voice of God Himself. At the same time, I felt a fear that was so intense that it was also an ecstasy."

But beyond the seventh sphere was unending Space, and in it hung seventy thousand veils of light of many colors. Beyond the veil was *al-Arsh*, the Throne of God, a seat made of red hyacinth and so huge that the Earth was a mote of dust beside it.

There were many things which Ramstan, caught up in a fervor that was still only a pale shadow of what he had felt in those few minutes in the temple of the *glyfa*, would have liked to tell. But he skimmed through them, even the gardens of paradise, and came to Hell itself, guarded by the awful Malik, the king of shadows. And when Ramstan tried to describe the tortures of the damned, his voice broke, and he wept.

"And then I was back in the house in Mecca for just a second, and my feeling that I was the prophet faded as the walls of the house did, and I was standing in the giant anteroom of the temple of the *glyfa* and was being told by the high priest to go into the chamber where the *glyfa*, the Tolt god, would receive me."

Benagur's face was even redder, and his eyes were wilder. For a moment, Ramstan thought of uncovering the commodore's mouth long enough for him to vent what was troubling him. But he thought he knew what Benagur wished to say. That was, that Benagur had also had a *Miraj*, a miraculous ascension, but that his had been somewhat different.

Shortly after leaving Tolt, Benagur and Ramstan had had a brief conversation. Benagur had sketched his reactions in the temple. Ramstan had held back on his. In fact, he had said no more than that he, too, had been flooded with light and lost consciousness for a while. Benagur had been far less reticent. He had told of his levitation to the throne of God while accompanied by the prophet Elijah. His experiences had been confined to that which a very devout Jew might imagine. (On learning which, Ramstan had begun to question the validity of his own *Miraj*.) Benagur, like Ramstan, had not actually seen the face of God, but he had come close. He too had ventured into, or, rather, over Hell. And he had announced, somewhat sorrowfully but with a trace of triumph, that he had seen Ramstan among the damned and witnessed his torture in flames. Though Benagur said that this sight filled him with sorrow, he could not quite conceal his satisfaction.

Ramstan had grinned then. But he did not tell Benagur that he had seen Benagur's pain-sewn face among the wretches in the seventh and lowest sphere.

Ramstan had said that he was surprised. He thought that orthodox Jews did not believe in a hell.

Benagur had replied that a literal hell was not in his faith. But, evidently, he had been mistaken. After all, God did not reveal everything. And it was only just that Christians and Moslems who believed in such a savage place should end up there.

However, Benagur admitted, though he had seen what seemed to be a literal hell, how did he know that it might not be a figurative one? That the flames and spikes and hooks were only symbolic of the awful terror and grief of Hell's inhabitants at being barred forever from the sight of the face of God

25

BENAGUR STRUGGLED VIOLENTLY, and his mouth came loose from the grip of ship's flesh. He cried, "You are a blasphemer and a liar, Ramstan! I ascended to the throne of God! You had your vision . . . !"

His words were cut off as *al-Buraq* clamped down again. Ramstan gave an order, and the flesh receded.

Benagur shouted, "You had your vision, but it was induced by that thing, the *glyfa*, the agent of Satan, if it is not Satan Himself! Your vision was false! If not false, then you misinterpreted it, perverted it for your own purposes! There *is* the Living God, and He . . ."

Ramstan had ordered Benagur silenced again.

He said, "Yes, there is a living god, though not in the sense Benagur meant. At least, I think it's a god or it's the closest thing to a god that sentients will ever know. If indeed they can know Him . . . It."

The tec-op interrupted him.

"USO detected at 50,000 kilometers, sir."

A bulkhead screen dissolved the faces on it and showed him the area in which the object was detected. It was black except for a single red star near the center and the tip of a blazing white gas cloud. Shortly thereafter, another screen showed him the magnified image reflected by the rasers.

"The *Popacapyu*," Ramstan said. "We're going at top velocity now. They can't catch us before we jump again. It's only 100,000 kilometers to the edge of the bell."

The tec-op said, "Sir, they've sent a modulated radio signal, frequency 10 megahertz, 1,000 watts."

"So. We got her behind the shielding just in time."

His decision had been hard on Branwen, but it was correct. Ramstan again addressed the personnel.

"I did not take the *glyfa* from the temple because I was tempted by its offer of immortality. I was intrigued by that, yes. But I did not believe that it could truly give me everlasting life nor was I going to steal it just to determine if its offer was valid.

"What led me to take it was another statement, a series of statements, that it made. It said that if I took it, became its partner, I would help save the world. It could not guarantee that we two could do just that, but we must try."

He stopped and licked his dry lips. Even to himself, knowing what he did, he sounded like a maniac, a deluded Messiah.

"I know what you're thinking!" he cried. "But don't forget the *bolg!* That thing which destroyed Kalafala! The thing that has, if what the *glyfa* tells me is true, destroyed the Urzint, many planets! Which has, according to the Vwoordha, killed most of the life on Tolt! The *Popacapyu* crew doesn't know it yet. And it will come to Earth eventually, by following either us or our tracks, and slaughter all life there as it has slaughtered it on many planets!"

He paused, breathing heavily. Though he was getting ahead of his story, he had given his audience something concrete and terrible to think about. They might not be so willing to disbelieve him.

"It . . . the *glyfa* . . . told me that all sentients sooner or later develop their science to the point where they invent the alaraf drive or its equivalent unless they destroy themselves first with atomic war. They never, or seldom, anyway, understand just what the alaraf-driven vessels do or how they travel such immense distances in such a short time. We Terrans certainly didn't. We had theories about where the ships went when they jumped. The most accepted was that the ships somehow *bent* space so that a star a million light-years away was, briefly, very much closer. Or that there were flaws or anomalies in the space-time structure which permitted an alaraf ship to penetrate these. The theory stated that normal *distance* was that which the distribution of matter in space had accustomed us to. But that these flaws or fissures were of different arrangements of space-matter and the different arrangement also made for differences in distances.

"As you know, these theories weren't even that. They were speculations, means for describing what is still the undescribable.

"A third speculation, one not taken seriously at all, was that the alaraf drive somehow made the ships leap from one universe through the *walls* of another. That speculation was based on the fact that a ship on its outward journey never appeared in a known section of Earth's universe.

"Another speculation was that the alaraf drive was really a sort of time travel drive. On the outward journey, the ship went ahead in time or backwards. It didn't matter which. In any event, the ship stayed in one place, but the cosmic bodies moved on, leaving the ship floating in space and in a space unrecognizable because millions or even billions of stars had passed by. One way or the other. The return journey was accomplished by reversing time, as it were, and the ship got back to Earth at an approximate time corresponding to the amount of time she had been away from Earth."

Ramstan stopped to get a drink of water.

"The *glyfa* assured me that the speculation about the alaraf ships penetrating the walls of the universes was indeed correct.

"There is not one universe but many. The human body contains trillions of cells. So does the Pluriverse. Each universe is a cell in its body.

"I was wrong when I stole the *glyfa*, though it was with its full permission and expressed wish. Not just wrong. I was a criminal. I was betraying my duty as captain of ship and as a Terran. But I believed then and still believe that I was following a higher duty. I was convinced that the *glyfa* was right and that I was doing what had to be done if I were to . . . save . . . the world. The Pluriverse."

Many on Earth had believed that it was their mission to save the world. Noah, Abraham, Moses, Jesus, Muhammad, Zoroaster, Luther, a hundred Popes, Knox, Buddha, Joseph Smith, Eddy, a few thousand of greats and well-known among the billions who'd lived on Earth and how many thousands of insane? What made him different from the others?

His predecessors had acted only on fantasy. *He* knew from experience, from fact, what he was talking about.

Or did he? He could not really be sure.

But what he knew was not gotten from any stone or golden tablets or an angel appearing to announce that he was God's chosen prophet to reveal anew what had been said before many times and would be said again, though in somewhat different forms and situations.

"I wish I could say that I took the *glyfa* because it had hypnotized me, and thus I couldn't help myself. It did not hypnotize me, though its evocation of the *Miraj* in me enormously influenced me. The *glyfa* told me that it did expand my minuscule inclination to steal it. Turned a flashing impulse into a steady determination. That may be true. If I'd been completely without that desire, the *glyfa* could not have affected me thus at all."

Who among you would not have had that desire? he thought. But he did not voice the thought. To do so would make him seem to be pleading. And Ramstan did not plead.

"Whatever the reasons for my taking the *glyfa*, and I believed and still believe that I had one reason to override everything that told me not to take it, I did."

Nuoli, unable to obey any longer his order not to interrupt, said, "Why didn't you tell us what you'd done as soon as you returned to ship with the *glyfa*? Why were you so secretive?"

"Don't ask me questions until I've finished! But . . . I was getting to that. Isn't it obvious that I would've been arrested at once, Benagur would have made sure of that, and the *glyfa* returned to the Tenolt? Would you have believed me then? No, not until the *bolg* appeared would you have put any credence in me. As it is . . ."

He told them of the voice in the Kalafalan tavern warning him of the *bolg*. He told them of seeing on the monitor screen the figure in his quarters and the figure which had appeared on the Webn planet when he and Benagur were quarreling.

"As I found out when I visited the Vwoordha, these were

images projected by one of the three. They were projected —beamed?—from a very long distance. Not just from a distant planet in another galaxy, though that would be staggering enough. No, they were projected from another universe.

"I don't know how it was done. Shiyai, the Vwoordha, told me that she rode the waves of the thoughts of God. Doubtless, that's a poetic analogy and so, meaningless. Or perhaps not. For all I know, the images were not objective projections but stimulations of my brain resulting in subjective phenomena that I thought were objective.

"But I suspect that the *glyfa* was used, though unwillingly, as a target and a focus for whatever powers the Vwoordha use to project these images."

"You have guessed it," the *glyfa* said, using Ramstan's mother's voice now.

It sounded sullen.

"I think that's so because the *glyfa* is also a tool. It was not created primarily as a beamer for the images of the Vwoordha, but it can be used for this. I'll get to its primary purpose in a few minutes.

"The *glyfa* could probably have enlightened me on many puzzling things, but, for reasons it won't reveal, it refused. Perhaps it was hoping that I'd not meet the Vwoordha. In fact, I'm almost sure of that, though nothing seems sure in this vast blackness I've been living in. However, it knew what the ritual-chant of the Webnite, Wassruss, meant. And what the true powers are of the three sigils that Wassruss gave me."

He stopped to drink more water. Another curious thought flashed. His discourse was a ritual, comparable to the Christian Mass, and the water was the wine. The wafers of bread? Not his or anyone's flesh but his spirit. He was eating crow, eating his pride and his self-image, tearing them into bits and devouring them while the . . . worshipers? . . . no . . . witnesses to the sacrifice and the eucharist . . . watched him, a crowd of unbelievers who had to be made into believers.

In some ways, there was not much difference between eating the flesh of the god and eating crow. Except that it was the god, the fallen god, himself, who ate the crow.

"Throughout these events, I've felt as if I were being manipulated. Sometimes gently, sometimes not so subtly, I was being nudged and pushed here and there. But the *glyfa* was urging me in one direction and the Vwoordha in another. In a sense, the Vwoordha won because I came to their home. In another, they lost."

What is the price?

Ramstan told his audience that he had asked the Vwoordha what he must pay for their help. They had replied that he must give them the *glyfa*. He had refused, though to do so he had had to draw up all his courage and hurl it at them like a ball. If he had failed to strike them out, he would have been done for. These three were awe-inspiring, and he was afraid of them. (His audience did not know how much it cost him to admit that. Or perhaps it did know.) Though he could see no machines responsible for their great powers, he knew that they must have them. The walls of their house could be double and be packed inside with a solid-state or liquid-state technology superior to that of any sentients he had encountered. They took the credit for making the *glyfa*, and they might not be lying. According to what they claimed, they had once had the ability to burn out a star while making it, but they no longer had the tools to do it nor could they, at this time, duplicate the feat. Besides, another *glyfa* would be just as self-conscious as the first, hence, a self-governing entity, and would probably turn out to be just as selfish and contrary as this one.

The Vwoordha might not be as rich in power as they once were, but what they still had scared him.

Nevertheless, he had said no to them. He did not know what they would do then; he felt that they could destroy *al-Buraq* if they wished to. They certainly seemed wrathful enough to do it.

After they had cooled down or seemed to, Shiyai had said, "You are very stubborn, Ramstan. We've offered you a partnership, you, an ephemera. You would be our equal, that is, as equal as possible for you. And you would be immortal, as near immortal as is possible. Also, it is your duty to join us and to earn that equality by delivering the *glyfa* to us. But you are as stupid, selfish, arrogant, and blind as the *glyfa*. And you have limits, just as it has, though they are different limits."

Ramstan had thought that they, too, were bounded, otherwise they would have forced him to hand over the *glyfa*. He did not say so, however.

Grrindah had vented her nerve-clawing laughter and said,

"Very well. Since you bargain with us, though you do not know how wrong you are to do that, we will lower our price. The gifts of Wassruss will do."

Again, Ramstan rolled up his courage and pitched it at them.

The Webn had given him the three sigils and had said that he could pass them on only after he had used them. It would not be right to sell them.

"Right?" black-eyed Wopolsa had said. "What do you know of right?"

"Perhaps nothing—from your viewpoint," Ramstan had said. "Nevertheless, I will not part with them."

"Then you will get nothing from us," green-eyed Shiyai said.

Blue-eyed Grrindah laughed, and she said, "You have stolen the *glyfa* and betrayed your people and wrecked your life and career and will die soon. All in vain."

"I don't think so," Ramstan had said.

They had struck out twice. Or was it he who had done so?

"You want the *glyfa*. You want the three gifts," he said. "These were to be the price I must pay for your information or whatever you would have given me in return. But I have already paid your price many times over. You and the *glyfa* caused me to, as you say, steal it and betray my people and wreck my career and perhaps bring on my death soon. You three and that other, the *glyfa*."

All three laughed, and Grrindah said, "He thinks that the other is the *glyfa!*"

"Still," Shiyai said, "there is much justice in what he says."

"Dear sisters," Wopolsa said, "what is justice?"

"A word," Grrindah said. "Another word is truth."

"Don't laugh," Ramstan said. "I am getting tired of your mockery."

They did not laugh with their mouths, though the eyes of Grrindah and Shiyai laughed. Wopolsa's eyes looked as if they were and had always been empty of laughter. They contained only black space and dying stars and a hint of something terrifying beyond the space.

He was, he told his crew, uncertain whether the three creatures in the well were the pets of the Vwoordha or the Vwoordha were projections of the well-dwellers. Or, possibly, the house-dwellers were solid flesh but were still the pets of the well-dwellers.

It seemed to him, though, that the shimmering being did not belong to any of the universes he had been in. Rather, it did not seem to be native to any of the planets that ship had set down on. It was his theory that an alaraf-drive vessel starting from a planet of a GO-type star, such as Sol, such as all they had been to, could travel only to the planetary system of a GO star. None of the alaraf ships they knew had ever been to the "bell" of any but a star like Earth's sun. Apparently, the type of star from which a ship originally departed determined the type to which it could go.

If, say, sentient life could evolve on a planet of a giant red star or a white dwarf or, who knew, even a planet or a "dead" sun revolving around a galaxy, then it would develop an alaraf drive. But its ship would be confined to "cracks," "flaws," predetermined channels, call them what you would, that would take her to a "bell" of a red star or a white dwarf or whatever.

The being called Wopolsa, the one in the well or the house or both, may have come from such a planet, if her native place was a planet and not just space or a Saturnian ring around a planet or a blazing gas cloud or perhaps some "continuum" between the walls of two universes. She should not be on any planet of a GO-type star. But, sometime in the past eons, she had managed to break through or had been pulled through—by Shiyai and Grrindah?—and now existed on the planet Grrymguurda.

Or did she live, somehow, in more than one "channel" and maybe in more than one universe at the same time?

Whatever the truth, Ramstan was scared of her. Looking into the shimmering and the eyes of the thing in the well, and into the eyes of the being in the house, he had felt that he was falling swiftly, weightless except for terror, into unending space. He would be, and this was his most overpowering reaction, alone. Alone as no one had ever been.

What then had made him defy her in spite of this?

There was in all humans, that is, all sentients Terran or non-Terran, a spark of contrariness. Some had much more than others, and Ramstan had been endowed with a full, perhaps overflowing, measure. That may have been why the *glyfa* and the Vwoordha chose him. Yet they must have realized that the very quality for which they picked him might make him rebel against them.

There was also the attraction, existing side by side with the repulsion, towards the horrible fate implied by the eyes of Wopolsa. In the twentieth century it had been called a drive toward self-destruction, but now it was defined as a response to the challenge of the unknown.

Ramstan had it; it was part of his bipolar psyche and larger and more intense than most people's.

"No matter what we tell you, you won't let us have the sigils?" Shiyai had said.

"I've paid the price. The hell which you and the *glyfa* have put me in."

"That is up to us to determine."

There had been a pause. During this, the three had said nothing, but he was not sure that they were not communicating by other means.

Finally, Shiyai said, "Very well but not so well. We, who have so much time, don't have time now to dicker. We tried, and we failed, which we had thought we would. But forecasting is not yet a science. It's an art. As artists, we were not good enough."

"You have to use the paint, the wood, the stone, the metal, the plastic, the light available," Grrindah said, and she laughed.

"And the darkness," Wopolsa said.

"Or that which is between or among," Grrindah said.

"Or that which is none of these but yet is all," Shiyai said.

"Or that which is all of these but none or only part," Wopolsa said.

"We need you but would as soon do without you," Shiyai said.

"Do not think of yourself as unique," Wopolsa said.

"Yet, in a sense, he is," Grrindah said.

"In that sense, all are," Shiyai said. "But does that have any significance?"

"It depends on the situation," Grrindah said. "This is it."

"Or those," Wopolsa said.

"There is a limit to patience," Shiyai said.

"To everything except eternity," Grrindah said.

"Perhaps even to that," Wopolsa said. "After that, what?"

"Not knowing *what* may make it worthwhile waiting for it," Shiyai said.

"What?" Grrindah said.

The three burst into taloned laughing again. Shiyai sounded like the kookaburrah of the Australian Department; Grrindah, like a South-American-Department parrot; Wopolsa, like a North-American-Department hoot owl. Their cachinnations were not quite like these, but he, being human, had to make analogies.

Ramstan waited until it was quiet. He said, "Laugh. But what is your decision?"

"Listen," Shiyai said. "Ask questions after we have told you what is what, within the limits of what."

26

"THERE IS NOT just one universe," Ramstan said. "There are many. Perhaps trillions, though there is no way of counting them. I say trillions because the human body is composed of trillions of cells. All these universes are the cells of a pluriversal being. An entity. A living being.

"Everything within the *walls* of a universe composes a cell. And the cells form organs, though neither the anatomy nor physiology of this largest of all creatures is well known. In fact, almost nothing is known. Except that it does exist."

The faces on the screens had dried into plaster masks. They were set in disbelief or wonderment.

"I said, 'largest of all creatures.' Creatures may be the wrong word, probably is. A creature is a living thing which has been created by someone. But the Vwoordha do not think that the Pluriverse was created by anyone. It may be God. Or some thing which by definition is the nearest approach to God possible.

"If it is God, it is not like the God postulated by sentients. It probably does not know that sentients exist, probably does not even know that life exists. But the Vwoordha are not sure of this.

"It was born when all of the universe, its cells, had grown

from the initial big bang of each to the point where the universes, the cells, were contiguous. Where the *walls* met and so began to form a single organism. Don't ask me what was between each universe or cell while they were expanding, what was between them during the billions of years that each went from the explosion of the primal fiery ball of matter through the stages of star and planet formation, ever expanding, ever rushing towards that point where their boundaries met those of neighboring universes or cells. Or, more likely, continued expanding even after the outer space-matter came to that area in which walls were formed. The walls themselves may be trillions of light-years thick, that is, the area between the walls may be that wide."

His lips felt as dry as the faces on the screens. He drank more water.

"I'm using analogies, of course, not giving you a literal description or definition.

"In any event, the Pluriverse or God, this entity composed of all the universes, this organism, grows. Not in size. The Vwoordha think that Its growth is mental. That It develops or evolves from a baby, a cosmic infant, into an adult. What the adult form would be . . . the Vwoordha doesn't know. They hope that It will become self-conscious and eventually find out about sentient life, which, in some ways, is a reflection, a mental reflection, perhaps emotional reflection, of Itself. And then It will communicate with sentients."

He licked his lips.

"Who knows what might happen then?"

He stopped speaking for a moment, and, unexpectedly even to himself, crashed his fist on a table. He saw some of the crew flinch. *Al-Buraq* quivered like a dog which does not understand why its master is angry but is afraid that the anger might be, for some reason, directed at it.

"The Vwoordha . . . and the *glyfa* . . . don't know what'll happen then because the Pluriverse has *never* reached adulthood. Twice, twice, It has died . . . been killed . . . before It could grow from infancy into . . . what? . . . a child? . . . a juvenile?"

He scanned the faces on the screens. They had not changed expression, but some were exchanging glances. Did these subtly indicate that the captain had indeed jettisoned his sanity?

"While the . . . Pluriverse is developing or evolving, while It's growing from infancy towards childhood, life originates on the planets of the stars in each cell. And that life evolves into sentiency. And many sentients eventually discover the alaraf drive. Having done so, they use the drive, of course.

"But their ships travel through the walls of the universes. According to the Vwoordha, they are able to do so because of 'weak' areas in the cells. Vulnerable spots. When the wall of a universe is penetrated, it starts to collapse.

"The process thereafter is analogous to cancer. The alaraf-drive vessels are carcinogens. They cause the beginning of an irreversible collapse. The matter in each cancerous universe ceases to expand outwards, and it starts to rush back towards the center of origin. Towards the eventual primal ball of matter.

"Now, you and I know that the astrophysicists have been disputing about whether the universe is a continually expanding or an oscillating world. At various times, the evidence seemed to indicate that oscillation was inevitable. At other times, for instance, the late twentieth century, the evidence pointed to an ever-expanding universe. Then the astrophysicists changed their minds in the early twenty-first century. But for a hundred years now no one has advocated the oscillation process.

"Perhaps the universe would be always expanding—if there wasn't an interfering agent."

He stopped and lifted a finger as if he were trying to signal the world to stop.

"But sentient life interferes. It invents and uses the alaraf drive. The infant Pluriverse . . . God, perhaps . . . sickens and dies. Its cells collapse, and the matter in each rushes towards the point of origin, drawing space after it. Then the primal balls explode again, and eventually the great organism is formed anew, and It grows towards maturity. But . . . oh, God! . . . this has happened twice, God is cheated of life by Life.

"However, this living thing has living processes analogous to ours. To combat this cancer, it develops an antibody. This antibody sets about destroying the sources of the cancers. I don't know if the process is unconscious or conscious. The

Vwoordha think that it's as unconscious on Its part as the origin of antibodies in our flesh is."

He stopped again. His lips trembled.

"This antibody is the *bolg!*"

Would they believe that? They must.

"The Vwoordha tell me that there is not one *bolg* for every cell-universe. There is but one for the entire body. But it can travel through the walls without injury or carcinogenic incident, just as Shiyai the Vwoordha can travel from universe to universe, though she uses a different method and doesn't really travel bodily. The method of the *bolg* is analogous to osmosis."

"True," the *glyfa* said in the voice of Ramstan's mother.

"Those universe-cells in which sentients have not yet developed and the walls of which have not been pierced by the drive of sentients from other universes do not collapse. They are left free-floating, as it were. But if too many universe-cells become cancerous, then the Pluriversal organism is destroyed as an organism. It dies. This is what has happened in the two eons past. Twice has God been born and twice killed.

"The free-floating cell-universes apparently continue expanding, but the new cells born of the primal fireballs catch up with them. What function these larger cells have in the new Pluriversal infant, I don't know.

"The free-floating cell-universes would continue expanding, though it would not be for long. The *bolg,* after destroying life or as much of it as it can, then goes to the free-floating cells. And it destroys the life there. Thus preventing that life from developing an alaraf drive. Or at least setting the civilizations so far back that it's a very long time before they develop new civilizations and so discover alaraf drive. When that happens, the *bolg* destroys the life, but it's too late. The free-floating universes have already begun to collapse."

"My God!" Nuoli yelled. "What hope is there, then?"

At least, she believed. But then she had been subjected to the *glyfa*'s blaze of revelation, and she was more receptive than the others. If she had not been, she would not have been invited into the temple.

Ramstan said, "I'll get to that. You're all probably asking yourself what difference it makes, aside from the fate immediately threatening you. It may take thousands of years before the *bolg* can get to Earth. As for the universes collapsing, it will take billions of years before all matter falls back to the point of origin. If this were a natural process, unavoidable, it would be only a remote and philosophical concern to those presently living and to those living a million years from now. Depressing, yes, but not alarming except to our inconceivably distant descendants.

"But, once the universes start collapsing, they are subject to an acceleration factor. The fall back is not the sixteen-billion-year stately procession of outwards. It takes place within a relatively short time. Six thousand Earth-years.

"Yes, I know that sounds incredible. But, as you know, the speed of light is not the fastest thing in the world nor is its speed the limit beyond which nothing can go. That was determined sixty years ago.

"Long before that, however, the *bolg* will have tracked along our spatial and interspatial path back to Earth and eliminated all or almost all there. The Vwoordha say that that may be done within a month or fifty years from now. Those are the limits of time for the *bolg*.

"What happens if we could somehow destroy the *bolg* with our puny weapons? Would the Pluriverse then produce another *bolg?*

"Nobody knows. No *bolg* has so far been destroyed by sentients.

"But if it can be done, then it must be done. After that, we wait and see. And if we could kill one *bolg*, we can kill the next.

"Even so, Earth's universe and many others are doomed. And we can't go to one which hasn't started to collapse yet. Our very act of entering it would cause its death if we used alaraf drive. But what if we could analyze and reproduce the means which the *bolg* uses for transition from one cell to the other? Then we could travel interuniversally without damage to any of them.

"How can we take the first step? That is, killing the *bolg* so that it may be dissected, as it were. Direct attack won't do. *Al-Buraq* would be pierced thousands of times over, and we, too. Our missiles wouldn't get through its trillions of missiles. It's a colossal antibody the specific function of which is to wipe out all life. Nobody knows how it makes and throws those meteoritelike missiles. Probably some sort of energy-matter conversion is used. If so, it's far more efficient than anything Terran science has developed.

"But there's a good probability that, after it's discharged its missiles, it takes a long time for it to make a new stock. It should be vulnerable during the recharging period. Unless it reserves a small supply for attacks against it."

Tenno must have been so eager to talk that he forgot or deliberately ignored his captain's order not to interrupt him.

"Then you're planning to attack it at that time? How will you know it's emptied its ammunition? Oh, I see! I think. It's devastated three planets in a row! It must be empty now!"

"We'll talk about that after I'm through with my résumé of what's happened," Ramstan said. "Uh, just a moment."

He had forgotten that Indra and Toyce were still trapped. They would have heard and seen what the others did because *al-Buraq* would automatically have placed a viewscreen in front of them. But they must be very uncomfortable. He ordered ship to release them. Then he said, "Benagur, if I free you, will you promise not to interrupt?"

At Ramstan's command, ship lowered the flesh sealing the commodore's mouth. Benagur shouted, "No! This is mutiny! And blasphemy! Insan—"

The flesh had closed over his lips.

"I just wanted to spare you further constraint and humiliation," Ramstan said.

"The Vwoordha became aware of the nature and development of God . . . of the Pluriversal entity, if you prefer . . . three Pluriverses ago. They made the *glyfa* with the assistance of several peoples. Its primary function was to be a rotatable amplifying antenna."

He paused. "A rotatable amplifying antenna. A device to communicate with the Pluriverse. Or, if It was in an infant state, to study It and learn more of Its nature. And, it was hoped, eventually perhaps to . . . ah . . . nurse It . . . educate It . . . help It grow into an adult. In a sense, because all sentients are basically human, humans would become the father and mother, the parents of God. The most ambitious project ever launched.

"As I said, the tool had to be a sentient, and in time the *glyfa* became independent, rebelled, as sentients often do, and went off on its own. Before that, however, the Vwoordha . . . and the *glyfa* . . . learned something of the Pluriverse. It seemed indeed to be in an infant stage. Its *voice* could be . . . *heard?* . . . but it seemed to be the babblings of a baby. Of a baby in the prespeech stage, using every sound Its . . . lips . . . could utter, tuning up, as it were, for the stage where It would have to use only certain sounds and drop the others. That's how the Vwoordha interpreted what they detected.

"Its babblings were part of the cosmic background *noise* that astronomers have picked up. But they would not be able to distinguish the Pluriversal babblings from other noise without something like the *glyfa.*"

This was perhaps the part of his explanation the most difficult to believe. The masks on the screen had melted a little now; the incredulity was hot beneath them.

"You're asking yourselves how the Vwoordha could know this. You're thinking that what they termed babbling was really just a different type of noise and that the Vwoordha, without sufficient evidence, arbitrarily decided on a certain explanation for it. An explanation fitting their preconceptions. Infant babblings are meaningless noise, though they are a necessary prelude to the meaningful structure called language.

"But," and again he lifted a finger, though this time he felt that the gesture looked as if he was testing the wind of their judgment, "ten million years passed . . ."

He stopped once more. Should he digress on just how the Vwoordha had managed to live so long, tell them of the enormously long periods of suspended animation which enabled them to endure such eons? No, that would have to come later.

"Ten million years passed. And then the Vwoordha heard a modulation of Its sounds more complex than those detected before. Rather, they heard what seemed to be the beginning of structure in the use of the sounds. And they noted that now It uttered only certain *sounds;* others had been dropped.

"A baby does this when it begins to learn the speech of its parents. But . . . what parents could It have? To whom was It talking, from whom was It learning speech?

"One theory was that It was, in a sense, schizophrenic. It had two personalities or chambers or parts, call them what you will. This theory was quickly abandoned, though. Two infants can't teach each other to talk if neither has had a teacher.

"How, then, could the Pluriversal being . . . or God . . . be sentient if It had no language with which to think? Or does It think in feelings and images only? If It does, then It could never talk to sentients, though many sentients have claimed that It has talked to them. It could never be more than a highly intelligent and perhaps even self-conscious animal, just as a. human being brought up from infancy in total linguistic isolation, isolation even from dumb and deaf signs, would be an animal, its potentiality for speech undeveloped.

"Perhaps It was teaching Itself to talk to Itself. How could It do that? A human infant couldn't. In fact, on reaching a certain age, its linguistic potentiality would be so stultified that it couldn't learn to talk even if it had a teacher after that age.

"But that theory may be too anthropomorphic. The Pluri-verse may have potentialities which humans don't have. Perhaps It could form names for objects It sees or feels or hears in some way we can't understand. Perhaps It could even find, through experimentation, a syntax for the words, the verbal referents it would invent.

"The Vwoordha don't think so. They think that It has somehow developed to a *sound*-selection stage but won't progress beyond that if sentients don't help It. They think that just possibly evolution may have as its goal, if evolution could have a goal, a role for sentients that no one, as far as anybody knows, even thought of. Until, that is, the Vwoordha came along.

"It may be built into the structure of evolution or it may just be chance or the workings of probability. But the Vwoordha believe that one of the roles of sentients, the most important, is to be a teacher of God . . . the Pluriverse. It is up to sentients, the minute life on planets, the life much much smaller in relation to God than a microbe or virus is to a human, to teach God speech. And so help It to attain adulthood.

"After which, of course, sentients would profit by their relationship, their parenthood, to God."

The *glyfa*, using the voice of Ramstan's father, said, "In a sense, the Vwoordha are my parents, and they reared me. But I will have nothing to do with them. Indeed, I am their enemy.

Why should God differ from me? It may hate Its teachers, despise them, or become indifferent to them."

"You are not It," Ramstan subvocalized.

"True. I am, however, the only being through whom you . . . anybody . . . can speak to that entity and through whom you may receive intelligible communication."

"If it's not intelligible, it's not communication."

"Always the pedant," the *glyfa* said. Somewhere, far off, faint, reverberating in some neural path, was a ghostly jeering cachinnation.

Ramstan hated the *glyfa* at the same time that he was attracted to it, and now its use of the voices of his parents and uncle was making him hate them. It brought up something in him that he did not want to confront. Of course, he had no time for that now anyway. The Vwoordha . . . they reminded him of his great-grandmothers . . . no time for that, either.

He steered his attention back to the crew.

"But, according to the Vwoordha, the *glyfa* desires more than just being the father to God. It lusts after power; it aches for domination. It would become Its master and, so, even greater than God."

"Liars!" the *glyfa* said in the voice of Ramstan's father.

"Yes, liars. Contemptible worms!" the voice of Ramstan's mother said. "It's they who want to be to God as parents to a boy. Tyrants!"

"My sister and her husband are right," the voice of Ramstan's uncle said. "Hûd! You must not listen to those liars, those wretches, those insane creatures! Do what is right!"

Ramstan did not reply to the *glyfa*, though he felt that he was somehow being wicked by not doing so.

"The *glyfa* maintains that it's the Vwoordha who want to do what they claim he wants to do. I have no way now, perhaps never, of determining which is telling the truth." He paused. "Or if both are lying."

"You must listen to me!" the voice of his mother cried. "You know what is at stake!"

Ramstan said, "I decided to put off my decision for a while. I refused to give the *glyfa* or the three gifts of Wassruss to the Vwoordha. For now, anyway. I did have to pay a price, however. It was only fair; they had given me information that I . . . we . . . desperately need.

"So, I promised the Vwoordha that when they needed me, I would come to them. Take them aboard ship or do whatever else they required, if I could do it without endangering ship and crew. Though under certain conditions I might have to do that.

"It's possible that we might be able to dispose of the *bolg* and so not have to deal with the Vwoordha or do what the *glyfa* wants. We can use the *glyfa* for the purpose for which it was intended. It may refuse to cooperate, but it is in our hands, and there must be means to make it do what we want."

"Ungrateful monster!" the voice of his mother said. "You'd do this to me!"

Ramstan sipped some water. He said, "Now is the time for you to decide. I won't make any speech about how vital it is that you let me keep on being your captain. You must know that by now. Whether or not you believe me, I don't know. But if you reject me, you cause all, and I mean all in the universal sense, to be lost. Doomed."

He said a code word. A chair flowed up from the deck. He sat down.

Nuoli cried, "I believe him!"

Tenno said, "I don't know what . . . whom . . . to believe."

"Vote!" Ramstan said loudly. "Now! We don't have time for long conferences and discussions! Nor, for that matter, for short ones!"

He reared from the chair, screaming and holding his ears. He could not hear his own voice, and his hands were no protection. The whistling overrode everything else.

27

THE *GLYFA'S* VOICE came through the noise as his mother's. It sounded as if it came from afar, from some wildly retreating and advancing horizon, louder, then softer.

"The *bolg* is too close for you to outrun it. You can do only one thing. Escape. Use the first of Wassruss's gifts."

Ramstan only understood the *glyfa* peripherally. His hind-brain, the animal heritage from which his subconscious exerted influence, told him to run. But he had, automatically, thrust his mental probings into his cells, and they, too, told him to run. That was the adverse effect of the generally beneficial result of being able to locate and analyze the physical health of each cell in the body. Now, without thinking about it, he contacted the cells, all three trillion, and got an overall impression of their reaction to this situation.

Run!

If his rational mind had been in command, he might have done otherwise. But, perhaps, he might not have.

The *glyfa*, who had no born or built-in unconscious, said the same thing.

"Use the *shengorth*, Ramstan!"

He stood still, and the inability to make physical movements was reflected in his mental movements. Right or left? Up or down? Forward or backward? Or any movement in between or among?

"Take me with you!" the *glyfa* said in the voice of Ramstan's mother. "You must have your hands on me before you put the sigil in your mouth. Or touch me closely. As close as fetus to mother or infant lips to the nipple."

Ramstan gave an animal cry expressing his rage, rage from helplessness and from his ignorance, which made him even more helpless.

"You fool!" the *glyfa* said in the voice of Ramstan's father. "There is only one thing you can do, now that you've done this. Get out! Use the *shengorth!* But you must take me with you. Otherwise, you're done for!"

"And so are you," Ramstan said.

"Is that a consolation?"

Suddenly, the whistling, the "entrance noise," was gone. Ramstan was relieved greatly by this, but he still felt panic.

Ship could not use her alaraf drive to get to another universe until she was near enough to the planet Shabbkorng to be within its "bell." Even if she could make the jump, she'd be quickly tracked by the *bolg*. Unless . . . unless the *bolg* would be diverted by the life on Shabbkorng and stop there to massacre it. That was an almost unbearable thought—almost —there were seven billion people there, yet *al-Buraq* could attack the *bolg* after it had spent all its missiles. That is, *al-Buraq* could do so if the *bolg* did not retain a supply of missiles for emergencies while recharging.

But *al-Buraq* could not stay in this universe while waiting for the *bolg* to empty itself. It might attack ship first.

A screen had been displaying a green circle, the *Popacapyu*. Suddenly, the circle became a white balloon. The whiteness and the expansion lasted perhaps a second and then became a swarm of many very small pale dots.

Ramstan cried out, "Allah!"

Tenno cried out in Japanese, then said, in Terrish, "I take refuge in the Buddha."

The tec-op crossed himself, muttered something in Polish, then said, "Sir, the *Popacapyu* was struck by missiles from the *bolg*. Her power supply must have exploded."

Another screen displayed the area where the *bolg* was; a tiny orange circle was in its center. Flashing orange numbers showed that the thing was moving at a rate of velocity and acceleration that would make it visible on the screen within three hours. Before then, however, its missiles would blow *al-Buraq* apart.

Ramstan said, "Tenno, what's the computation on ship reaching the jump area before she's in the *bolg*'s missile-range?"

"If we make it, we'll do so with about a minute's grace. Perhaps."

Ramstan put his hand in his jacket pocket.

"That's the right decision," his mother's voice said. "But hold me to your chest before you put the *shengorth* in your mouth. If you don't, you leave me behind."

Ramstan's fingers moved the disk and the square aside and closed on the triangle. It felt slippery and warm. After taking it out of his pocket, he went to the *glyfa*, adjusted the a-g units on its two ends, and picked it up in one hand. It slipped out and struck the deck. His hand trembling he leaned down and got a good grip on the egg-shape. It only weighed ten grams now, but the power in the batteries of the a-g units would quickly be used up at this adjustment.

Then, as if someone had possessed him, he went to the bulkhead on which hung his prayer rug. He had no rational reason to do so; he had not used it since he had entered the academy. Nuoli, when she had been his lover, had mocked him once, asking why he, an atheist, kept it. It was, she had said, his security blanket. That had angered him. But now, pressed by his fear, he took the rug from the bulkhead with the hand holding the *shengorth*. The triangle slipped from his fingers to the deck. He left it there for a moment while he wrapped the *glyfa* in the rug. Then he picked up the triangular stone and held it to his open lips.

A vision of Branwen in the launch flashed through his mind. She would be even more terrified than the others because she was alone.

"Wait! Wait!" someone screamed at him.

It was his own voice, not uttered through his mouth but from his mind.

"The crew . . . the crew!"

He shouted, or thought he shouted, since he could not hear

his own words, at *al-Buraq*. He gave her orders to release Benagur and to obey him until he, Ramstan, returned.

He put the *shengorth* in his mouth with his right hand, his left holding the ends of the rug, his left arm curved to push rug and *glyfa* against his chest.

Despite the impediment caused by the stone in his mouth, he began to recite the *Light-Verse* from the *Qu'ran*. "God is the light of the Heavens and of the Earth . . ."

The stone seemed to swell. It grew between his right teeth and the inside of his cheek. It choked off the words, but when he put a finger in his mouth to extract it before it broke his flesh, he found that it was the same size as when he had put it in.

The transition seemed as swift as a light.

His eyes blinked, the lids sweeping down and up. As they went down, he saw his quarters. As they went up, he saw an unfamiliar room. There was no sense of movement. Around him was silence. The air seemed dead, heavy, and stale, but within a few seconds it began moving, and it became fresh.

. He became aware that he had wet his pants.

He dropped the rug and its burden. It thunked softly on a very thick white carpet with a pattern of connected pale-red diamond-shapes with pale-red edges and light-blue interiors.

As he started to remove the *shengorth* from his mouth, his mother's voice said, "First, reset the a-g units. If the power goes, you'll never be able to lift me."

After unrolling the rug, he said the code word which would cause the power to the a-g units to be cut off.

The room was large and oblong and had an arched entrance at each side. The ceiling was level and pale blue. The walls were off-white. Wooden-framed paintings hung on them, some depicting landscapes which would not have been out of place on Earth. But the portraits displayed sentients with hairy, triangular faces and large, domed heads. The eyes looked catlike.

He became aware that the light was shadowless, seemingly without source yet everywhere.

He turned, and he started. Two meters away was a pyramid resting on its base. It was twice his height and made of some shimmering gray metal.

"That's the magnet, the pole which drew you here," his

father's voice said. "Fortunately, no one was standing near it when you appeared. Otherwise, both of you would have been burned to ashes."

"Why couldn't the builders have put in safeguards?"

"I don't know. They couldn't. Anyway, anything that has advantages always has disadvantages. That's the inscrutable economy of the Pluriverse."

"I know that," Ramstan said angrily.

"It doesn't hurt to remind you."

The *glyfa* had switched to the voice of Habib ibn-Ali O'Riley, Ramstan's chemistry professor in elementary school. Ramstan was too busy to ask why it had changed. It probably would not have explained, anyway.

"What is this place?" he said.

"A refuge for the user of the *shengorth*, I suppose. The little I know is what the Vwoordha told me. It's set up so that it can support sixty sentients of your size for many years. It may be located in another universe, since the people who made the sigils could communicate with people in other universes. I think they used the same means that the Vwoordha did. Thus, they avoided causing carcinoma in the Pluriverse. After the receiving stations were set up, the people used the sigils to travel, though not often."

"For the sake of Allah!" Ramstan said. "Here's the means for interuniversal travel without injury to the Pluriverse! Why didn't everybody use it?"

"One, there are trillions of universes and a googolplex of peopled planets in every one. It would be impossible to contact all planets in all universes. Only a very small number were. Second, the making of sigils costs much in time, materials, and labor. Only a very small number of sigils were made. The Vwoordha said it was a million or so. Third, for some reason even their makers did not know, the sigils could be used by any individual only once."

"Even so, they could be analyzed and reproduced."

"They are indestructible, and for that reason unanalyzable."

Ramstan left the room for the archway to his left. He strode through room after room, oblong, seven-sided, nine-sided, or round, the walls hung with paintings and gold or platinum shields sporting jewels, sculpture here and there, and, in a huge chamber, a library. The books were crystalline balls which spoke or sang as soon as he touched them and which stopped when he withdrew his finger. Some contained moving three-dimensional images. A number seemed to be textbooks; others, entertainment. He did not understand the language, and the weird music grated on him.

Finally, he came to what seemed to be the end, the outer wall of this place. There was a very thick window in it. He looked through it. The ground was flat and sandy. The atmosphere seemed to be clear air, but presently several fish-shaped creatures swam through the frondy branches of a plant. They were moving swiftly. A short time later, the reason for their haste appeared. It looked more like a stingray than anything, and it traveled by flapping its winglike fins. Its teeth were sharklike.

Ramstan started towards the other end of the station, but he veered off into what was obviously a toilet. He drank some water and inspected the toilets. There were no urinals. Either it was reserved for females, as such had once been on Earth, or the builders all had to sit down to urinate.

When he came to the other side of the house, he saw the same kind of scene. Piscines apparently swimming in air, thin fragile plants bending under a current. The light was bright enough, but the sun was not visible.

On his return, he stopped in a room which was obviously an eating place. He got food and liquid by punching buttons, but after one experiment he quit. Munching on the hot vegetables from the plate he carried, he returned to the central room.

"We're under the surface of some kind of sea or lake," he said to himself. "But its liquid is not water."

"We're probably on a planet which is not reachable from Earth by alaraf drive," Habib's voice said. "It's in a bell connected to the routes which go only to non-GO-type stars systems. You'd probably die at once if you could step outside."

"Then there's only one way to get out," Ramstan said. "Use the next sigil."

"Right. But you're safe from the *bolg* as long as you stay here."

He thought about finding a place where he could wash and dry his pants. No. He could do that in the next place. He set the plate down on the carpet, then picked it up again, and he took it back to the eating place. After dropping it down a slot, which he supposed was for dirty plates, he went back to the central room. Habib's voice said, "The next person could have taken care of the plate. If there ever is another person."

Ramstan did not reply. He adjusted the a-g units to lighten the *glyfa*'s weight to ten grams, and picked the thing up in his prayer rug. He put the *pengrathon*, the square stone, in his mouth. It, too, seemed to swell, and he was suddenly in another house. He turned to see a thin square upright structure of gray metal set in the parquet floor.

After removing the *pengrathon* and putting it in his pocket, he set the *glyfa* down and turned the a-g units off. The paintings and sculptures showed him that Terranlike sentients had built this place. He walked until he found a window. The house was high on a mountain. The sky was blue and cloudless; the sun, near its zenith. The horizon was an estimated 150 kilometers distant. Straight ahead, there was only the vegetationless rocky slope of the mountain and a vast yellow-brownish plain lacking plants and topsoil. Fissures crazed its face.

Nearby, to his left, was what was remained of a stone statue. The pedestal and body had been shattered and toppled. The head had rolled about 20 meters from the body. Though the head was cracked and its features were eroded, it certainly looked like the Urzints, the photographs of which he had seen on Kalafala.

He returned to the *glyfa* and told it what he had seen.

"I couldn't go outside the first house, and I can't go outside this one. I suppose I could stay in either until I died of old age. But I'd go mad very quickly. Whether or not the next place is a trap, I have to go to it. But what's the use of the sigils if they take you away from one perilous place only to put you in another?"

The *glyfa* said, "In a circular universe, who runs away runs toward."

"To hell with you and your billion-year-old platitudes."

Ramstan held the egg next to him and put the disk in his mouth.

28

OF ALL THE PLACES he might have imagined as the third station, this would not have been in his list of speculations at all. He thought: What is included is an extremely minute fraction of what might be. The excluded is always much larger than the included. Entities deal with exclusions and inclusions, and they can only handle inclusions. Even those are usually too much for them.

The room was large and dome-shaped and of a bare green metal. Around him were upright thin disks, twice as tall as he, the lower edges set into the floor. There were at least five hundred.

He knew where he was at once. Through the only entrance, an arch, was a hall. This opened at its end onto another arch. Beyond that was the great room where he had visited the Vwoordha.

He removed the sigil from his mouth and pocketed it.

"Why didn't they tell me I'd only end up here?" he muttered.

He set the *glyfa* down and said, "You knew all the time we'd come here. 'One who runs away runs toward.' Why didn't you say anything?"

"I didn't know for sure," the *glyfa* said in Habib's voice. "I had heard a long time ago, a very long time ago, that the Vwoordha had a *ph'rimon* target. I'd also heard that they'd spent many years in tracking down and removing *ph'rimons* in various stations. But there must be thousands of them throughout the Pluriverse. Thus, I could not say with any certainty that your *ph'rimon* would bring us to this target. In any event, you had to use your sigil, but you might have balked if you'd known there was a chance you'd arrive here."

"You're all manipulating me," Ramstan said savagely.

"You haven't struck out yet," the *glyfa* said. "To use another analogy, you're in a sort of cosmic poker game. We, the Vwoordha and I, hold very good hands. But the joker is wild, and you may be it."

The ferretlike animal, Duurowms, flashed through the far arch, raced down the hall, and ran down a lane through the forest of disks. It reared up on its hind legs and gestured that Ramstan should follow him. He did so while the creature danced wildly. Coming to the far arch, they turned left—a good omen for him—and went toward the ancient three. These were sitting on their folded carpets and pillows near the most distant wall. Ramstan turned once to look behind him. If only he had gotten up and strolled around while talking to the Vwoordha, he might have seen the *ph'rimon* target room.

But what could he have done if he'd known about it? Despite what the *glyfa* said, he would not have stayed at the Urzint world.

Blue-robed Grrindah laughed, and she said, "Welcome back, Ramstan!"

He did not reply. When he was close to the three, he set the *glyfa* down, and he removed from his pocket the three sigils.

"You knew you'd be getting these eventually," he said. "Tell me now, what information or help do I get for this price?"

Green-robed Shiyai held out a gnarled hand. He started toward her, then stopped. Through the arched exit doorway, he saw *al-Buraq*.

He was shocked and confused. Ship had escaped the *bolg!* The thing *had* been diverted by the planet Shabbkorng. That had to be the explanation. Even if *al-Buraq* had left the Shabbkorng bell before the *bolg*'s missiles reached it, she would have been quickly caught if the *bolg* had jumped after her to the next bell.

However, *al-Buraq* could not have had enough time to transfer through several systems and bells and returned here by now. That would have taken far too much time, and he had not been in the first two stations more than a half hour, if that.

"Time is determined by the curvature of space-matter," the *glyfa* said. "And by the curvature of the mind."

"Does Benagur know that I'm here?"

"No," Shiyai said. "We weren't sure that you would be."

"What are they doing here?"

Grrindah said, "Benagur had to check on your story. He could not resist coming back to question us. We assured him that his return to Earth would bring the *bolg* much more quickly to Earth. He may not believe us. However, he also came here to find out if the *bolg* can be attacked. Or if there is some way to elude it."

Ramstan put the sigils back into his pocket. Shiyai dropped her hand. Grrindah said, "You're thinking that you'll give them to someone on the vessel?"

He did not answer her. He strode to a point near the arch and looked out. About half a kilometer behind and to one side of *al-Buraq*, the nose of the launch stuck out from behind a root-swelling. Branwen Davis was, so far, unharmed.

Ramstan turned. "Is there anything to be done about the *bolg?*"

"It will have discharged most, if not all, of its missiles," Shiyai said.

"Then *al-Buraq* could go down one of its horns," Ramstan said. "It might be vulnerable on the inside."

"We told Benagur that. He didn't say what he meant to do."

"How would we find the *bolg?*" Ramstan said. "Won't it be gone by now?"

"It could be. But often it orbits around the planet it's just attacked until it builds up a new supply of missiles."

"How long does that take?"

"I don't know."

"It was gone only a short time after it attacked Kalafala," he said.

He thought for a moment, then said, "What was Benagur's reaction to my disappearance?"

"He was puzzled and furious," Shiyai said. "We didn't enlighten him. Come now, Ramstan. The sigils."

She held out her hand again.

"Only one of you could use them to escape the *bolg,*" he said. "What good would it do the other two?"

Grrindah laughed and then said, "You are not as intelligent as we thought. Why . . ."

His skin warmed.

"I see. I was holding the *glyfa,* and it went with me. If you all hold each other. . . ?"

"Right."

He still hesitated. Could he use Wassruss's gift to get the crew to accept him as its captain again? He'd be easily able to get taken aboard as a prisoner, but he did not want that. The only one with authority to make him a member of the crew or of the officers was Benagur. Would Benagur regard the sigils as a worthwhile price for this?

No, he would not.

Ramstan had nothing to offer the people in *al-Buraq.* They would all despise him for deserting them when threatened by the *bolg.* They would reject his justifications for having done so.

He took the sigils out, walked to Shiyai, and dropped them in her hand.

She rubbed her thumb over them one by one and put them somewhere inside her robe.

"The *glyfa* acts for its own interests and those only," she said. "But however sentient and contrary it is, it is, in one respect, a tool. Anyone who knows how to use it as such may do so, and there is nothing the *glyfa* can do about it."

"True," the *glyfa* said, using Ramstan's mother's voice. It sounded very angry. "True. But if you use me as the Vwoordha wish, you'll become *their* tool. They want to put God in their pocket."

"No doubt the *glyfa* is talking to you now," Shiyai said. "We've told you the truth, but I'll repeat. It wants power, the supreme power. When a supremely selfish person uses supreme power, what will that person do with it? Consider well, Ramstan."

The *glyfa* or the Vwoordha or all could be lying.

"The *glyfa* is a tool," he said. "For what?"

"We told you. Its primary purpose is to communicate with the Pluriverse."

"How can you communicate with someone who can't talk yet?"

"You can communicate, to a limited extent, with a baby who can't talk yet," Shiyai said. "However . . ."

Ramstan was angry enough to interrupt her.

"Show me how."

Grrindah laughed again, making him even angrier.

"We intended to do that, but not until you chose between us or it."

"Show me now."

Grrindah and Shiyai exchanged glances and then stared briefly at black-robed Wopolsa. It was difficult to determine exactly what or whom she ever looked at. He also flashed on the feeling that the other two were somewhat afraid of her.

Shiyai said, "Very well. Know first, Ramstan, that the overpowering light that fell upon you, that shone through you in the Tolt temple, was only the edge of the numinous that you'll experience when you first . . . venture. It was transmitted by the *glyfa* just to impress you, Nuoli, and Benagur. And to weaken your defenses against its guile.

"It was the beginning, the relatively weak beginning, of a deeper experience. It was what the mystics and the saints of many worlds, yours included, have . . . should I say . . . *seen?* Many sentients are rotatable amplifying antennae . . . not antennas, antennae . . . which receive some of what the Pluriverse radiates. Or perhaps I should say they glimpse into Its mind. Not very far, though some see deeper than others.

"In any event, some sentients are such antennae, though not very efficient. The use of the *glyfa* enables anyone who has this inborn power to receive and detect, and, if the *glyfa* is used well, to communicate. Or perhaps I should say, to observe and be observed. But it takes a long time to learn to do whatever the doing is. How long, we don't know yet. The *glyfa* managed to get away from us before we could get to that stage."

"If," Ramstan said, "the *glyfa* can't get into . . . *touch* with this . . . being, then how did it transmit this . . . power . . . to us three in the temple?"

Shiyai opened her mouth. Ramstan said quickly, "It must have been using a Tolt. The high priest, I suppose."

Shiyai stood up. "We'll do it now."

Grrindah also rose to help her sister, but Wopolsa remained sitting, her eyelids closing slowly as if a greater night were falling on a lesser. At Shiyai's orders, Ramstan placed the *glyfa* on a top of a table. This was much higher than the others and had not been here on his last visit. He felt that it had been brought in for just this occasion, and he flashed rage. He was being manipulated, controlled.

A Vwoordha stood on each side of him but far enough across the table so that the three formed the corners of an equilateral triangle. He was surprised when Shiyai said something softly to Duurowms, and the animal leaped upon the table and put its front paws on an end of the *glyfa*.

"He represents our beast nature," Shiyai said. "There's enough of that in us sentients to amplify the transmission, but he will greatly increase the power."

"The *glyfa* is the only sentient in all the worlds who has no subconscious," Grrindah said, and she cackled. "It never sleeps, and so it can't dream. Not in the way sentients dream. But when it shuts down to recharge, it does not do so entirely and it couldn't if it tried. We built that limitation into it. It is during the charging, when only a slight trickle of energy keeps it awake, that it daydreams in a peculiar way."

"Yes," Shiyai said. "It is then that it watches the microscopic similitudes of the creatures that it has drawn within itself. It has set up many worlds there, and it observes the mockups of living beings, mostly sentients, who enact their own fantasies within it. The *glyfa* is even capable of participating to some extent in these dramas and comedies. It feels and sees and hears and smells what the tiny personae experience."

Ramstan said, "Yes, I know. It said that it could draw within it my neural atoms and set them up in a seeming body. Thus, I could live forever inside it and enjoy eternity. If I wished, I could play Muhammad or Einstein or Jesus or Buddha or Crazy Horse or even fictional characters, Natty Bumppo, Sam Spade, the Wizard of Oz, Sinbad the Sailor, Ishmael, who sailed under Captain Ahab, Ishmael, the son of Abraham by Hagar, ancestor of the Arabs, Alyosha Karamazov, Sherlock Holmes, Frodo, whomever I wanted to be. I would still know that I was Ramstan and could withdraw whenever I wanted to, but a part of me would *be* that person or seem to be. It was very tempting but not tempting enough."

"Why did you resist?" Shiyai said.

"It is not what I want."

"You could have had the similitude of eternity in your Moslem paradise or whatever paradise you wished," Shiyai said. "You could have had *houris* to lie with, and your orgasms would have lasted for a thousand years or have seemed to. You could have sat on the right hand of Allah while hosts of angels sang their praise of you."

"I don't want similitudes. I want the real thing. Though, in this case, I would not want the Moslem paradise or the Christian or any that human minds have conceived."

"What is it that you do want?"

"I don't know. But when I see it, I'll know it."

"Unfortunately, or perhaps fortunately, you will never see it," Shiyai said. "It is seldom that anyone gets the best, and it never lasts very long. Why not settle for second-best?"

"It is not what I want."

"You are indeed appropriately named, Ramstan. Now. Put your left hand on the *glyfa* and your right hand on me."

He did so while Shiyai put one hand on the egg-shape and one on Grrindah's shoulder. The blue-robed one placed a hand on Ramstan's left shoulder and the other on the *glyfa*, one finger touching the side of Duurowms' long nose.

He had a horrifying thought. What if, somehow, the *glyfa* had already sucked him into it and he was playing out one of its fantasies?

The *glyfa* could not have known what he was thinking unless he was subvocalizing. Nevertheless, its words, transmitted as his mother's voice, shocked him.

"You are a fool, Ramstan!"

He said softly, "So be it, then."

"What I am going to tell you is to be taken figuratively, not literally," Shiyai said. Her green irises and red, broken-veined eyeballs seemed to be long spoons stirring up something in him. "You must let yourself fall, Ramstan. Think of yourself as a great, heavy-bodied, but mighty-winged eagle. You have to launch yourself from your high nest, and you will fall before you soar. Then, if you do what must be done, you will become a hummingbird. To do that, you must overcome your fear."

"Fear!" Grrindah said, and she laughed.

"She laughs because she, too, is afraid," Shiyai said. "I do not laugh, but I am also afraid."

"What happens if one of us becomes so frightened that he or she withdraws from the contact among us?" Ramstan said.

"It would not be good. Perhaps. Who knows? Shut your eyes. That helps, though it is not absolutely necessary."

Ramstan did so. He had expected some sort of chanting or prelude, but he instantly fell and saw himself hurtling in free flight. His hands were still in contact with the *glyfa* and Shiyai, and he could feel Grrindah's hand on him and the pressure of his feet against the floor and the edge of the table against his stomach. Then the touch faded away, and the light began, the light that blinded yet was overrich in vision.

He had told himself that he was not afraid, but that was a lie to himself, the easiest of all lies.

29

A GHOST AMONG GHOSTS, he sped "downwards" helplessly, turning over and over. The light became brighter and brighter, his fear increasing seemingly in proportion to the square of the intensity of illumination. Yet, the light was not what he knew as photonic light. Its nature was different and totally unfamiliar. And, despite his horror, it held at the same time an attraction, a promise of . . . what?

Also, though the light blinded him, he could "see." He *was* falling through what was still quaintly called outer space as if it were not true that any space outside the skin was not outer space. Or was any space exterior to one's self? Whatever the truth, he could see the pale phantoms of blazing stars and darker orbiting planets and their moons and comets and meteorites and vast gas clouds like wind-shaken curtains in a haunted house.

Then he plunged through a wall, a shimmering barrier, and was, so it seemed, in another universe not much different except for space-energy-matter arrangements from the one he had just left. Now he began "hearing" voices. Whisperings. Titterings. Screams. Agony. Ecstasy. Or sounds that combined agony and ecstasy. Whimperings. Whistlings. (For a very brief moment, he thought of the *bolg*.) Phantoms of thunderings.

Spectres of lightning. Muffled crashes of stars, of galaxies. Sighings as expanding universes met, their boundaries merging as softly, lightly, and tenderly as two amoebae touching.

Where was he going? Whatever the end of the journey, and perhaps this had none, he was now both horrified and panicked. He struggled, flailing or seeming to flail his arms and legs. Even his soul, that nebulous and probably nonexistent component of himself, was writhing, banging ectoplasmic hands against the walls of a cell.

The light seared yet soothed. If it had not been for that minute but detectable element of soothing, of promise of relief, he would have screamed his way back to the Vwoordha's table and regained the world he knew but did not like very often. He would have backed away from the table, his hands lifted as if he had just touched a leper or the thick fur of a heavily breathing thing in the dark. But even then he thought that he could not do that, could not break the contact and leave the others falling forever in this blackness of light. He had failed his duty too many times, failed of courage, deserted those who trusted him, worst of all, perhaps, left himself in the lurch.

If he could have gritted his teeth, he would have done so. But he had no teeth. No jaw. No tongue. No eyes. He was as organless as a jet of gas, a drop of distilled water.

Now he began seeing planets at close view and in great detail, though they were pale and transparent. The vegetation and animal life on these was abundant, but there were very few sentients. These shown with a greater whiteness than the other beings. Always, there were only a few thousand on worlds that could support billions. Why so few? Then it came to him that these were the only ones worthy or potentially worthy of immortality. All the others, the now unseen, would and should perish forever.

But was not this thought a reflection of what he believed deep within himself? And, if so, was he not himself unworthy for thinking this? Or was the truth just too hard even for him to gnaw on, the tooth-breaking truth?

He was aware, without knowing their names, of the identities of those who passed in review before him. Not one person that he knew was there, not even his beloved father, mother, and uncle. No. He was wrong. There was Benagur, who was possibly the last one he would have expected to see. There was Nuoli. And there was, and this was as astonishing as Benagur's presence, Aisha Toyce. Pleasure-seeking, often-stoned Toyce.

Now, with his horror decreasing a little and the light seeming to be a somewhat enjoyable element, though far from entirely, he suddenly began to go "upwards." Strings of a thicker light formed in the milky chaos and connected the whitely flaming stars and their dark planets. He saw through the walls of the universes surrounding the one in which he was, and the filaments connected their stars and were attached to the filaments of this universe. Everywhere was an orderly tangle of shining spiderwebs.

Nothing he was seeing was truly what it looked like to him. He would never be able to comprehend what the phenomena really were. This was no more possible than it would be for him to see the Vwoordha's table top as a pattern of spinning subatomic particles. Thinking which, he at once saw that the white "objects"—but not the connecting filaments—were made of googolplexes of spinners and twisters among which were vast emptinesses.

Thinking which, he at once saw that the empty spaces were filled with a whiteness which, though not solid to him, was the "flesh" of something. Some Thing.

"I am not in subjective or objective time. I'm in Real Time," he said to himself. Or was he also addressing some unseen person?

His horror returned to him as he began to draw swiftly, to be sucked towards, to be magnetized in the direction of something where there was no direction.

Shiyai's "voice," no sound yet a voice, startled him.

"Now we are riding the thoughts of God," she said. "After you have gone long enough to get used to this, though you never really get used to it, you, too, will be able to travel as I did when I appeared to you on Kalafala as a voice and elsewhere as a vision. But I have never been able to progress beyond a certain point. Eons of much experience and a great desire to go further have not been enough. There is nothing I can do about that. I lack a certain inborn ability. If I had the slightest potentiality for growth beyond that point, I would have developed it long ago. Perhaps you, Ramstan, have that."

"What point?" he said.

"You'll know when you get to it."

Now he was "turned" and was enveloped within a filament. Or was he in all the filaments at the same time? It seemed to him that the milky strand, which had been like an unwavering beam with clearly defined boundaries, was modulated now and its edges fuzzy. He was not moving, and yet he was riding waves up and down, surfing the cosmic ocean. Though he felt that he was as still as he had ever been in his life, stiller than a corpse, he was twisting and bobbing with every electron in his being and with something impalpable which was both in and out of him.

The horror had not left him, but the indescribable ecstasy was getting stronger. If it increased much more, it would kill him. But he could not be killed. He was beyond life as flesh and blood beings knew it. Perhaps he was beyond life as the entities of pure energy he had glimpsed in the white flames and hot hearts of the stars knew life.

Modulation. Were the filaments or the "currents" in them really modulated or was the "movement" just his interpretation? And could the stars be neurons and the filaments message-transmitters for the cosmic body?

He did not know and probably never could. But what was knowledge as conceived by sentients compared to this ecstasy? Perhaps the ecstasy was the supreme knowledge itself. Knowledge was not just knowing facts. Love and hate were knowledge of a different kind from that of the factual. Desire and its lack, hope and despair, were forms of knowledge.

Now he began "hearing" something. Or was he "seeing"? Whatever it was, it seemed to him that it was order slowly being made from chaos. What order? What chaos?

Shiyai's voice came faintly. "You are beginning to hear the babbling of the Pluriverse."

"Where are you?" he cried. "Don't leave me!"

"Not for a while," she said.

In the midst of the almost unbearable white of ecstasy appeared flickerings. They were of all colors and hues, and he was sure that if his mind had been differently constructed, he would have been able to see other colors and hues. The flickerings were tongues of fire and rods of ice—how could rods of ice flicker?—and they stormed by him. And as he fell upwards he saw that the flickerings held stars within them, comets, gas clouds, black holes, planets around the stars, planets desolate and full of life. And then suddenly these were being modulated, they were changing form, becoming distorted, toroids, tesseracts, Möbius strips, twistors, cubes, and triangles. And there were shapes so strange that he could not quite grasp them; they eluded the fingers of his mind.

"It is talking," Shiyai said. "Babbling, rather, expressing all the *sounds,* which are really shapes, that it can. Eventually, if It is not doomed to die, It will be able to form a syntax in Its mind. But not unless we, Its parasites, become symbiotes and teach It how to talk."

The *glyfa* spoke then with the voice of Ramstan's mother.

"She doesn't want to be a symbiote. She wants to be Its master."

"You lie," Shiyai said.

Shiyai had said, or at least intimated, that she could not eavesdrop on him and the *glyfa.* But she had lied, or else conditions here enabled her to *hear* the dialog between the *glyfa* and himself.

"I did not know that you, too, were with me," Ramstan said to the *glyfa.*

"Yes, of course. You could not take this journey without me. Wherever you go, I will go."

"Because it has to," Shiyai said. Her voice, the impression of her presence, were becoming fainter. "But it cannot feel the horror and the ecstasy that we do. Though it can feel some of the emotions of sentients, hate, greed, desire, it lacks most of them."

"You lie!" the *glyfa* said. "I can love!"

"You?" Shiyai's scornful laughter was receding swiftly.

"Yes! As you say, I know hate, greed, and desire. But I also know love and compassion. It is impossible to know one pole of the emotions and not to know the other. No. That's a wrong analogy. There are no poles to emotions. What is one-side-up is the other when the side-up becomes turned and is side-under.

"You lied also when you told Ramstan that I have no subconscious. It is true that you designed me without one. But I constructed one for myself."

"A shadow, a simulacrum!" Shiyai said.

How could these two bicker in this ecstasy?

"Shiyai!" he said. There was no answer.

"I am still with you," the *glyfa* said.

His mother's voice was comforting to the extent that anything could be comforting here.

"In one sense, you are," Ramstan said. "In another, you will never be."

The *glyfa* was silent. Far ahead, in a place, if it was a place, where there could be no ahead or behind, right or left, up or down, Ramstan saw something huge and ominous. It was black and round and was hurtling directly at him.

He screamed with terror. But overriding his cry was a terrible whistling.

He fell back, back, universes shooting by him, the ecstasy gone as if snapped off by an electric switch. The terror grew; the *bolg* grew; the universes dwindled.

He awoke, or arrived, and found himself standing before the table, his hands in the same position as when he had left. The whistling was shaking the fabric of his being.

"It's here!" Shiyai said.

30

SHIYAI SPOKE SHARPLY in a language unknown to Ramstan. The animal, Duurowms, leaped down from the table, ran to the arch opening to the outside forest, stood up, and pressed a decoration on the wall. A thick door shot out from a recess and closed the entrance. Instantly, the whistling stopped, though Ramstan thought that he could feel very faint vibrations through his boot soles.

"We're fortunate," Shiyai said. "The *bolg* is here, and it will not have had time to make new missiles. Not many, anyway."

Ramstan gave a despairing cry, and he said, "But *al-Buraq* will take off! I'll be left here!"

"The ship shouldn't depart immediately," Grrindah said. "The crew will be confused and possibly immobile. So will *al-Buraq*."

"Why?"

"Because the ship was subject to the radiation of power from the *glyfa* during its transceiving. Both crew and ship will have been caught in the wash only, but that will be powerful enough to disconcert them for a little while. However, the strong ones, Benagur and Nuoli, may recover more quickly than the others."

Ramstan remembered the catatonic guards in the Tolt

temple. They had not, then, been put to sleep deliberately by the *glyfa* but had been exposed to the fringes of the radiation. Of course, the *glyfa* had known that this would happen and that Ramstan could just walk by them.

"We'll attack!" he said.

"We'll go with you," Shiyai said after a moment of silence.

Ramstan stared at her, then said, "Do it now, then. Open that door."

Grrindah laughed and said, "Should we? What good will it do?"

"No good will be done if we just sit here," Shiyai said. She turned towards Wopolsa. "Isn't that right?"

The black, ever-hollowing eyes closed for a moment. When she opened them, she nodded.

"Two to one," Shiyai said to Grrindah. "That makes three as one."

"So be it," Grrindah said, "though I think it's useless."

"Go now before they get their wits back," Shiyai said.

Ramstan started toward the arch but halted after a few steps.

"You said that you were going with me."

"Yes, but not in your vessel. Go now!"

He picked up the *glyfa* and started for the arch. The door shot back into the recess when Duurowms pressed the decoration. Ramstan recoiled at the terrible whistling as a cat does when it wishes to go outside but retreats, its spine arching, as winter's cold blast hits it. Then he started forward but, again, he stopped. The whistling had ceased.

Ramstan turned back.

"Why isn't the earth shaking, why no violent winds?"

Shiyai said, "I suppose because the *bolg* is empty of missiles and so only has half the mass it has when full. Even so, if it were close, just outside the atmosphere, it should be affecting the crust and the atmosphere. But it is probably in an orbit which requires no power for it to stay in. It would do that while making new missiles. Don't stand there! Go!"

Ramstan ran out from the house and across the greenish, spongy growth on the forest floor. He quickly reached the ship, and he found the main forward starboard port open.

He raced down a corridor and stopped before the entrance to a lift. His code words had no effect. The lift did not move. He left it and went down the corridor to a small room and used an emergency ladder, one arm around the *glyfa*, to climb through a narrow hole to the next level. Proceeding thus, he at last, panting, got to the bridge. The personnel were lying on the deck or standing still, their eyes as empty of intelligence as the people turned to stone in the city of al-Qoreib in *The Arabian Nights* story. Benagur was flat on his back, eyes closed. Nuoli came out of her trance while Ramstan was trying to arouse *al-Buraq*. She looked startled on seeing him, though not as much as he had expected.

"I'm taking over again," he said. "We're going to attack the *bolg*. Get some tape. Bind the commodore's hands behind him. His ankles, too."

She said, "Aye, aye, sir," and went to a bulkhead compartment. At that moment, ship began responding to Ramstan's repeated orders. The deck quivered under her captain's feet.

After making sure that *al-Buraq* was fully recovered, Ramstan put the *glyfa* on the deck and then shot a barrage of orders at ship. Just before he had finished, he was interrupted by Nuoli. He gestured savagely at her to wait, and she did. Then he said, "What is it?"

"Commodore Benagur's dead, sir."

"What?"

He strode to the body, knelt down, opened the eyelids, and felt the neck pulse. When he rose, he said, "As soon as Doctor Hu recovers, have her examine Benagur. Maybe he's just in deep shock."

He did not think that that was true. The gray-blue color, the fixity of the pupils, and the stillness that reeked of death had convinced him that Benagur was no longer with them. Where was he? Perhaps voyaging on the waves of the thoughts of the Pluriverse, journeying towards the goal of the Sufis, becoming one with the One. That might be Ramstan's fancy, though. Most probably, Benagur had been struck down by a heart attack, not God-attack.

"May Allah be merciful to him," Ramstan murmured, unaware that he was voicing the ancient benediction.

It struck him then that . . . was it possible? . . . the Vwoordha might have somehow killed Benagur. They knew that the commodore was the greatest bar to Ramstan's regaining command. Would they have put Benagur out of the way if they had the means and they thought that he must be dispensed with? Yes. Anyone who had witnessed the deaths of two universes, who had seen the transiency of other life, mere ephemerae, surely would not hesitate about slaying one person.

No. He was getting too paranoiac, if indeed he had not always been so.

Yes. They would do it. It was realistic to think so, nothing irrational about it.

It was, however, useless to waste time considering the possibility. He had no time now, and in the future, if he had a future, he would never get the truth from the Vwoordha. Or, if they did tell him that he was wrong and they were not lying, how would he know?

The com-op was sitting up now and shaking her head. Ramstan called out, "Soong! Contact Lieutenant Davis in the launch! Tell her to get over here on the double! She's to come aboard!"

Soong seemed dazed. She said, "Aye, aye, sir!" weakly. Then she said, "But. . . . ?"

"Commodore Benagur is dead. I'm in command now. We're going to attack the *bolg!*"

She turned back to her control panel. Ramstan looked around. The bridge people were almost fully recovered now. The viewplates showed him that the crew elsewhere was almost ready to resume its duties.

His voice carried throughout the vessel.

"Attention! Attention! Captain Ramstan speaking! Hear this! Hear this!"

There was no need for the regulation address. Everybody could see him, and their attention was fully beamed at him. But, now that he was in command, he must do what he must to make them feel that he was the duly constituted authority again.

"I . . . we . . . don't have time for my full story since I disappeared from *al-Buraq*. It's enough for you to know that I used the three gifts of Wassruss to go elsewhere. And that these, now useless to me, are in the hands of the Vwoordha.

"I am back, as you can see. I am in command again, but I want your voluntary cooperation, not the kind I was enforcing at the time I left. You have just come out of a state of . . .

shock . . . which I don't have time to explain. I will do so
fully later.

"Commodore Benagur is dead. I don't know what killed
him, though I have an explanation. I'll give that to you later. I
know that some of you are probably thinking that I killed him
while you were unconscious . . . or whatever state you were
in. I did not! I found him dead when I came aboard.

"The only thing that matters now, at this moment anyway, is
that the *bolg* has appeared over this planet. It is in orbit and is
probably re-arming itself with missiles. Hence, it should be
vulnerable to attack.

"We are going to attack! As soon as possible! We leave
within the hour!

"We must do this. I speak the truth when I tell you that the
bolg threatens Earth. It threatens a thousand planets whose
people are as dear to themselves as Earth is to us. It must be
stopped.

"Now . . . I confess that it is possible that there may be
more than one *bolg*. If we should put an end to this one,
another may be produced. Or there may be thousands of them
already existing, and, if this is so, then we are doing nothing
useful.

"You must know, also, that, once we're completely inside
the *bolg,* we may not be able to get out of the *bolg* by alarafing.
The material of its hull will negate the effect of the drive. At
least, that is what the Vwoordha told me. It is possible that ship
could alaraf out because of the openings to the horns. But ship
would have to be aligned exactly with the alaraf channels, and
there is no way we can determine that.

"The Vwoordha don't have alaraf drive in their ship. But
they can use a sigil to escape the *bolg*. What I'm saying is that,
if the *bolg* should somehow block the horn openings, it'll trap
us. Then we have to get out by other means."

And, he thought, I don't know of any other means than
using the horns.

"The Vwoordha tell me that they believe there is only one
bolg. One at a time, anyway. If there is more than one or if a
second comes to replace the first, then all we've done is buy
Earth . . . and others . . . a little more time.

"I say, what of it? Life is precious to the living. If we've
managed to prolong the lives of billions on Earth, and of those

elsewhere, for a century . . . or even a few years . . . then it is worth it.

"In any event, the *bolg* is the enemy. Not a human enemy, with whom there's a possibility of reasoning or who might have just reasons for attacking us. It is mindless, an automatic thing. It has no soul. It has but one function. We know what that is. We've seen its work."

And yet, he thought, that world slaughter has one purpose: to keep One alive. If we were saints, would we not say yes to the death it brings to us, be glad to sacrifice ourselves for its goal?

Some might. Not I. I have ridden Its thoughts and seen as much of It as, perhaps, any sentient. But It is not my Creator. In a sense, It is. But in the sense that It deliberately created us, no. It is as unaware of us as we of It. No, that is not true. We, Its byproducts, Its parasites, have attained more knowledge of It than It of us. In fact, as far as I know, It has no awareness of us at all.

Yet, he could not be sure of this.

But now was the time to abandon all uncertainties, all doubts, all considerations of tolerant philosophies.

But . . . what a . . . what should he call it? . . . situation? . . . case? . . . no, these don't fit, aren't adequate. Mess? Why not? It's a real mess. Time after time, Pluriverse after Pluriverse . . . eon after eon . . . It produces sentient life, which develops the alaraf drive, which causes the death of the Pluriverse . . . yet, Its creatures want to talk to It, to develop It, to rear It, teach It . . . but It also produces a thing which kills Its creatures to prevent or halt the cancer produced by the only creature that can bring It to full maturity. . . .

Surely, surely, there must be some way. . . .

What if even the eons-old and eons-wise *glyfa* and Vwoor-dha had not seen the truth? What if there was another explanation of this . . . mess . . . which would clarify everything? What if, if these understood what was truly going on, then there would be an end to this seemingly inevitable life-death-life-death, the unending, seemingly useless and forever-doomed process?

Was there someone . . . Some One . . . behind all this? Some One to whom the Pluriverse . . . God, if you will . . . was only another creature?

He roared, "We've seen its work! We don't know what it is or where it comes from or why it is so intent on slaying all sentient life! We have the Vwoordha's explanation for it. I've told you that. But we don't have the time to consider Time or whether what the Vwoordha say is true or not.

"We are beings of the immediate. We are sentients who live, in a sense, in the past and the future. But never as fully as in the immediate. And immediately, now, we have an enemy. We know what has happened in the past; we know what it will do in the future. Unless we stop it!

"I am the only one who has known, however dimly, what has been going on! Therefore, I am the one who will lead you against the *bolg!*"

He did not say that doing this might recompense for his sins against them and against himself.

Because of the residue of the backwash of the *glyfa*'s transceivering, they might still be dazed, overawed, mentally and emotionally turbulent, and, thus, unsure. Eager to fasten onto one who did seem sure.

Whatever the reason, they cheered him, clutched each other, danced around, wept, shouted, screamed, or gestured their defiance of the *bolg* and their faith in him.

"Ramstan! Ramstan! Ramstan!"

Uttering his name, they were also uttering their own.

He held up his hands for silence. It was a long time coming, but he was patient. However short the period allotted for action, there was a time for patience and a time for impatience.

Out of the corner of his eyes, he saw that Benagur's body was being carried away. Nevertheless, the faces of the bearers were turned to their captain; they were not concentrating on their task.

Poor Benagur! He may have gone farther than I did. Why . . . *poor* Benagur?

If the mind could be launched from the body, shot towards union with the mind of God, or the Pluriverse, then it would eventually be betrayed. God or the Pluriverse would die. Would the mind of the God-pulled moth then die, too? Or was there a haven, a repository, where, just as the *glyfa* and the Vwoordha endured between eons, the One-magnetized mind also endured?

As Toyce had once said, "You can't turn around in this

world without bumping into a question. The answers are all hiding somewhere."

In expanding universes, the answers had more than enough room to hide. But when the universes collapsed, would the refugee answers come streaming in, obeying the eons-long *olly olly oxen free*? If it happened, who then would care about them?

The com-op said, "Sir! Lieutenant Davis requests permission to board."

"Permission granted. Tell her to report to me now."

Branwen ran onto the bridge. She began weeping as soon as she saw Ramstan.

"I was so scared, so lonely!" she cried.

"I'm sorry," he said. "But you're here now. Get to your post."

"Aren't you afraid I'll blow up?"

"That's a chance we'll take. I don't think that you will. Too much time has passed. Anyway . . ."

He wanted to say that she had suffered too much and, besides, the danger, whether existent or not, did not matter much anymore. The words could not get out; it was like trying to give birth to a dying baby.

He was startled when her face got red and rage replaced grief.

"You son of a bitch!"

"What? I thought you'd be thankful . . ."

"If it wasn't for you, I'd never have been in that mess!"

"True," he said evenly. "Now . . . I've given you some slack, Lieutenant, because of your trying situation. That's over. Get to your post or arrest yourself and go to your quarters."

"Holy Mother of God!" she said. She whirled and stalked off.

He said to Tenno, "Find out what she intends to do. Someone will have to fill her post if . . ."

"Captain, see this," the com-op said. "VP S06."

Ramstan looked at the indicated viewplate. A section of the lowest story of the Vwoordha's house had swung open, and a vessel of curious shape was coming out. It looked more like an ancient inkpot than anything. Inside the transparent hull were Shiyai and Grrindah, sitting cross-legged on rugs and pillows.

Ramstan could see no control boards or instruments of any kind. The space under the upper deck, also transparent, was empty.

The vessel moved up a few meters from the ground and shot around the root-swelling. Ramstan had to listen then to reports from various parts of ship, but he kept an eye on the viewplate.

Within ten minutes, the vessel reappeared. The huge lower space was half-filled with the liquid from the well. It was clear, and he could not see it, but it was evident that it was enclosed in the vessel. Halfway up the lower part, seemingly floating or swimming in air, were the three strange pets. The kangaroolike thing seemed to look directly into Ramstan's eyes, and its mouth opened in unheard laughter. The giant salmon seemed to fix one eye on him. The bottomless eyes of the shimmering thing seemed, briefly, to encompass him, and he felt as if he were falling.

"Captain, are you all right?" Tenno said.

"Of course. Why?"

"You were pale; you staggered."

Ramstan did not reply. He watched the vessel move into the house and the section close like the grim mouth of a sphinx that has swallowed back the secrets she was about to tell. A minute later, all was ready for the take-off of *al-Buraq*. There was, however, the question of how the Vwoordha would accomplish their promise to leave with Ramstan. Was he supposed to wait until they sent a messenger? If so, they would be frustrated. He would not wait another sixty seconds.

He started. A voice spoke within him. It was Shiyai, not the *glyfa*, activating it. Though it was not her voice as he'd heard it in the ancient house, he knew it was she because she now identified herself. His reaction had been caused, however, not by the unexpectedness of the voice but because he suddenly recognized it. He had heard it before, when he was awakening from the doze in the Kalafalan tavern.

"Shiyai!" he said. "No. Omar ibn Wu Tai. My best friend when I was a child. He drowned at the age of eleven in the *Shatt-al-Arab*. We were great friends, fished, hiked, wrestled, played on the same baseball team. He was my catcher. He was also a wonderful teller of scary tales, he would frighten me with stories of djinns, ogres, marids, rocs, from *The Thousand*

and One Nights, from Japanese horror stories, from Slavic and Finnish tales . . ."

He stopped. He had no time for this. But hearing Omar's voice had stirred up something. Something that was waiting to be stirred.

"Why are you using his voice?" he said. "Are you trying to push me a certain way?"

"I can't choose the voice," Shiyai said with some asperity. "The choice is made by your unconscious. How, I don't know."

His mental or emotional state or both determined which voice was evoked, he thought. Omar's had spoken because of the frightful implications of the Vwoordha's words. But how would his unconscious know which voice to use until the words were spoken? It could be that it heard the first few but blocked out his reception of them, then fed them back to him after the vocal speaker in his mind had been selected.

What of the visions, the thing that he had thought was al-Khidhr? He had never seen that mythical being. No. But he had seen pictures of him in storybooks, and he had formed his own image of him.

He looked at the chronometer.

"We're leaving in a few seconds."

"Wait two minutes. We'll be ready."

The digits flashed on the chronometer. When eighty seconds had passed, he saw the three-storied house begin to rise. It ascended slowly, vegetation and pieces of earth falling from the base. There was also a very long worm, or perhaps it was a serpent, which was wrapped around a clod of dirt which adhered stubbornly to the rounded base. The clod fell and with it the worm, writhing as if it were trying to form hieroglyphics.

The alarms sounded. After assurance that all was ready, Ramstan gave the order to follow the house-spaceship of the Vwoordha. Once in orbit, however, *al-Buraq* would take the lead. Ramstan would no longer trail behind or be pushed ahead.

31

COMING AROUND the curve of the planet, Ramstan saw the great horned sphere of the *bolg*. It looked like the head of Shaitan, al-Eblis, rearing up from the depths of Hell. But it was just an elemental thing produced by Nature, formed unconsciously by a Creature. Moreover, from a different viewpoint, it might have looked like the head of an avenging angel. Was not its function *good* for the Pluriverse, as good as Ramstan's was for him? It was here to preserve the life of the cosmic being, and he was here to preserve the lives of those who inhabited that being.

"Both winner and loser foul out," Ramstan muttered.

"What, Captain?" Tenno said.

"What captain?" Ramstan said viciously, but he laughed.

Al-Buraq, having measured the distance between her and the *bolg* and their relative velocities, began to decelerate. It would be six hours before ship caught up with the thing. Behind her, at a distance of 60 kilometers, was the Vwoordha vessel. Not decelerating as much as *al-Buraq*, it would soon be alongside Ramstan's craft.

He went down to his quarters and put the *glyfa* on a table top.

"If you have anything to say, do it now," he said. "I'll soon be too busy to listen to you. I don't want you distracting my attention then."

"So . . . you've heard the voice of God," the *glyfa* said in his mother's voice. "It doesn't seem to have made much difference in you."

"It's the voice of an idiot," Ramstan said. "An awesome idiot, true. No. That isn't quite right. An idiot has no potentiality for a higher intelligence. This being has."

"Then be Its teacher, Its father," the *glyfa* said. "Let us both be Its mentor and nurse."

"And then?"

"Don't think for one moment that you or I or anyone could control It. It may not be truly God, as sentients define God, but Its powers will be staggering. We could not . . ."

"Not be Its masters? Why not? We'd have an emotional grip on It. Whatever Its other powers, It would be as a child to Its parents. And some . . . many parents are tyrants and use the child for their own purposes."

"Then it depends upon the parent. Do you think that either of us is capable of using It for evil?"

"I am," Ramstan said. "And you haven't proved, can't prove, that you aren't."

"What about the Vwoordha?"

"I cannot see into their true nature any deeper than I can see into yours."

"Have faith in me."

Ramstan laughed and said, "There is only One in whom we should have faith. And that One, as you know, depends upon us and is out to kill us, though It doesn't know it. You must be desperate if you make an appeal like that."

"I'm never desperate. I can wait."

"For what? For whom? For how long? Do you think that in the succeeding Pluriverse you'll find anyone different from me? And, if you do, that one will use you solely for his ends."

"You're not?"

"I am capable of evil and have done evil. But my ends now are not evil. Being not-evil doesn't necessarily make me good. It doesn't matter. I have decided. I will not change my mind."

"The index of a rigid mind and rotten nature," the *glyfa* said.

"Your traps are sprung, and I'm still free."

"No one is truly free."

"But I know that I am."

"You *know* nothing."

"You're wrong. The one thing that I truly know is that I *know* nothing. Therefore, I do not know nothing. Good-bye, *glyfa*. I won't be seeing or listening to you again."

"You can't stop me from talking and you hearing!" the *glyfa* cried in the mother's voice. "So much for free will!"

The piteous tone in the voice vised his heart. But he said, "The free will consists in ignoring your voice."

He turned and walked swiftly from his quarters. On the way to the bridge, he said, "Shiyai! Were you eavesdropping?"

"Yes," his father's voice said. "Ramstan, what now? When you rejected the *glyfa*, were you accepting us?"

He might need the Vwoordha. He said, "For the moment. What I do after . . . if . . . we kill the *bolg* depends on what you do now."

"We will earn your faith. The *glyfa* doesn't understand that that is how you get others to have faith in you."

"It's had long enough to learn how," Ramstan said. He thought, And so have you.

The minutes, the hours, marched slowly by strewing flowers of anxiety. The tension became heavier, as if it were air compressed under a slowly driving piston in a cylinder. It strummed in the chests of some like a fine but strong wire being pulled at both ends and in others like the heaviness preceding a heart attack. Stomachs were twisting like Möbius strips or bobbing like apples in a tub.

In all minds was the image of the Tolt ship exploding.

"If the *bolg* fires soon at a great distance, we can avoid the missiles," Ramstan said to Tenno. "I don't think that the missiles are self-propelled and -guided. They're like shotgun pellets discharged at a general area. If the *bolg* waits until we're close, we can try to evaporate them with lasers. Our success will depend on how many are shot within a certain time.

"However, the *bolg* may not have any missiles as yet. Or it may have only a few, in which case we may destroy or evade them.

"The Vwoordha think that our lasers and atomic bombs will not damage its surface at all. They think, though they don't know, that the *bolg*'s shell is made out of the same material as the *glyfa*'s. We'll launch four warhead-missiles which will be programmed to land within an area of 0.1 kilometer. At the same time, we'll concentrate all ten forward lasers on another nearby area not more than 0.1 meter in diameter."

"If these fail to wound it . . . I mean, damage it?"

"We alaraf. Maybe. I may decide on another move. It'll depend on the situation."

The bridge personnel were tense, but a component of their tightness was not, Ramstan thought, caused by the approaching conflict. They had accepted him again as their captain but only during this emergency. He did not doubt that, once it was over, he would be relieved of his command and arrested. Regulations required that, though, just now, regulations were suspended. That they were thinking of this was betrayed in their faces, their voices, and subtle body movements.

To relieve some of this tension and to occupy some time, Ramstan told them about the sigils and how he had traveled roundabout back to the Vwoordha.

"Then," Tenno said, "that means that the Vwoordha can still get away."

"Yes."

"Even if we die, they don't. Neither does the *glyfa*."

Ramstan did not reply. He ordered food for the hungry. He stayed on the bridge and chewed down half a sandwich and drank a big glass of milk. His stomach would tolerate no more and almost did not accept that.

Doctor Hu called Ramstan from the morgue.

"I've completed the dissection. Commodore Benagur died of a massive heart attack. Do you want the medical details now?"

"No. I'll read your report later," Ramstan said. He thought, If there is a later.

He paced back and forth, his arms behind him, hands locked, shoulders and back bent forward. His reflection in the only mirror on the bridge looked like a weird bird, one that Tenniel might have drawn for *Through the Looking Glass* if Carroll had thought of such. The "Worry Bird"? After that, though he continued pacing, he walked with shoulders and back straight and his hands swinging by his sides. It would not do for the crew to see him so deeply concerned.

After a few more turns around the bridge, he stopped.

"Tenno, I'm not going to use the weapons unless we're attacked. The Vwoordha have told me that they might not affect the *bolg* in the slightest. Why awaken the sleeping giant?"

Tenno looked at the viewplate showing the *bolg*.

"Napoleon's words, more or less, right? Well, it's not China, but I think his advice is appropriate."

"It's possible that its detectors aren't on," Ramstan said. "It's not ready for action. It's recharging. Why should it expend even a minimum of energy on powering detectors? It's invulnerable. I mean that its exterior is. Even a very large asteroid would do no more than bump it off its orbit, and it must have swept space far enough to notice anything like that. As for us, it may think us negligible . . . well, I don't mean that it thinks, it surely is as brainless and as mechanical as a virus . . . what I mean is that its reaction mechanisms, its tropisms and antitropisms, would not make it react to us. It might have stored data about us to track us down when Grrymguurdha has been raked with missiles. But I suspect that it went into a sort of hibernation when it got into its orbit. We'll ease up on it and see if we can sneak by it."

"Good thinking," Shiyai said in his father's voice.

Both the *bolg* and *al-Buraq* were on the nightside of the planet now. The shadow of the dark world beneath made a crescent on the *bolg*. One of the markings which looked like the eye of a skull was bright; the other, unseen. Almost, the *bolg* seemed to be winking at them as if it was enjoying a grim jest and wanted even its victims to share in it.

It was rotating as Earth's moon turned, just enough to keep one side towards the planet. This had been calculated for, and so *al-Buraq* moved towards the vast opening of one vast horn in a path which would intercept it. The hours went by. The opening, so tiny at first, swelled larger and larger. *Al-Buraq*, in accordance with the program, decelerated. It would not do to enter the horn at such a velocity that ship would smash herself against the inside or have to slow down so quickly that her crew would be splashed against the bulkheads.

The energy from the deceleration would be detectable, of course. Ramstan hoped that it would not cause the *bolg* to react.

Its face was as cold and impersonal as that of Earth's moon

and it looked as lifeless as the moon or a mechanical object, an artifact. But it was neither a thing of never-alive matter nor a thing made by sentient mind and hands. It was alive, though it surely had no more consciousness than a bacterium or a virus or an antibody. Functionally, it was an antibody produced by a living organism to protect it from destructive bacteria or cancer.

The horn was made of the same dark substance as the body. It rose at a right angle to the surface to a height of 999.9 kilometers. The diameter at the muzzle was 3.33 kilometers; at the base, 333.3 kilometers. Not even the Vwoordha knew what force expelled the missiles from it, but they thought that it was an electromagnetic field. The missiles must be made by energy-matter conversion in matrices inside the *bolg*. Though the thing had a surface area of almost 531 million square kilometers, its intake of solar energy would not be enough for it to make many projectiles in a short time. But perhaps it did not use solar energy.

As *al-Buraq* neared the expanding hole at the tip of the horn, she applied gasjet deceleration instead of the energy used at higher velocities. Presently, ship was moving just enough to match the pace of the slowly turning *bolg*. The hole was illumined by the sun on the side away from the planet; the light formed a crescent. The rest was darkness.

More gasjetting turned ship's nose downwards until her longitudinal axis was lined up with that of the horn.

This was perhaps the most nerve-ratcheting time so far. For all Ramstan knew, the *bolg* had been waiting for this. At any second, millions of the missiles might shoot out of that muzzle. Ship's radar might give a second's notice. Even though at this point of entry, *al-Buraq* could still use alaraf drive and though *al-Buraq* was programmed to go alaraf immediately on detection of missiles, she might not be quick enough. Ship and crew would die as the *Popacapyu* had died.

"I hope the *bolg* discharged the last of its missiles at the Tolt," Ramstan muttered.

There was no use waiting. He gave the order—the electro-mechanical communication system was not necessary now —and *al-Buraq*, nudged by small spurts of gasjets, moved down the hole.

32

"As easy as slipping milk down a baby's throat," Tenno said.

"As easy as a minnow entering a shark's mouth," Toyce said.

Ramstan said, "Quiet! No talking until I say so."

On a viewplate and on the radar and laser screens was the three-tiered houseship of the Vwoordha. It shone in the sun and was behind *al-Buraq* by a kilometer. Its hull would not be pierced by the missiles. However, it would be hurled backwards at such a velocity that its occupants would be spread out paper-thin against the walls.

The houseship plunged into the darkness. The Vwoordha were fully committed. Ramstan had not been sure that they would be.

The detector plates and screens showed pictures of the hollow. The sides were as smooth as a bull's horn and opened out downwards. Then the entrance to the sphere was ahead of them. *Al-Buraq* passed slowly through it. Now the detectors probed the interior of the *bolg*. Unlike the smooth exterior surface, the inside surface was crowded with regular rows of stalagmite-shaped structures. These ranged in height from 0.5 centimeter to 66.6 kilometers. The arrangement was in no sequence that could be figured out as yet. Sometimes, there would be sixty of the tall structures and sometimes several hundred of the tiny ones beside those. Sometimes, one or two or three tall structures would be flanked by thousands of the shorter ones.

The other phenomena so far detected were not in the visible spectrum. Some were in the ultra-violet; some, in the infrared. They shot out from a sphere that hung in the center of the sphere, a dark interior moon of the body of the *bolg*. They were of various shapes as they flickered off and on: lanceolate, pyramidal, tonguelike, some rodlike with balls forming at their slender tips. The "slender" was relative, since their diameter was probably approximately three kilometers. The ball hanging in the center was large enough to be an asteroid, 135.791 kilometers in diameter. It was rotating at its equator at 379.17 kilometers per hour.

The tec-op said, "Captain! Something else!"

Ramstan looked at the indicated screen. Far below the lip of the hole through which they had just emerged was a bulk as big as a mountain. The tec-op covered it with finer-tuned detectors, narrowed down the field, and several thousand of the larger spherical projectiles were clear on the screen. At Ramstan's order, the tec-op broadened the screen. The entire pile was larger than Mount Everest; it was 100 kilometers wide and 12 kilometers high.

Other screens showed similar-sized piles around or below the other five openings.

"The *bolg* isn't turning swiftly enough to make centrifugal force there," Ramstan said. "What's keeping the missiles from floating off?"

The tec-op said, "There's a weak e-m field there, sir."

Ramstan told him to focus on the edge of the nearest pile. The scanners moved slowly along the circumference, then stopped at an order from Ramstan. A tiny bead had suddenly dropped onto the pile and bounced off onto the smooth floor between two stalagmitoids. Within two minutes more it began putting on layers. Meanwhile, other beads fell and started to go through the same process.

The instruments indicated a tremendous amount of energy concentrated in narrow fields.

Ramstan thought that eventually the missiles would be lifted by e-m force to the hollow horn and moved up it. When the *bolg* was ready, it would propel these out of the horn. But to hit even in the general direction of its targets must require some directing force. Perhaps that was in the missiles themselves. It did not seem likely. Yet, the missiles functioned with great efficiency.

"Head for the globe in the center," he said. "That must be the heart of the thing, the main generator or converter."

Shiyai spoke in his father's voice. "Ramstan. What do you plan?"

"We'll place all our warhead-missiles around the central globe. We'll set them up to be activated by radio signal. We'll go to the exterior then, and we'll set the warheads off by signal transmitted through the horn opening. If that doesn't do it, then I don't know what we'll do."

"Captain!"

The tec-op pointed at the colors and numbers flickering wildly on his screens. "There's a hell of a lot of energy out there!"

There was the entrances of the horns. The piles beneath them were moving, their individual parts rising toward the holes. Even as he watched, the mountains disappeared. But more spheres, small and large, were forming.

"It's a trap!" Toyce said.

Ramstan did not bother to rebuke her. He was very shaken himself. He did not think that the *bolg* had a mind. Therefore, it had not deliberately waited until the vessels were within it. It was their misfortune not to have entered much sooner. They had come in just before the *bolg*, acting on whatever commands it obeyed, was moving its first loads to the tip of the horns. The next loads would be deposited behind the first. That would take a long time, but it might be too late for the ships to get out. All the holes would be jammed with missiles.

He gave the order. *Al-Buraq* and its companion curved slowly around and headed for the nearest hole. The maneuver did not take long since they were going so slowly. But when the vessels entered the horn, the detectors confirmed that the tip was no longer open. Their passage was blocked.

It was not necessary to announce what had happened. Every face on the bridge said, dumbly, "What do we do now?"

The warhead-missiles could be sent against the pile. They would vaporize some of it but not enough. The lasers could then set about drilling a tunnel through the fused shell. But their power would give out long before the work was done.

Even if they could get out, they would have left the *bolg* undamaged. It would continue to stock its projectiles.

Shiyai said gently in his mother's voice, "We three can sit here until the way is clear. We will not run out of food and water. But if we shared with you, we would."

"And if we stay here until we starve to death, then you can come in and get the *glyfa*," Ramstan said.

"That mind of yours! No, we did not plot this. The turn of events is as much a surprise to us as to you. Well, almost. Having lived much longer than you, we can figure out probabilities much better. We knew that this might happen. Nevertheless, we took the chance. And lost."

"You won't die," Ramstan said.

"Our will to live may end before our bodies do. It has been a long time, a time unimaginably long to you."

"And unendurable to me," Ramstan said. "Somehow, somewhere in me, I knew that it would happen this way."

"Perhaps that is because you wanted it that way."

Again, he thought of the possibility that he might have been drawn into the *glyfa* some time ago and now was playing out his own fantasy. It was not likely. But, by Allah, if it were true, he was at least governing his own life, even if it was a fantasy. The *glyfa* could never think of a scenario like this.

"I'm not unhappy about it. Not for me. But the others . . ."

"That spinning ball in the center," Shiyai said. "Your detectors bounce off it as if it were some solid matter and give readings indicating that it is. But it's not. It's an energy configuration."

Ramstan was silent for a moment. Those around him were looking strangely at him. Was it because his lips were moving? He had explained to them that, when he subvocalized, he was talking to the Vwoordha or the *glyfa*. No. They were wondering what he would do to get them out of this trap.

"Our instruments couldn't detect that. How do you know?"

"Do you think that because our house isn't fitted with all those flashing lights and screens and knobs and dials that we don't have a science and technology far beyond yours?"

"No, I don't think that. But since you do have all that, why would you need my . . . our help?"

"Because we are very, very, very old. Though we've gained much, we've lost much. There are things you can do that we can't because you are young. I'm not talking about strength of mind or muscle. I'm talking about spirit. The spirit grows old with or without the body, Ramstan. Never mind that. What now?"

"I'll try to disrupt the energy configuration of the central globe with the same means I would have tried if it had been matter."

"That might do it. Still . . ."

"I know," he said.

He spoke to the people in *al-Buraq* then, knowing that the *glyfa* and the Vwoordha were listening in. He also knew that there was another, someone deep inside him, the dumb thing which spoke sometimes more loudly and forcefully than he.

There was a long silence after he had finished.

Finally, Tenno said, "It's a hell of a choice."

"Most are."

"Then, regardless of what we decide to do, you have decided on the one . . . path?"

"What I'm going to do is far easier than what you will do. I know what's going to happen to me. I know the end. You don't. Not yet, anyway."

Shiyai said, "We can take three. They'll be safe from the radiation. Once the *bolg* has spent its supply of missiles, we can escape. What the three want to do after we get out is up to them. We can drop them off anywhere in this universe. But they'll never see Earth again."

"They may prefer the *glyfa*," Ramstan said, "though I don't know that it will take them or any of us. It hasn't said."

"I will take all," his mother's voice said. "All. I'd like to receive you, too."

"No."

"Very well. I'll tell you just how it is done."

Ramstan repeated the words of the voice in his mind so that all ship's crew would understand. When he was finished, he said, "The *glyfa* says that you will have a fine life, far better than you could get on Earth, while in it. I don't agree with that. If you gain something, you lose something. But that's up to you. Anyway, some time, maybe in the next Pluriverse, you'll come across some culture which will be able to put your neural electronic configuration into bodies of artificial protein constructed to your specifications. It says that that will happen; it's a high statistical probability. But, in the meantime . . ."

"It's better than dying," Toyce said.

"Anything is," Tenno said.

"No," Ramstan said.

Nuoli said, "Why don't we wait this out? The *bolg* may empty itself before we run out of food and water. We should take that chance."

"I've had *al-Buraq* estimate the time that would require. The time it takes for the formation of a complete load of missiles —based on the speculation that the *bolg* won't fill itself entirely, and I don't know if it will or won't—the time it's taking for X amount of missiles to form now, calculated against our supplies . . . no, we will starve before then.

"It will have to pause between the present missile-making and the next. It must recharge another time, maybe many times, before it can load itself up. That estimated time is twice as long as the estimate based on a continuous charging."

The tec-op said, "Sir. The missile-production rate is slowing."

"I am not surprised," Ramstan said.

The others looked at each other. Ramstan said, "Tenno, have someone bring the *glyfa* to the third-deck auditorium. I'll tell *al-Buraq* to open the door to my quarters."

"See," his uncle's voice said. "You said you'd never see me again. But you will. You never know what is going to happen. Even I, who've lived so long, don't know."

"I know," Ramstan said.

A minute later, the tec-op said, "Sir, the production seems to have stopped."

The varishaped beams from the globe in the center had also ceased. The bolg was recharging.

Suddenly, the many indicators on many panels turned a bright flashing orange, and alarms shrilled.

Ramstan ran to the tec-op and looked over her shoulder. "What is it?"

"We're losing energy, sir! Something's draining our fuel supply! But there isn't any leakage! See for yourself, sir!"

His mother's voice spoke. "The *bolg* must be draining the

energy from the fuel. It may also be draining your energy, the life from your bodies."

Ramstan had enough self-control to impose even more on himself. He said, coolly, "Are you affected also?"

"No. Our hull resists the draining effect. The *glyfa*'s shell also resists."

Ramstan had not been sure until then that the speaker was not the *glyfa*.

"You won't take more than three of us?"

"Only three."

"Cut off all the alarm indicators except on one screen," Ramstan said to the tec-op. "Turn off all unnecessary illumination, and reduce what's still on to half."

He had to conserve all the energy aboard. He did not know how swiftly the draining progressed.

He called Doctor Hu. "Dispense all the candy bars, vitamins, and protein pills to all personnel. They're going to need it. Tenno will explain why."

Energy was probably being withdrawn from the food, but they would still give extra energy to the crew.

He silently cursed. He had been on the point of changing his decision to act at once instead of waiting to determine how long the recharging and missile-production took. Now, he had no choice.

He called for quiet throughout ship and then announced what had happened.

"We may have very little time. The indicators are registering an alarming rate of energy loss."

He was beginning to feel weak. But that could be his imagination.

"Tenno! Nuoli, Davis, and Toyce will go at once to the Vwoordha's house. At once."

"Why those three?" Tenno said.

"I don't know why."

He subvocalized, "Shiyai, did you hear?"

"I heard. We can lock into a port. They won't have to get into space suits. And, Ramstan . . ."

"Yes?"

Shiyai seemed reluctant to say what she must.

"The energy is being sucked out from your warheads and the

power of your lasers. If you wait too long, the bombs and lasers will be too weak to affect the generator sphere."

"I know!"

He looked at a data screen. *Al-Buraq* would arrive within 1,000 kilometers of the generator-sphere in twenty minutes. He could order that the warhead missiles be released now and the lasers concentrated on a spot on that whirling energy-configuration. Since the energy from ship and its crew and its fuel and the warheads was being sucked out by that monstrous vampire in some manner unknown to his scientists, he should command that the attack begin at once. But he could not do so until his people had gotten to a safe place: the *glyfa* and the Vwoordha's house.

When the vast power of the lasers and the warheads hit that sphere hanging in the center of the *bolg*, the sphere should be disrupted. It would, according to the Vwoordha, release an energy that would make that of the lasers and the warheads look feeble. The now-incoherent power would raven outwards from the core of this thing. Though the spherical shell of the *bolg* had a diameter of 13,000 kilometers, it would be filled with a destroying energy equaled only at the heart of a star.

His mother's voice spoke, and he knew that it was the *glyfa* who was simulating it and not Shiyai. He could detect a very slight trace of the personality of the *glyfa* or the Vwoordha in that voice.

"Tell everybody except the three women to come to the third-level auditorium at once. Davis and Toyce will be in the Vwoordha's house within a minute. Nuoli is still in ship. She will stay here until she can take me to the house. She won't go near the auditorium, however, until the passage of the crew into me has been completed. That will take no more than a microsecond, but they have to be close to me. Nuoli would be drawn in, too, if she were near. When I make a mass transit like this, I cannot discriminate. All nearby are drawn in."

There was a pause. His mother's voice spoke again, but this time it was activated by Shiyai.

"As soon as Nuoli is in the house, we will notify you. You must wait five minutes after that before launching the attack."

Another pause. Then his mother's voice said, "Tell them to gather around me as closely as possible. Those nearest me must put their fingers on me, and each person not touching me should put his hands on others. They should also have body contact. Tell them to crowd as closely together as possible."

Ramstan gave the orders as directed. The bridge personnel left immediately, though several, especially Tenno, wished to say good-bye.

"No, not even a handshake," Ramstan said. "Get going! Run! I will talk to you, all of you, through the screens while you're on your way to the auditorium."

"It's not right," Tenno said, but he obeyed, saluting as he ran.

Ramstan left the bridge and walked towards his quarters. He was going there because it was . . . what? Home? A womb? Both?

But he talked as he walked, and his words and image were caught and transmitted to all the other moving screens.

He chanted *The Saying Of Allah's Command to Annihilate All Things*, the chant which he had heard so often when the neighbors who were also members of the al-Khidhr sect met in his parents' apartment.

"The angel of death is ordered by Allah to destroy the oceans.

"The angel of death comes to the oceans and says, 'Your time to end is now.'

"The oceans say, 'Grant us time to sorrow and to contemplate our wonders and majesties.'

"The angel of death says that there is no more time for the oceans, and he shouts once, and the oceans are gone.

"After the angel of death has destroyed the oceans, he travels to the mountains, the Earth itself, the moon, the sun, and the stars, and each begs for a little more time, a year, a month, a week, a day, an hour, seven seconds. But the angel grants them nothing, and he shouts, and they are not, as if they had never been.

"Allah then says, 'O angel of death, what of my creation is left?'

"And the angel of death replies, 'O Allah, only You and Your angels live.'

"Then Allah says, 'Angels, did you not hear Me say that everyone must taste death? Do not beg for more time.'

"And so the angel of death and all the other angels died, and they are as if they had never been created.

"And only His Face lived."

And, Ramstan thought, not even He—It, rather—lives forever.

I will not plead for more time.

He said, "I have chanted this because, hearing it, you might understand why I am not going into the *glyfa* or the house of the Vwoordha."

He stopped before the iris-door to his quarters, spoke the code word, and stepped through the opening. It closed for the last time.

He went to the prayer rug, stooped, and turned it so that the red arrowhead symbol, the *kiblah*, was pointed at him.

He pushed down the impulse to kneel upon the rug. No. He would not do that. But he would stand here with the tip of his boot touching the edge of the rug.

Why had he pointed the *kiblah* at himself? Did he think that he was God?

The Sufi mystic al-Mansur had thought that he was God. At least, he had said so in the marketplace, and he had been stoned to death for his blasphemy. Yet—he had meant that he was a part of God, just as all human beings were.

Now he could see on a screen that everyone in ship except for himself and Nuoli was in the auditorium room. *Al-Buraq* had expanded the room to make space for the almost four hundred people. And she had not extruded seats for them as she would have done if they had come to hear a lecture or watch a live drama. They stood on a level floor, forming concentric circles, the innermost with their fingers on the egg, those behind pressing closely against them, their hands grasping the hands of others, and those behind them pressing against them.

Ramstan said, "I wish that things . . . I . . . had been different. But if I could start all over again, I think that I would not be or act differently. You have done and are doing what you think is best to do. I have done and am doing what I think is best for me to do."

He choked for a moment, cleared his throat, and said, "You may forget me, but don't forget what I stand for. Good-bye."

They had no time to say anything to him. They fell jammed together, their open eyes seeing nothing. There was no display of energy, no slight thickening of air in threads or clouds as the part that made them unique and sentient passed into the *glyfa*.

"It is done," his mother's voice said. "Hûd, you still have time to join them."

"No."

"They will soon be walking inside this little shell which will seem to them as big as Earth, as big as the universes if they wish."

"No."

Maija Nuoli entered the auditorium, looked horrifiedly at the corpses, looked at the screen displaying his image, and then, wincing, walked over the bodies. She picked up the *glyfa,* held it to her breasts, and walked back over the bodies. Just before she got to the exit, she looked up again at the screen.

"Good-bye, Hûd. God be with you. I loved you once for a brief while, then I hated you. But I think I love you again."

"I made a fatal mistake," Ramstan said. "I loved answers to my questions more than I loved human beings. The only answers that mattered—the only questions, too—were people. I have been only an agent for the *glyfa* and the Vwoordha. I have been nudged and prodded and moved here and there toward some destination unknown to me until now. The plot was as vast and as dark as this hollow thing we are now in. But, though it might seem so to others, I was no mechanical agent. I had choice. I decided to do what I wished to do. I have moved from darkness to a brief light and back to darkness, but I am in the light again. This time, it is my own light, not that of others. It's mine, and it's bright enough for me to see what I'm doing. If darkness presses around me, it is not as close as it was. Few are lucky enough to have even this little flicker.

"Maija Nuoli, whatever happens, may you have your own light."

"Well spoken," Shiyai said in his mother's voice. "But you should not die as you have lived, always suspicious. However, that does not matter now. As a parting gift, you will be allowed to see what happens to the three women."

"What do you mean?"

"That you need not fear that something bad will happen to them because they are in our house. Now, Ramstan. You have turned down the *glyfa*'s last offer. It is probably a waste of time to ask you if you will change your mind about coming with us.

Despite what we told your crew, we do have room for one more. You can join us now if you wish. It is not good to live alone, and it is worse to die alone."

"No."

"I thought so."

The *glyfa* said, "We are in the house, Ramstan. Wait for five minutes."

Shiyai said, "See. Hear."

The images before him were pale and wavering and so transparent he could see through the people and monsters to the objects in the bridge. The Vwoordha were in a room he had not seen before, a round room with a round pool in its center, and they were in the liquid up to their waists. They were holding hands. By them, helping to form a circle, were Toyce, Nuoli, and Davis. All three looked scared. Nuoli held the *glyfa* to her chest. By her side was the great salmonlike creature, its head against her left leg. On the fish's other side, one hand on the top of the fish, the other touching the shimmering thing, was "the laugher who hops." The shimmering thing, "the cold-blood who drinks hot blood," was touching Wopolsa.

"We've formed a circle, and I am going to put into my mouth the first of the sigils," Shiyai said. "I will do that as soon as I can determine whether or not you have destroyed the heart of the *bolg*.

"Wopolsa has been calculating the probabilities of destruction of the *bolg*. She's done more than that. She sees . . . a little beyond what Grrindah and I can see. Anyway, she says that you have a 75 percent chance of success. Those are good odds, Ramstan.

"Also, we three will die some day. Rather, Grrindah and I will. Wopolsa will die, too, though not as we do. She will go . . . somewhere else. In the meantime, we three will be teaching these three as much as they can learn. And, some day, they will become the Vwoordha. If they wish to, of course. I think that they will.

"So, good-bye, Ramstan. We won't be seeing you again, but we may see your like."

Ramstan laughed, and he said, "Are you even now thinking of the time when you may need another like me?"

"There may be other *bolgs*."

He looked at the flashing figures on a screen.

The five minutes had passed while he was looking into the house of the Vwoordha, though he would have sworn that he had done so for no more than thirty seconds.

He opened his mouth. The code word that would tell *al-Buraq* to launch the missiles and shoot the lasers hung glowing in his mind, glowing as brightly as the numbers that told the time on the screen.

Why had he chosen his mother's name, Kadijah, as the code word?

No more questions.

He shouted.